# SAVING ERIC (SPECIAL FORCES: OPERATION ALPHA)

### SAVING SEALS, BOOK 2

JANE BLYTHE

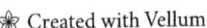 Created with Vellum

Dear Readers,

*Welcome to the Special Forces: Operation Alpha Fan-Fiction world!*

If you are new to this amazing world, in a nutshell the author wrote a story using one or more of my characters in it. Sometimes that character has a major role in the story, and other times they are only mentioned briefly. This is perfectly legal and allowable because they are going through Aces Press to publish the story.

This book is entirely the work of the author who wrote it. While I might have assisted with brainstorming and other ideas about which of my characters to use, I didn't have any part in the process or writing or editing the story.

I'm proud and excited that so many authors loved my characters enough that they wanted to write them into their own story. Thank you for supporting them, and me!

READ ON!
   Xoxo
   Susan Stoker

*I'd like to thank everyone who played a part in bringing this story to life. Particularly my mom who is always there to share her thoughts and opinions with me. The wonderful Cat Imb of TRC Designs who made the stunning cover. And my lovely editor Lisa Edwards for all her encouragement and for all the hard work she puts into polishing my work.*

# CHAPTER 1

December 21<sup>st</sup>
9:23 P.M.

The usual calm he felt when he was on a mission eluded him tonight.

His pulse drummed faster than it should, and his heart felt tight like worry had wound itself around it like a python and was slowly constricting. His skin felt overheated, and the beginning of a stress headache drummed at the base of his skull.

Nothing about this mission was normal.

In his career as a Navy SEAL, Eric "Night" McNamara had performed plenty of rescues, many of them in Afghanistan—where they were about to land—but not a single one of them had involved someone he knew.

Until now.

Six months ago, he and his team had found his little sister, who had been missing for over a year, during a rescue of some abducted children, but that was different. They hadn't known Abigail was there, his best friend—who was now Abigail's husband—had stumbled upon her by accident.

This time he knew exactly who was suffering at the hands of men who had no moral compass. Men who wouldn't only not hesitate to torture and kill her, but who would also revel in it.

Tension flowed through him leaving him antsy. He wanted to be there, he wanted to be moving, he wanted to find Lavender and the other hostages and set them free. What he didn't want to be doing was sitting on this helicopter.

The flight felt like it was taking forever. In reality, Night knew that it wasn't, they were traveling at the same speed they always did, but every second it took them to get to Lavender was another opportunity for someone to hurt her.

"You need to calm down."

Night looked up to see his best friend since childhood, fellow SEAL, and now brother-in-law, Ryder "Spider" Flynn, watching him with concerned blue eyes. "I'm calm," he muttered the lie mostly under his breath.

Spider barked out a laugh. "And I'm the Queen of England. Look, man, we all want to find Lavender before she's hurt, but if you don't calm down and pull it together, you become a liability. To yourself, to her, and to all of us."

His friend was right.

He had to pull it together.

For Lavender.

"You think I'm not feeling the same urgency?" Spider asked. "We all know her, and Abigail is out of her mind with worry. You think I like leaving my pregnant wife with a promise that I'll bring her friend home, knowing there's a very real possibility I won't be able to do that?"

Night knew this mission was going to be hard on all of

them. Lavender had moved to California four years ago and taken a job as a waitress at one of their favorite hangouts. The bar served the best burgers he'd ever eaten, had a great atmosphere, and there were plenty of women around tripping all over themselves to bag a SEAL.

However, it was quiet Lavender with her long red hair and sad gray eyes that had caught his attention.

The two of them had never had sex, but next to the men on his team—who were like his brothers, he was closer to them than he was his own sister, although that was changing —Lavender was the best friend he had.

They talked about everything.

Lavender was the only one who knew how badly he had messed up and how guilty he still felt about how selfish he had been.

Still, he shot his friend a reproachful glance. "You shouldn't promise her that, you know we can't guarantee we'll find Lavender or get her back in one piece." He had messed up his relationship with his little sister, but he was trying to be a better brother, and that meant looking out for her, even if it meant protecting her from her own husband.

Spider let his head drop into his hands, elbows propped on his knees. "I know, man, but she's pregnant and she cried. Abby never cries. But she cried and begged me to bring her friend home, and the words were out of my mouth before I even thought."

While it wasn't wise to make promises like the one Spider had given Abigail, as far as Night was concerned, his friend's promise was further motivation to bring Lavender home.

"Landing in two," Owen "Fox" LeGrand announced.

Just like that, Night was able to shove away his fear for his friend and finally slip his mind into SEAL mode.

This mission and the lives of the people he loved depended on him getting it together. He was no good to

Lavender, or his team, if he allowed the fear he felt for Lavender to mess with his head.

Under the cover of darkness, the helo touched down, and like the well-oiled team that they were, Night, Spider, Fox, Charlie "King" Voss, Logan "Shark" Kirk, and Grayson "Chaos" Simpson, all grabbed their packs and jumped out.

Feet on the rocky ground, Night scanned the area. There was no movement, no signs of torches, no gunfire, no shouts or voices. It was just him and his team.

The helo took off, the sound quickly fading into the night. Assuming everything went to plan, it would return to collect them, Lavender, and the four other aid workers taken with her before the sun rose. The other hostages, a sixty-year-old pastor who had dedicated his life to working with victims of war, his fifty-five-year-old wife, and a forty-eight-year-old woman who had also been an aid worker for the last two decades. Lavender was both the youngest and the newest worker, making her particularly vulnerable. The things he'd seen men like the ones who had taken Lavender do to women were some of the worst things he had seen in his career as a SEAL.

Determined that Lavender wouldn't be their next victim, he took point and started in the direction they believed the group—who had claimed Taliban allegiance—had gone. The abduction was a fairly standard one, militants had arrived at the aid camp armed to the teeth, killed half a dozen of the workers before grabbing their hostages and leaving. They'd sent photos of their hostages to the US government demanding a ransom and then no doubt hiked off into some remote village where they were unlikely to be found.

At least that was what they thought.

But he and his SEAL team had done this before, they were the best of the best, and they weren't leaving here without Lavender and the others.

Yeah, okay, he was as bad as Spider because he definitely would have made the same promise to his sister, whether it was a good idea or not.

Seamlessly, they wove their way through the harsh terrain. An informant in the area had reported seeing a group of Taliban with several Americans moving through, and while they didn't have an exact visual on the area, how many men there were, what kind of firepower they had, Night was confident that whatever they were up against his team would come up victorious.

They'd been dropped off about 3 klicks from where they believed the Taliban were holed up, on the other side of a small mountain range. They'd chosen the spot because not only would it hide their approach, but it would give them time to do a little recon before they crossed the mountains and rescued the hostages.

It was cold out, but the winter's night was comparatively mild, which he hoped was a good sign. The last thing they needed was a snowstorm to limit visibility and make it harder for the helo to return to extract them.

As they made their way up the mountain, they didn't encounter any hostiles, which he again interpreted as a good sign.

In and out.

That was how he was hoping this mission would play out, but if he had learned one thing in his years as a SEAL, it was that their motto of 'the only easy day was yesterday' was, more often than not, accurate.

They'd covered about one klick when he spotted a heat signature with his night-vision goggles.

Someone was about a hundred feet ahead of them.

Holding up a hand, his team halted behind him. Indicating the person ahead of them with the help of a few hand signals, his team spread out to approach the unknown person from all sides. It could be a local out here tending their livestock, it could be a kid wandering out on their own, or it could be one of the Taliban out patrolling the area.

Whoever it was wouldn't see them coming until it was too late.

If it wasn't anyone to be concerned about then they wouldn't see them at all.

For six very large men, all of them over six feet tall and pure muscle, they all knew how to move like a ghost. If it was a Taliban out patrolling, they'd interrogate him and walk in with the advantage. At this point, he wasn't above doing anything that would help him get Lavender out of that hell-hole and back home where she belonged.

10:00 P.M.

The cold was going to kill her, but it had one benefit.

It numbed her.

Thanks to the bitter Afghanistan winter, her broken leg's pain was dulled, and since she didn't have a very high pain tolerance that was a blessing.

It was also a blessing that the winter was comparatively mild, and she'd been wearing her coat, scarf, and mittens when she'd been tossed down here, so she hadn't already succumbed to hypothermia.

She would though.

That was a given, it was only a matter of time.

What had she been thinking coming here?

Right in this moment, Lavender Vaile couldn't remember what had possessed her to decide to volunteer for an aid agency to help deliver food and medical supplies to remote villages in Afghanistan.

She'd thought it was time to start doing something good with her life, something that wasn't just her being selfish. She'd done that for long enough, and she'd realized that the only way she might be able to find redemption would be to dedicate her life to helping others.

So that had been the plan.

She'd signed up to become an aid worker, fully prepared to give up everything—her family, friends, home, and job—to make this her life. This was going to be her future and now look at her. On her very first trip, she'd seen a dozen people gunned down in front of her, been abducted for ransom, and then thrown down into this hole.

Where she was going to die.

If she was lucky.

While none of the men who had taken her spoke English and she didn't speak either Dari or Pashto they had made their intentions perfectly clear with their crude gestures. They had thrown her down here because she wasn't to receive the same fate as the others.

Even if the ransom was paid she wouldn't be going home.

No, they would wait to get the money then come back and get her and use her to fulfill their own sick and twisted desires before killing her.

The best Lavender could hope for was that hypothermia took her first. It was a relatively painless way to die as far as deaths went and certainly better than whatever the men who took her had planned.

Well, there was one other option ...

No.

She had told herself she wasn't going to hope for it because hoping and having those hopes dashed was too much to bear.

But if he knew …

No.

There was no way to know that the terrorists who had taken them had made contact with the US government, and even if they had, there was no way to know what their response would be. Did they pay to get US citizens returned unharmed? If they didn't, would they send in the SEALs to …

Stop it, she reprimanded herself.

He wasn't coming.

No one was coming.

Her life was going to take one of two routes. Either hypothermia killed her or the men returned, raped, and tortured her, then killed her.

That was it.

It was one or the other, there was no third option.

If he could, she was sure that Eric and his team would come and get her, or one of the other teams, she knew a lot of the SEALs, but she and Eric had a special friendship.

He was probably the closest friend she had.

Him and his sister Abigail, who was married to another SEAL on Eric's team.

They'd become her surrogate family since guilt had driven her away from her biological one.

Lavender and her twin sister Marigold had grown up mostly raising themselves. Their parents had divorced, Dad hadn't wanted custody, Mom had decided traveling and dating was more fun than raising kids, and she and her sister had been left to their own devices.

Only she'd taken advantage of Marigold.

While she'd gone to the mall with friends, dated, and gone to parties, she'd let her sister deal with the day to day running of the home, making sure they had food to eat and clean clothes to wear to school the next day. Then she'd pretty much abandoned Marigold to travel the world, finishing school through a foreign exchange program in another country, then housesitting her way across the globe.

After a horrific incident about four years ago, her guilt had grown too much, and she'd fled to the opposite side of the country.

It hadn't helped.

The guilt was still there.

She was starting to think it would never go away.

Was it possible to do enough good deeds to wash away the ones you regretted?

If her current predicament was anything to go by the answer to that question was a resounding no.

Lavender tried to shift in the small space, but it was difficult. The hole—or what she thought was an old well that had been partially filled in—was only wide enough for her to sit with her legs straight out in front of her. When her bottom got tired of sitting on the hard ground, she carefully rolled onto her side and curled in on herself, trying to conserve as much warmth as she could.

If she hadn't been dressed warmly to pack supplies into the truck ready to take them to the surrounding villages, she would probably already be dead.

She didn't like the cold, so the coat she'd bought when she was preparing to come here was the warmest one she could find, and that along with her hand-knitted beanie, scarf, and mittens, were warm enough to keep her alive.

For now.

Until the snow came.

Sooner or later it would.

The mild weather couldn't hold indefinitely, and she hoped that change came before her captors returned for her.

With an uncomfortable wriggle, Lavender tried to find a more comfortable position. Thankfully, the bone in her leg hadn't snapped through the skin when she landed on it, but the broken bone still hurt with a sharp, stabbing sort of pain.

She'd never been good with pain.

The slightest sign of a muscle cramp, or headache, or toothache, and she immediately dosed herself up with painkillers.

But there were no painkillers out in the remote Afghanistan hills.

There was nothing but her and her pain.

At least when the men had tossed her down here they'd thrown down some food and a few bottles of water. They didn't want her dead. They wanted her alive and ready to use for their pleasure when they returned.

She'd eaten most of the food and only had half a bottle of water left, maybe she'd die of dehydration before the cold froze her.

Lavender cast another wistful glance at the top of the hole a good ten feet above her head. It wasn't a huge distance, and even with her broken leg she'd tried to climb out, but she hadn't been able to find enough finger and footholds to get further than about a foot off the ground.

Even without the broken leg she wouldn't have made it.

She hated being this vulnerable, having to just sit down here and wait for someone to come for her. She wanted to save herself and had already decided that when the men did come for her, and they pulled her out, she was going to make a run for it. It didn't matter that she would be outnumbered and that they would be armed and she wasn't, it didn't even matter that her leg was broken and she could barely stand on it let alone run on it, she wasn't going to just let them take her.

She was going to fight.

Fight with everything she had.

The sounds of footsteps on the rocky ground had her stiffening.

Was someone up there?

They'd held her and the others for ten days then walked for almost twenty-four hours before they'd come across this old, abandoned well and stashed her in it. She remembered how hard it was to walk across the rocky ground with her hands tied behind her back. More than once she had lost her balance and face planted, cutting and bruising her cheeks and forehead.

What she'd heard just now was the same sound of feet walking across the rocks as her and the others trudging across the treacherous terrain.

Someone had to be coming.

Was it time already?

She was pretty sure she'd been down here about two days, but she'd thought she would have longer, more time for her leg to heal so she at least stood a chance at making a run for it.

It was too soon.

She wasn't ready.

Panic flooded through her veins leaving her lightheaded and dizzy, she tried to look up into the night to see who was coming for her and how many of them there were, but all she could see was the cloudy sky above.

It was dark, she was injured, and she had no idea where she was or where she could go to find help and safety.

She was doomed.

∿

10:13 P.M.

. . .

Their target didn't seem to notice that he wasn't alone, which Night was grateful for. With Lavender out there somewhere, the last thing they needed was to be wasting time.

As he crept closer, he could hear the man talking, to whom he wasn't sure, he could only see one heat signature with his NVGs, but there was obviously someone else out there.

The man spoke Dari, and since Night was near fluent, he could understand every sickening word the man said.

"You are very beautiful, I will enjoy this." Lust was heavy in the man's voice, and he seemed to be looking down at something below his feet. A hole of some sort, he had to have a woman down there. "The others don't ever have to know that I had a little sample before them."

Obviously, this woman was being held against her will, while his body itched to keep moving to find Lavender, there was no way he could walk away and leave this woman to her fate.

Neither could any of the other guys.

Protectiveness ran deep in SEALs.

Withdrawing a little, he spoke softly into his comms. "He's speaking to someone, a woman, must have her down in an old well or something. I can't see if he's armed but no doubt he is. I'm going to cause a little distraction, get him to move away from the woman. We need to take him down before he makes a sound because he just said he intends to sample the woman before the others."

"You make the distraction and King and I will take him out," Fox ordered. "Night, you then circle back and find the woman, Chaos, Spider, and Shark you keep watch, make sure these others he's referring to don't return."

Orders given, Night didn't hesitate to act them out.

Moving close enough to the man that he would hear, he

let his next footfall land on a rock, sending it crunching into the surrounding rocks.

The man, about forty feet in front of him, froze and stopped what he was doing, turning in a circle to scan the area.

Night let his next step make a similar noise, and the man lifted his AK-47 and aimed it directly at him, although Night could see the man wasn't wearing NVGs and couldn't actually see him.

"Who is there?" he asked in Dari.

Of course Night didn't answer, but he did turn and start running away from the hole this man had stashed his captive in, knowing that the man would come running after him.

As soon as he heard footsteps following him, he immediately stopped, having done his part, he was ready to rescue this woman so they could resume their mission.

Leaving Fox and King to deal with the man, whoever he was, Night kept his movements silent as he backtracked to the hole. Several bottles of water were on the ground beside a stone ring that looked like the remnants of an old well. There was obviously someone down there, and from the looks of things the man had intended to leave her there.

Why bother?

Why not keep the woman wherever he was living?

Who was the man?

Who was the woman?

As he looked over the side of the well, Night expected to see the terrified face of a local Afghani woman—or girl—looking up at him.

Instead, the face he saw was Lavender's.

Glowing green in the glow of his NVGs, she almost looked like a creature from another planet.

A very frightened creature.

She cowered in the bottom of the well, her arms wrapped

around her middle, and from the look on her face she had no idea who he was or if he was here to harm her or help her.

Given what that man had been about to do to her it was no wonder.

"It's Lavender in the hole," he murmured into his comms before lowering his weapon, and removing his NVGs so she could get a better look at his face, covered in paint though it may be. "It's me, Eric," he told her.

Lavender gasped, her hands flying to her mouth, and she shook her head as though she hardly dared to believe it.

"It's really me, Lavender, I'm here, and I'm going to get you out of there." Already he was running through a plan on how to make that happen. First, he needed to get down there to check her for injuries, then he had to get her out. They'd need whatever information she could give them because she was alone, the other hostages nowhere in sight. Then they'd get her onto that helo and back home where she belonged.

"Assess Lavender, perform any first aid needed, we'll see if we can get our friend here to talk," Fox said through their comms.

"You got him?" Night asked.

"Yep, and soon he'll be singing like a raven," King said.

"It's sing like a canary," Night muttered.

King just laughed before the comms went silent.

On his own for the moment, Night focused his attention on Lavender. He knew Chaos, Shark, and Spider were keeping watch and that they would alert him to anyone approaching them, so he didn't have to worry about his six.

"Lavender, I'm coming down," he said, keeping his voice calm even though he wanted to grab her, haul her out of there, then find every single man who had participated in her abduction and make them suffer before slitting their throats.

Telling Lavender that wasn't going to keep her calm though, so he kept his thoughts to himself. This mission was nowhere near over and if he wanted to get himself, his team, Lavender, and the other hostages home alive then he needed to make sure Lavender didn't lose control. A hysterical woman—even if she had every reason to break down—wasn't going to help them achieve that goal.

The man who'd been about to assault Lavender had thrown a rope ladder over the edge of the well which made his job that much easier. Keeping his pack on his back, he quickly scaled down the side of the hole and dropped down in a crouch at Lavender's side. The space was small, barely enough room for the two of them, and Lavender was still watching him like she expected him to disappear at any second, so the first thing he did was reach out and cup her cheek in his hand. She was dirty, there were fading bruises on her forehead and both cheeks, so he let his thumb brush lightly across her skin before leaning down to rest his forehead against hers.

"It's going to be okay, sweetheart," he whispered. Usually, he was the last of the guys on his team to step up and offer comfort to a victim, tears and hysterics freaked him out, he never knew what to say or what to do, but this was different.

This was Lavender.

The woman who he had spent countless hours sitting beside on the roof of the restaurant where she worked, talking about anything and everything.

For her, he would deal with tears or hysterics.

"Y-you're really h-here," she said, lifting her hands and running them over his face before clutching at his BDUs.

"Yeah, honey, I'm really here," he assured her.

"H-he was g-going to … to …"

"Yeah, I know," he said, not wanting her to have to say the words. "But he didn't, and he won't, we won't let him."

"We?" she said, looking up to the top of the hole. "Your team is here?"

"Yeah, interrogating our prisoner and keeping watch over us so I can look after you. Here, drink some water," he said. He shrugged out of his pack and squeezed it onto the ground behind him, then pulled out a bottle along with a protein bar. "Eat this, small bites, take your time," he said, unsure when she had last eaten.

Lavender took the canteen and unscrewed it, taking several gulps of water before she opened the protein bar and began to nibble at it. While she ate, he ran his hands over her body in search of injuries, taking note of the fact that she was shaking. He'd thought it was because she was afraid, but the skin on her face was cold to the touch, she was hypothermic.

When he got to her legs, Lavender cried out when his hands touched her left lower leg. His gaze darted to hers, pain in the gray eyes that looked back at him.

"Lavender?"

"I-I think it's b-broken," she stammered.

His heart sank.

That wasn't what he needed to hear right now.

He and his team couldn't be two places at once, they couldn't leave Lavender alone, injured, and vulnerable, but he could hardly take her with them as they rescued the other hostages, and now he found that she had broken either her tibia or fibula meaning she wasn't ambulatory. They were going to have to carry her out.

10:34 P.M.

From the look on his face, Eric didn't like the news she had just given him.

Lavender knew that the fact she'd broken her leg when

she'd been thrown down here was going to be a problem—although she'd thought it would prevent her from running when she was eventually taken out of here—but seeing the concern on Eric's face made her heart race.

"I-I'm sorry," she told him. She couldn't seem to stop shaking, she'd been cold before but ever since she'd looked up to see the scary-looking man staring down at her that cold seemed to have consumed her, covering her in an icy cloud that she couldn't seem to escape.

"No, sweetheart, don't be sorry, we'll make it work," Eric assured her. He took one of her hands and held it while she nibbled at the protein bar and tried not to let her shaking fingers lose their hold on it. "Lavender is hurt," he told his team, "hypothermia and a broken leg, she's dehydrated too, I need to get her out of here and treat her." He paused and listened, whatever his team was saying he obviously didn't like if the expression on his face was anything to go by.

She tried not to worry, Eric and his team were here now, she'd been rescued, only it didn't feel like it. They still had a long road ahead of them, starting with just how he thought he would get her out of this hole.

Did he expect her to climb up the ladder?

She could do that no problem without a broken leg, but with it …

Right now, she couldn't see that happening.

She was exhausted, she'd barely slept because besides the pain and the cold, fear was her biggest enemy. She knew they were coming back for her, she knew what they were doing when they did, and Lavender found that every slight noise had her jerking awake if she did manage to drift off thinking it was her abductors.

"Hey, you doing okay?" Eric asked, his attention on her again, as he ran a hand over her tangled red locks.

"I w-want to g-go home," she murmured. The tremors

coursing through her body increased, it was like the more she tried to calm them the more she shook. "I can't s-stop sh-shaking."

"I know, honey, you're hypothermic and in shock. We need to get out of here so I can do something about your leg and warm you up some."

There was something in the way he spoke that said there was something else he was worried about. Something he wasn't prepared to share with her yet. Lavender might have worried about it, but right now she had bigger concerns. "I c-can't climb up th-there."

"Yeah, you can."

Eric said it with such conviction that she started.

Did he really believe that she could climb up a rope ladder with a broken leg?

Because right now it seemed impossible.

"We'll do it together."

Not giving her any more time to dwell, Eric put his pack back on, then gently put his hands under her arms and drew her up with him. He took most of her weight so that it didn't hurt her leg too much, but it was the first time she'd stood up since those first few hours she'd been in here, and she immediately felt light-headed, sinking back into Eric's arms.

Eric tightened his hold so her back was pulled up against his front, his arm around her waist, the other across her chest. "You okay?" he asked, his voice low as he spoke close to her ear.

He'd done that the whole time, kept his voice quiet. Was he afraid that they wouldn't be alone much longer?

The man who'd brought her food and water had been taunting her, and while she might not have understood his words, she could clearly read the expression on his face.

He'd come to rape her.

The thought had her shaking intensifying.

She'd been assaulted before, she still had nightmares about it.

"Come on, honey, you got this," Eric said. Again the confidence in his voice managed to make a tiny crack in her terror. Enough that she was able to get it under control—for the moment at least—and focus on the task that had to be done. She wanted to go home, she wanted the others who had been taken with her to go home, she wanted Eric and his team to go home, and to make all of that happen she had to do her part.

She had to pull it together.

"I'm okay," she assured him.

"Never doubted it for a moment," Eric said, and she could tell he was smiling down at her. She knew him better than she knew almost any other person on this planet, including her twin sister. She and Eric both suffered from guilt that impacted every aspect of their lives. It made them kindred spirits, and that had solidified their friendship.

"So h-how do we g-get up th-there?" she asked through chattering teeth.

"One step at a time," Eric replied. "I'm going to stay like this, right behind you, taking your weight, all you need to do is move your arms and feet and let me do all the work."

She could do that.

She hoped.

So long as Eric did most of the work then she was sure she could. It wasn't like she had a choice anyway, they had to get up there and the only way to do it was to climb out, so she would do it. Who cares if it hurt her leg? At least she was alive, and she knew how good these guys were, they would get her home.

"L-let's d-do this," she said, forcing everything else from her mind.

"That's my girl." Lifting her off her feet, Eric moved her

so she was standing on the ladder's bottom rung. "One step at a time, remember, that's all you have to do. We can take this slow, no need to rush."

Curling her numb fingers around the rung closest to her face, Eric kept one arm around her waist as his other hand closed around the rung above the one she'd grasped. Urging her up, they slowly took each step while Lavender tried to keep her balance on her good leg.

It took much longer than it should have, but finally they neared the top, and then hands were reaching down, closing around her biceps and lifting her up, swinging her into a pair of strong arms. She was carried a short distance away before being laid down on a reasonably smooth rock.

"Abby said you better not die," Spider said with a grin, his blue eyes studying her as he straightened.

His words brought a smile to her lips. "I'll do m-my best."

"You'll do it," Eric said as he dropped to his knees beside her. He lifted one of her wrists to take her pulse, peered into her eyes, and gently probed the bruises on her face before he turned and rummaged through his pack for his first aid kit. "You sore anywhere else?"

"No, j-just my l-leg," she assured him.

Producing a bandage, he carefully pulled up the leg of her jeans and wrapped it around her calf. Lavender tried not to whimper, she knew that the bandage would help support her leg if she had to walk on it, and she *would* walk on it if the guys needed her to.

Spider stood beside them with his weapon ready, guarding them so that Eric could tend to her, and the gratefulness she felt warmed her a little. These guys were risking their lives for her, and she could never repay them for it.

"Do you know where the others are?" Eric asked as he pulled out some heat packs.

"N-no. We were t-together for a w-while, but then th-

they threw me d-down into the h-hole. They were g-going to come b-back for me l-later, I guess th-they took the o-others with th-them."

Eric nodded like it was what he was expecting her to say. "Were they injured when you last saw them?"

"They h-hit us a b-bit, knocked u-us around, but they c-could all still w-walk."

Eric pulled off one of her mittens and put a heat pack on her palm before pulling the mitten back into place. He repeated that with her other hand, then unzipped her coat and reached inside the neck of her sweater to place more heat packs under both of her armpits before zipping her coat back up.

"That should help to warm you up, and I'll give you a shot of painkillers."

"No morphine," she said firmly. She knew they were far from out of the woods and she wanted to be as lucid as she could be so she could pull her weight.

Although his brow furrowed, Eric nodded and switched out the medications, putting a few pills into his hand and offering them to her along with some more water. "You're dehydrated, we need to get some more fluids into you."

She took the painkillers then drank a few mouthfuls of water, the heat packs were warming her up but also making her drowsy. She wanted a warm bed, a hot meal, a cup of steaming coffee, she wanted to know that she was safe and this nightmare was over.

As though reading her mind, Eric leaned in close. "I know you're exhausted, but I need you to hold on a bit longer, soon I'll get you somewhere where you can close your eyes and sleep for a bit." He touched his lips to her forehead and the resulting flush of warmth and fluttering in her belly had nothing to do with the heat of his breath.

This man was strong, fearless, and sexy beyond words, he was her hero.

~

10:59 P.M.

Keeping one hand on Lavender's shoulder, Night's thumb stroked the skin behind her ear, partly because he needed to keep contact with her to remind himself that she was alive and it was his job to keep her that way, and partly because he wanted to reassure her, remind her that they were here now and they would get her out in one piece.

He hoped.

"Night, can you handle Lavender on your own? Get her as close to the extraction spot as you can while still remaining hidden, so the rest of us can go after other hostages?" Fox asked. "If you think you need someone else, Spider can go with you. Lavender isn't ambulatory so it's fine if you need back up, the rest of us will make it work."

Night immediately shook his head. "You need everyone you can get if you're going to get the hostages out. According to the intel we got from the man who was here to feed Lavender, there are more than fifty men in the camp where they're holding the others. Spider should definitely go with the rest of you, I can handle getting Lavender somewhere safe."

Lavender having a broken leg and not being able to walk would make it difficult, but not impossible. He could handle her and his weapon, and they had the advantage of the kidnappers believing she was still safely tucked away in the old well and no idea that a SEAL team was closing in on them.

It also seemed suddenly extremely important that he be the one to stay with Lavender, get her to safety. Night wasn't going to examine too closely why exactly it seemed so imperative that he not let her out of his sight, he was just going to make sure he kept her safe.

"Are you sure?" Fox asked.

"We definitely stand a better chance of getting the others out with the five of you." While it was only the difference of one person, that one extra person dramatically increased the odds of this going off successfully.

"I can walk on my own," Lavender piped up, he had thought she'd drifted off to sleep, but it was clear she had been following their conversation. "If I walk on my own then the five of you can go after the others, and Eric can make sure no one comes after us without having to also worry about carrying me."

Night wasn't sure that she could walk on her own, but he appreciated her bravery and willingness to be a team player. "Honey, I don't want you to push yourself too hard, a broken leg shouldn't be walked on."

"I can do it," Lavender said firmly.

Fox gave a nod of agreement. "Another team is on the way here, they just finished up on another assignment so since we have to split into two groups it's better to have another team come and join us. Night, you can get Lavender somewhere safe, meet the other team when it arrives, the rest of us will go after the other hostages. All right, let's move out," Fox ordered. While the others stood and headed out into the darkness, Night fixed his attention on Lavender.

"I *can* walk," she said before he got a chance to say anything.

"You don't have anything to prove," he assured her.

Sadness crossed her features, and she gave a small shake of her head. "Actually, I do. It's why I came here."

He knew her reasons for coming here, they'd discussed them at length the first time she had brought the idea up almost two years ago. It was shortly after Abigail had gone missing, and he and Lavender had been talking late one night up on the roof in their special spot, and she had told him that she was thinking of joining an aid organization.

His first instinct had been to talk her out of it, he knew the dangers lurking in the countries she would be working in, especially as a young, beautiful American woman. He knew that being taken hostage and ransomed was a possibility. Just like he knew that the chances were high if she did get grabbed, she would be tortured and raped. But he had also known how important it was to Lavender that she feel like she was making a difference in the world, so he had been supportive of her choices while also educating her on the dangers involved.

Unfortunately, she had been just a hairsbreadth away from the worst happening.

"You're wrong," he said softly, cradling the back of her head in his hand. "You made some mistakes, but you learned from them, became a better person, and you know what?" Night waited until her eyes met his. "I think you're a pretty amazing person." He turned his voice brisk because he didn't want her to get too introspective and get herself bogged down in emotions they didn't have time to deal with right now. He needed her focused. "All right, we'll get you on your feet, but the ground is rocky and uneven, I'm not sure you're going to be able to make it far on your own."

Fire flared in her silvery eyes which glowed green in the light of his NVGs, and he fought back a smile. As long as he kept this a challenge, he knew Lavender would rise to the occasion.

"I can make it as far as I have to," she bit out.

"We'll see," he said pragmatically, knowing he was antagonizing her but confident it was the best way to handle her.

"Yeah, we'll see," she muttered under her breath.

Night held out a hand and Lavender hesitated, no doubt not wanting to admit to needing his help, but then took it and allowed him to pull her to her feet. He didn't take the heat packs back, the ones under her arms would fall when she started moving, but they would stay inside her sleeves, which she had tucked into her mittens, so they would still provide warmth, and the last thing he needed was for her to lose consciousness due to low core body temperature.

While Lavender took a couple of tentative steps, wincing each time her bad leg took her weight but able to stay upright and moving, Night scanned the area. Not seeing anyone approaching, he positioned Lavender in front of him and pointed her in the direction of the mountain where they would find a cave to hide out in until the other team arrived. With him behind her, he was between her and where he suspected an attack would come from should some of the Taliban that had abducted her come looking for their missing friend.

Before they started moving, Night slipped an arm around Lavender's waist, brought her up against him, and whispered close to her ear. "I will get you home, Lavender, trust me."

She pressed closer. "I do."

He whispered his lips across her cheek. "Hold onto that faith, sweetheart. Okay, let's move out."

It was slow going, he knew that each step Lavender took was agony, but she didn't complain. A couple of times he had to reach out and grab her elbow to steady her as her feet slipped on the rocks, but otherwise she plowed on like a trooper.

They'd been walking for maybe fifteen minutes when he felt it.

That tingling on the back of his neck that said that trouble was coming.

Night didn't think, he didn't question it, he simply trusted in the intuition that had saved his life on more than one occasion.

Lunging forward, he managed to curl an arm around Lavender's waist and take them both to the ground, rolling so that he took the brunt of the impact.

Mere milliseconds after they hit the ground the shots came.

If he hadn't acted they'd both be dead by now.

They had landed behind a rock, and he propped Lavender up against it, making sure her head was beneath the top of it, and said in a harsh whisper, "Stay here. Don't move."

"Eric, wait." She grabbed at him as he went to move, intending to draw their attention away from Lavender as he took out their attackers.

"What?"

"Give me a gun. I know how to shoot. I've never shot at a real person before, but I can be a distraction. They know we're behind here, let me keep shooting, that will keep their attention here so you can circle round and take them out."

Night hated that her plan made sense.

"Don't get yourself shot," he warned as he shoved a gun into her hands.

She shot him a grin. "I won't, don't want to get on Abby's bad side. No offense, but between you and your sister she is the scarier one when she's mad."

He huffed a chuckle because she wasn't wrong. His little sister could be a force to be reckoned with, and hopped up on pregnancy hormones as she was right now she could definitely be scary.

Praying he was making the correct decision in splitting up and leaving Lavender alone and as the bait to keep their would-be killers' attention, Night slipped away silently to eliminate the threat and get her to safety.

～

11:26 P.M.

Someone was shooting at them.

Lavender wasn't sure why she was surprised about that. She was, after all, in the middle of Afghanistan, where she had been taken hostage at gunpoint, been left in a hole in the ground, and almost raped. Why was she shocked that someone would be shooting at them?

Eric had her on the ground and safe—well, relatively safe —behind a rock, before her sluggish brain had even registered what was going on, but as soon as it started functioning again she knew that she could help. After being abducted by a man she thought she was falling in love with— unbeknownst to her, he had targeted her specifically to get to her twin sister—she had decided she never wanted to feel vulnerable again. Top of her list had been learning how to shoot a gun and taking self-defense classes.

Although he looked like he didn't like the idea, Eric passed her a gun before he disappeared.

She wanted to beg him to stay but shook off the idea. If he stayed, they might both die, and she wasn't going to be responsible for anyone else getting hurt. So she gritted her teeth and did her part knowing that the sooner Eric could eliminate the man—or men—trying to kill them, the quicker he would come back to her.

It was dark, and she wasn't wearing night-vision goggles like Eric was—nor did she have the innate ability to see in the dark that Eric possessed, the ability that had gotten him his nickname—but she supposed that it didn't really matter whether she aimed at the shooter accurately or not, all she had to do was keep their attention fixed on her so Eric could do his thing.

Ignoring the pounding pain in her leg and the headache that was attempting to steal what little vision she had, Lavender twisted so she was balanced on her knees, and quickly lifted her head over the top of the rock so she could fire off a few shots.

Gunfire immediately lit up the night, and she ducked back down as bullets flew at her.

This was insane.

It was hard to believe that this was really her life.

Waiting a few moments, she darted up again and fired in the direction the shots had been coming from. She could make out at least half a dozen men with torches stalking towards her, and when they fired on her she could feel the bullets whizzing by, mere inches away.

Lavender huddled back down and dragged in a steadying breath, her pulse raced, and her head spun, she was beyond exhausted, but she couldn't rest until they took care of these men.

"You can do this," she whispered, giving herself a pep talk.

Before she could let the terror that constantly ebbed at her, threatening to claim her and wash her away at any second, take control, she got back up and fired off the last of the bullets in her gun.

That was it.

She was done.

It was all on Eric now, and she prayed that she had done enough to help him.

Sagging down onto her bottom, she rested heavily against the rock and waited to see what would happen next.

Silence.

Nothing.

No footsteps, no gunshots, no anything.

Then she heard it.

Footsteps.

Approaching her.

Then seven shots were fired in quick succession.

Was that Eric?

Had he got them?

Tears threatened to burst out, but she chewed on her bottom lip and forced them to stay in. Sitting here on the hard ground, rocks sticking painfully into her backside, cold, hungry, thirsty, and more tired than she had ever been in her life, she felt close to breaking. How much more could she take?

Lavender was afraid that the answer to that was that she had already reached her limit.

Something crunched, and she opened her eyes and asked, "Did you get …" her question trailed off when she didn't see Eric standing before her but a man with a vicious smile and a machine gun aimed at her head.

He said something to her in a language she couldn't speak, but the message in his eyes was clear.

He was here for her.

He was going to hurt her and then he was going to take her back to the others.

Where was Eric?

Had this man killed him?

The man reached for her, and she shrunk away from him. It couldn't end like this, it couldn't. She'd been starting to accept the fact that she wasn't going to survive this ordeal, but then Eric had appeared like an avenging angel, pulling her out of the well, helping her cross the countryside, and she had started to hope.

Now that hope was gone.

With the weapon trained on her, his other hand was about to curl around her arm when something suddenly sprayed across her face, and the man's eyes went wide right before he dropped.

Lavender just stared, frozen, at the face of the man who would have viciously tortured and raped her before ending her life.

"Are you hurt?"

The words floated through the air as though attached to balloons, but she couldn't seem to find them. They were like gibberish, another language like the one her would-be tormentor had spoken.

"Lavender."

Her name was said harshly, as though the speaker were worried, but she still couldn't break her gaze with the man's eyes.

Was he dead?

Was that why he hadn't touched her?

Her brain couldn't seem to focus and the darkness of the night seemed to seep inside her very soul, taking it over and transporting her to another place.

"Oh no, don't you dare pass out on me." A new face suddenly appeared right before her, close enough that she could feel the warm breath against her skin. "Did he touch you? Are you hurt? Did you get shot?"

The questions were fired at her too quickly, and she had trouble processing them.

"Come on, honey, come back to me." Someone shook her, and a finger tapped lightly at her cheek.

The touch somehow broke the hold of the darkness, and she blinked slowly as she recognized Eric crouched before her.

"Is he …?" she asked, not sure she could say the word.

"He's dead," Eric said with a nod. "Are you hurt?"

Was she?

No.

She didn't think that she was.

Slowly she shook her head.

"Okay, good, I'll check you over but not until we get somewhere safe. Anyone could have heard those gunshots and come to check it out. We have to put as much distance as we can between us and here."

As though talking more to himself than to her he picked up her hand, which clutched the gun, and pried it away from her. He then grabbed her arms and pulled her to her feet, steadying her until she got her bearings.

Her leg hurt, but complaining about it wasn't going to change anything. She had to walk out of here, Eric was right, the gunshots were like a beacon telling anyone in the vicinity where they had been, they had to get away.

"Can you walk?" he asked, his mouth close to her ear.

"Yes," she said, hoping that if she said it like she believed it then it would be true.

"All right then, let's move out."

They began walking. It took hardly any time for exhaustion to start pulling her down like a weight around her neck. Her whole body shook, and she stumbled more and more often.

One time she went down hard onto her knees, pain spearing through her broken leg, she knew all this walking on it wasn't a good idea, but it wasn't like she had a choice.

Using Eric's hand for support, she somehow got back onto her feet and they resumed their walk.

Lavender started counting their steps as a way to keep her mind off the pain. The numbers rolled on and on, into the hundreds, and then the thousands. She wanted to stop, wanted to lay down and sleep, she doubted the rocky and uneven ground would be enough to keep her awake.

She had no idea how she was still on her feet, but she wasn't giving up, she wouldn't do that to Eric.

She would keep walking until her body physically couldn't keep going.

She was into the five thousands when it happened.

Her bad leg rolled on a small rock, her exhausted body unbalanced easily, and she landed hard on her hands and knees.

She was trembling, putting all her effort into getting back onto her feet, but she couldn't.

She physically couldn't.

"It's okay, honey, I got you, not much further to go, you've done amazing, I can carry you this last bit," Eric said as he easily lifted her onto his shoulders. He didn't even sound winded, and she'd be jealous of his peak physical condition if she wasn't so tired. First thing she was doing when she got back home and her body healed was hit a gym, she was going to work out until she could handle hikes like this without batting an eye.

Eric walked for a little longer, managing to navigate the rocky terrain and the steep incline easily, and soon after he was setting her down.

"I'll be right back," he murmured in her ear, and true to his word he returned a moment later to pick her up, cradling her in his arms as he carried her into a small cave.

It was quiet inside, still, and a little warmer away from the wind, and when Eric set her down in a back corner of the cave, she sighed in relief. He gave her his canteen then rifled through his pack and pulled out a thin-looking blanket that he spread over her and she found to be surprisingly warm.

Once he had her tucked in, he brushed his fingertips across her cheek. "Sleep now, Lavender, you definitely earned a rest."

"Can you lie down with me?" she asked, somewhat tentatively. She knew he was here to protect her, but right now what she needed was to feel safe, and Eric gave her that, she wanted his arms around her.

"Sure, sweetheart," he said. He stretched out at her side, wrapped an arm around her, and pulled her against him, then covered them both with the blanket.

They lay like that for a few minutes before she spoke, "You're my own personal superhero."

A laugh rumbled through his chest. "Superhero, huh?"

"Mmhmm," she agreed, a smile curling her lips up. "You'd look really good in spandex, it would show off all those muscles of yours."

"You been checking me out, sweetheart?" Eric asked in a sexy voice that made her body clench despite her pain, exhaustion, and fear.

"Maybe. You wouldn't need anything to make you look like you've got muscles, you have the real thing. I didn't even know eight packs were a thing until I saw yours."

"We should get you hypothermic and hurt more often so I can get more compliments," Eric said, sounding amused.

Lavender giggled.

"What would my superpower be?"

"Seeing in the dark, just like your name, Night," she finished softly then yawned.

"Close your eyes now, sweetheart, you need sleep."

"Eric?"

"Yeah?"

"I'm scared."

His grip on her tightened. "I know you are. What scares you the most right now?"

"Waking up and you'll be gone, that this is all just a dream or a hallucination." If that was all this was, Lavender wasn't sure she could handle it. Everyone had a breaking point and she was precariously close to reaching hers.

"This isn't a dream, Lavender. I'm right here." His thumb and forefinger found her chin and tilted her face up, then he leaned down, and his lips whispered across hers.

The kiss was light, brief, but it went further in warming her than anything else had. With the feel of it lingering on her lips sleep finally claimed her.

# CHAPTER 2

December 22<sup>nd</sup>
3:49 A.M.

Night shifted slightly so he could touch the back of his hand to Lavender's forehead. Her skin was still cool to the touch, but she had definitely warmed up over the last few hours.

Confident that she was doing as well as could be expected given what she had been through, he rested his head back against the hard ground and tucked Lavender closer against his side. After she'd fallen asleep, he had slipped out of the cave to make sure he had sufficiently covered their trail before returning to find her still sleeping peacefully. Exhaustion had Lavender in i's grip, and other than him waking her once to give her some water and feed her another protein bar while he checked her vitals, she had slept deeply.

She'd need a lot more than a few hours of sleep in a dark, cold cave, where the enemy roved somewhere out there in the darkness. She needed IV fluids, warm blankets, morphine, and proper medical care. Still, at least for the moment, she was relatively safe and still in one piece.

He lay with Lavender in his arms for another fifteen minutes before carefully easing her off his chest. He'd dozed a little while keeping both himself and Lavender tucked under his emergency blanket so that his body heat could help keep Lavender warm, and she had slept draped half across him, her head pillowed on his chest. It was time to go for another perimeter check. He'd gone out twice already since they settled into the cave almost three hours ago.

Night had tucked the blanket back around Lavender and picked up his weapon from where it had been lying beside him when he heard it.

Footsteps.

Someone was close by.

He knew it wasn't the other team coming to assist in extracting Lavender and the other hostages which meant it was either a local or one of the Taliban come searching for them. They had to know that he was out here somewhere and that he had Lavender with him. They'd killed the man at the well when they'd first found her, and he'd killed eight of them last night. There wasn't time for him to do much with the bodies which meant they knew Lavender had help.

Sooner or later someone *would* find them here hiding out in the cave. It would be another hour before the other SEAL team was on the ground, so he would have to decide if he felt like he and Lavender were safe here or if they needed to move further up the mountain. It would make it harder to get back to the exfil spot, but it would keep them out of sight until reinforcements were there to help. Night wasn't sure how much longer Lavender could walk on her broken leg. She'd been pushing it last night, and watching her take each painful step had made him feel like he was walking across a bed of knives. He hated that she was hurt, hated that he couldn't just whisk her away to safety, hated that she had been made to suffer.

Nothing else was happening to her on his watch.

Quietly, he slipped out of the cave and quickly located two men about a hundred yards from their hideout.

Not wanting to do anything to paint more of a target on their back and light a path straight to their doorstep, he decided that shooting them was out.

Instead, he pulled out his knife and circled around until he was behind them.

The two weren't very smart, they were bickering with one another. One of them apparently thought that he and Lavender had gone this way while the other was adamant that he believed they'd gone in the opposite direction.

Between their arguing and the fact that they carried torches they were easy to spot, and he had no idea how they had thought they were going to sneak up on them, they were practically advertising their arrival.

They were about to round a large rock, and he readied himself to make his move.

The first one came within striking distance, and he moved behind the man and slit his throat in one smooth, clean motion.

The other man startled but was too slow lifting his weapon, Night threw the dying body of his friend at him and while the man raised his hands to knock the body away from him, Night struck, plunging the knife into the man's throat, severing his carotid artery.

There was no way to hide the blood, but he could at least do something with the bodies and hope that when more men came looking for them they wouldn't notice the blood. There was a pile of rocks not far away so he dragged the two bodies over to it and moved the rocks so they covered the bodies.

Not wanting to waste any more time, the need to get back

to Lavender and make sure she was okay was strong, and almost …

Nope, not going there.

Lavender had worried him coming out to such a dangerous place, and then learning of her abduction had thrown him into a tailspin, but that was all there was to it. There were definitely no feelings involved. Nothing beyond friendship anyway.

Not sure he believed himself, Night did a quick check to make sure these two were the only ones out there, then returned to the cave to find Lavender still fast asleep.

He hated to wake her, but it wasn't like he had a choice. Kneeling beside her, he removed the blanket, folded it up, packed it away, and then got his pack on before he gently placed a hand on Lavender's shoulder.

"Wake up, honey," he called softly.

She stirred but didn't wake.

"Come on, honey, time to wake up." He brushed the back of his knuckles across her cheek.

Lavender groaned, and then blinked open heavy eyes to stare up at him. "What time is it?"

"It's still early, dark out, but there were men out there looking for us." When Lavender gasped he quickly added, "I killed them, but they'll keep sending more, we need to move higher up the mountain."

To her credit, Lavender didn't complain, just carefully climbed to her feet, allowing him to help, then stood ready and waiting for further instructions.

"We're going to be heading up, the same direction we went in last night. If I tell you to get down and hide you do it without arguing."

"I did everything you told me to last night," she reminded him.

"I know you did, honey, but they know we're out here.

The rest of the team will be moving in shortly to get the rest of the hostages out, they will be scouting out here trying to find us."

"I promise, Eric, I'll do whatever you tell me," she assured him.

"I need you to promise me one more thing." He suspected this one would be a harder promise for her to make. When her gaze met his he continued, "You need to tell me if your leg gets too sore to walk on." He cut her off with a frown when she opened her mouth to protest. "I mean it, Lavender, if you can't walk any further you need to tell me, I can carry you and still watch our back at the same time."

Her gaze dropped to look at her leg which she held stiffly, her good one supporting her weight, but then she sighed and looked back up. "Yeah, okay."

Satisfied, he led her to the cave opening and once he had cleared the area directed her to start walking.

For the next thirty minutes, they climbed steadily higher, the couple of hours of rest seemed to have done her some good, and she was able to keep her footing. Night knew that wouldn't last. She was exhausted, she needed uninterrupted sleep and medical care, she needed to stop living on adrenalin which was what had kept her going over the last two weeks. Sooner or later she was going to crash completely, but he prayed he had her to safety before that happened.

Another ten minutes passed before Lavender stumbled and went down hard, crying out in pain.

He was crouched at her side in seconds, helping her turn so she was sitting and propping her up against his bent knee. "You okay, honey?"

"My leg just collapsed under me," she said, and he could tell she was close to tears, her eyes were watery and she was chewing on her bottom lip. "I'm sorry, Eric, I don't think I can walk anymore. I'm sorry, I don't want to be a burden, I tried, I tried to keep going, but I don't think I can. I'm sorry," she said again.

"Would you stop apologizing?" He curled a hand around the back of her neck and drew her forward so her forehead rested against his shoulder. "You're fine, better than fine, you've done better than I could have asked for. I'll carry you for a bit, and then we'll find another cave to hide out in, and you can get some more rest."

"I don't want to make this harder for you. You're here to rescue me, and I don't want you to get hurt because I broke my stupid leg," she said, and he could feel her tears start to fall.

"Don't worry about that, honey. It's not the first time I've had to carry someone and still watch for threats. We'll be okay."

No sooner were the words out of his mouth than he got that feeling. That sense of no longer being alone.

Someone else was coming.

Sensing the change in him, Lavender lifted her head. "What is it?"

"Someone is coming." Scooping her up, he ran a few yards away to where there was a rocky outcrop. He deposited her then said, "Stay here, I'll be right back." Pausing before he stood, he touched his lips to her forehead, then silently made his way back the way they had come.

Hiding behind a rock, he watched and waited, wanting to know what he was up against before deciding on a course of action.

Someone rounded the rock he was hiding behind, and he swung his weapon to point at them before relief had him sagging against the rock. "You are a sight for sore eyes," he said as the back-up SEAL team appeared before him.

~

5:34 A.M.

Lavender shifted uncomfortably on the small rocky outcrop she was perched on. She wanted Eric to come back. She felt safe when he was around, safe in a kind of way that she had never experienced before. With just his presence, he made her feel like everything was going to be okay, like the ground —that had felt so shaky when she was sitting alone in that well waiting for those men to come for her—was suddenly stable and secure. She knew he would gladly give his life if it meant getting her home alive, and while she didn't want that to happen, knowing what a fearsome warrior he was warmed her inside.

Despite the pain in her leg and the lingering headache, despite the dull aches and pains that littered her body, despite the hunger and the thirst, the nausea and the biting cold, snuggled in his arms she had felt completely safe to let go and fall into the deepest sleep of her life.

What would she do if he didn't return?

She was injured and unarmed, if those men killed him then she would either die out here, a victim of the elements, or her kidnappers would find her and rape and torture her until she was begging them to end her life.

Fear had her stomach churning, and she inched further backward, away from the opening where they entered and out onto a ledge. It would be hard for them to reach her here, the space was narrow, and those men would be bigger than her, making it harder for them to pass the rocks that now partially blocked her from view.

To her right was the rocky mountain, but to the left was probably a forty foot drop, not a straight drop, this was a sharp decline, dotted with large rocks and the occasional scrubby bush. There was no way you would survive the fall.

There were too many things to hit on the way down, and the landing would be solid rock and hard-packed dirt.

Lavender gulped and pressed her back firmly against the side of the mountain. This little hidey-hole no longer felt so safe, and all she wanted was to be back in Eric's arms. She'd gladly keep walking, doing her best to ignore the constant pain in her leg if only he would return.

"Lavender."

She shrieked at the voice and sudden presence in front of her.

"It's only me, honey," Eric said, smiling at her.

She went to smile back when she became aware of the fact that they weren't alone. Had he caught someone? Did he have a prisoner he intended to drag along with them? Or was this some sort of trap? Had he been captured and told that he had to lure her out so they had both of them?

Lavender whimpered and shuffled further back away from the man who had made her feel safe just moments ago.

"It's all right, honey, it's the other team," Eric told her, remaining where he was as he obviously interpreted her fear and realized he needed to handle her carefully.

"The SEAL team?"

"Yep."

"Which team?" She knew a lot of the guys in the SEALs, they were regulars at the restaurant where she had worked, and while she might be closest with Eric, who she had formed a close friendship with and his team, she liked a lot of the guys and their families.

"It's Wolf's team."

Matthew "Wolf" Steel was a good guy, she liked him and his wife, Caroline. The rest of his team consisted of Christopher "Abe" Powers, Hunter "Cookie" Knox, Sam "Mozart" Reed, Faulkner "Dude" Cooper, and Kason "Benny" Sawyer. The team had been through a lot as had their women, she didn't know the details, but she knew Caroline, Alabama, Fiona, Summer, Cheyenne, and Jessyka had all survived their own hellish ordeals and she respected every single one of them.

Eric wouldn't be lying to her. If he said the other team had arrived then she believed him, still she couldn't help leaning sideways just a little to peer around Eric to see who was standing behind him. When she saw both Wolf and Dude, she relaxed a little more.

Now that it wasn't just her and Eric, they definitely stood a better chance at getting out of here alive.

She shifted a little more, intending to get up onto her feet and move back onto the main outcrop so she could join the others, but the soft, gravelly dirt beneath her began to shift, making her fall sideways, close to the edge.

"Lavender," Eric cried out, reaching out a hand toward her. "Take my hand, honey, your bad leg is making you unstable."

Trying to get both legs beneath her, she reached out to grasp Eric's hand, it wasn't far away, but as she moved her broken leg shook and collapsed, taking the rest of her along with it, and then she was falling.

Falling.

Eric's eyes grew wide, and he lunged toward her, but it was too late.

Gravity had already taken over.

The last thing she saw as she disappeared over the edge was Eric's terrified face which seemed to glow in the pre-dawn light.

Everything seemed to happen in slow motion.

Time slowed down.

She fell slowly.

Her eyes scrunched closed. She didn't want to see the rocks that were going to bash her body to pieces on the way down or the ground coming up to meet her in the moments before her death.

The feeling of weightlessness made her feel sick, and if she wasn't about to die then she was pretty sure she would have thrown up the little she had eaten in the last few hours.

Her life flashed before her eyes.

Regrets taking center stage.

There was so much she wished she had done differently.

So much she still wanted to do.

The landing was hard, and pain shafted through her chest where she had taken the brunt of the landing.

Was she dead?

She didn't feel dead.

Lavender sucked in a harsh breath and opened her eyes, instead of finding herself at the bottom of the mountain, she was balanced about one-third of the way down on a large rock. It was barely big enough for her chest to rest against, her legs dangled over the edge, and she clawed at the rock with her hands, trying to find finger holds that would keep her perched there.

One wrong move and she would fall.

Again.

And this time she didn't think she would be as lucky as to land on the only rock big enough to support her.

"Lavender, don't move. I mean it," Eric called down to her. "You move, you'll fall, just stay right where you are, I'm coming for you."

She made the mistake of lifting her head to look up at him, the movement had her slipping until she was holding on with just her arms and the very tip of her chest still on the rock.

"Lavender," Eric said sharply. "Close your eyes, don't move a muscle. I'm coming, but it's going to take me a moment to get hooked up to the rope and get down to you. I have to move slowly because I don't want to send any other rocks showering down onto you."

His voice would be soothing, but she could practically feel his fear even from down here. Knowing he was worried had her own anxiety ratcheting up.

"Lavender, hey, sweetie, it's Wolf. You're doing amazing, Night told us how you walked on your broken leg for over an hour last night, and then again today for almost an hour, you are strong and tough and you got this, okay?"

Wolf's calm tone went a way to soothing her and she forced her wildly beating heart to slow down. If she didn't move she would be okay, and Eric was coming for her. She trusted him.

"I-I'm o-okay," she called up.

"Course you are," Wolf said like he hadn't thought anything else was a possibility. "We're getting Night into a harness right now and getting the ropes ready, then he's going to climb down to you. When he gets to you he's going to put a harness on and bring you back up."

Up until then, Wolf's steady voice and explanation had her clinging more tightly to calm, but the idea of having to climb up the mountain with a broken leg had her panic surging back.

"I can't climb up," she sobbed. She was seconds away from a full-blown meltdown, and she was sure she couldn't keep holding on and have a panic attack at the same time.

"You won't have to do any of the work," Wolf promised, "all you have to do is keep calm and let Night do everything else."

It felt like an eternity, but probably wasn't more than ten minutes or so when she felt Eric's presence. Risking a glance, Lavender opened her eyes and turned her head, keeping her cheek pressed to the smooth, cold rock, and saw him just a few feet above her.

"Almost there, honey, won't be much longer now," he said when he saw her looking at him.

Not trusting herself to speak, she just nodded then kept her eyes locked on Eric and his slow progress until he was just beside her. Now on the same level as her, but still out of reach, he moved sideways as easily as though he were walking on the ground and then he was there, moving into position behind her, his strong arms encircling her in a little bubble of safety.

"You're here." She breathed in relief.

"At your service," he said, shooting her a grin, but she could see the worry in his eyes. "I don't want you to move, but I'm going to strap this harness around your waist and your thighs, and then I'm going to clip it onto the rope."

"I have to put a harness on?" She had no idea how she was supposed to do that clinging to a rock twenty-five feet above the ground.

"Relax, hon, I'll do all the work," he assured her. His hands circled her waist and then she felt him slip something around her, his hands then moved to her thighs, and a moment later, she felt herself strapped into a harness. "All right, now the guys are going to help us get back up. All I want you to do is let go of the rock and lean back against my chest. You don't need to hold onto the rope, you don't have to try to use your legs, you just have to hang there. And, Lavender, I suggest you keep your eyes closed."

She was down with that.

Letting go of the rock was a lot harder than it seemed because despite the fact she was attached to a rope along with a SEAL, with two more SEALs to help them get to safety, her mind couldn't seem to let go of the fact that she was dangling twenty-five feet above the ground.

If it wasn't for Eric's strong hands gently prying her off the rock, she likely never would have moved.

Taking his advice, she allowed Eric to sit her up and prop her against his chest, and kept her eyes firmly closed as they slowly ascended back up to the outcrop she had fallen off.

When they were close enough, strong arms grabbed hold of her, unclipping her and passing her off to someone else who carried her away from the edge of the mountain and gently laid her down on the ground.

"How you doing, sweetheart?" Dude asked, taking her chin between his thumb and forefinger and tilting her face so he could see it better. His fingertips ran over her cheek, and she winced, she'd obviously hurt it in her fall. "Lavender, I'm going to need you to open your eyes and look at me." Dude's voice was strong and commanding, and she complied immediately. She'd been intimidated by Dude's intense persona when she first met him, but seeing the way he doted on his wife, Cheyenne, treating her like she was the most precious thing in the world, she had come to realize that he was intense but sweet underneath.

Dude knelt above her and nodded approvingly when he saw her eyes open, he checked out her face before running his hands up and down her body checking for injuries. Lavender winced when he touched her ribcage, and Dude frowned when he realized she was hurt there.

Now that she was safe—for the moment at least—the tears she had fought back earlier threatened to spill out. She glanced around, seeking Eric, he was her rock, she needed him, needed his arms around her, holding her tight.

As soon as she saw him she choked on a sob, and then he was there beside her, holding her against his chest, rocking her gently as he held his lips to her forehead. Lavender clung to him as she wept, never wanting to let go of him. Never wanting him to let go of her. In that moment, something changed inside her. Eric suddenly became a whole lot more important to her than he had ever been before.

~

9:18 A.M.

"I want to walk for a bit," Lavender said, lifting her head from where it had been hanging limply against his shoulder.

It was the first time she'd spoken since that dive off the side of the mountain that had shaved a decade off his life.

Night still couldn't get the image of her disappearing from view out of his head. The look on her face, the horror in her eyes as she realized she was plummeting to her death, believing that was the last time he was going to see her alive. Her scream as she fell through the air, and the deathly silence that followed her landing. He had lunged for her as she started slipping but had been too slow getting to her and he knew that if she had died, he would never have forgiven himself.

Or the men responsible for putting her life in danger.

Suicidal or not, if Lavender had died, his next move would have been sending Wolf's team on their way while he backtracked to find wherever the Taliban were holed up where he would have killed as many of them as he could before they overpowered him.

Avenging Lavender's death would have been his final action, but he wouldn't have regretted going out like that. He had long since come to terms with the idea that there was a very real possibility that one day he wouldn't return home from a mission, and nothing would have stopped him getting vengeance for the sweet woman who had flung her arms around him and clung to him while she cried.

"Honey, now that Wolf and the others are here, you don't need to walk on that leg anymore," he reminded her. They had been carrying her ever since he'd pulled her up the side of the cliff. She'd withdrawn, retreated inside herself, allowing them to pass her from man to man without protest, but when he wasn't the one carrying her he could feel her eyes on him.

The same way he found it difficult not to keep her in his line of sight when one of the other guys was carrying her.

The only thing forcing him to remain focused was the knowledge that if he failed, Lavender died.

"I know, but I just need to move by myself for a while, unless I'm going to be putting you guys in danger," she quickly added.

That her worry right now was the rest of them had his respect for her soaring. She'd just lived through most people's worst nightmare, and yet she was more worried about them than she was about herself.

"We'll be fine if you want to walk for a bit, right, Wolf?" he said to the other man, everyone had stopped walking when he had.

Wolf nodded, and the other guys spread out around them to keep watch while he carefully eased Lavender down and kept an arm around her waist while she got her balance. Her hands rested on his forearms, and he was struck by how small they looked. Lavender was around five-two, maybe five-three, a good foot shorter than he was. He knew she worked out because they sometimes went to the gym together, he knew she was well trained in self-defense and that she was a pretty good shot, but she was still small, and she provoked a strong protectiveness in him.

"You okay?" he asked as she tentatively took a step, wincing as her bad leg took weight. He probably shouldn't allow her to walk on it any longer, now that there was no need for her to, but she seemed to need to take a little control over herself and her situation, and he found he couldn't say no to her.

"Yeah, I'm okay." She turned around and shot him a smile, her eyes were twinkling, and despite the bumps and bruises on her face, not to mention the ones he couldn't see that were hidden by her clothes, she seemed to be in reasonable spirits. "Can I go behind a rock and … you know … go to the bathroom?"

"Sure, but don't wander far away," he told her. So far they hadn't seen any more of the extremists, but they were out there, and he knew they would be hunting them. They were working their way up over the mountain and down the other side to the exfil point. The helo wouldn't be coming until late tonight so they still had between twelve and eighteen hours to make their way through enemy territory before they made it to safety.

That was a lot of time for something to go wrong.

He watched as Lavender hobbled over to a large rock and ducked around it, and fought the urge to follow her and stand guard, but she deserved a little privacy while she did her business.

"So you and Lavender, huh?" Abe said as he came to stand beside him.

"Me and Lavender what?" he asked, turning to look at his friend.

"You're together, right?" Abe asked, looking confused now.

"Together, like a couple?" He and Lavender were friends, but he'd never thought of her beyond that. Yeah, he'd kill for her, yeah he'd die for her, yeah she brought out that same protectiveness that he felt for his little sister, but that was it.

"Yeah, a couple." Abe rolled his eyes. "Were you two trying to keep it quiet?"

Night shook his head. "We're not a couple. We're just friends."

"Yeah, friends," Abe said the word like he was making air quotes.

"No, really, we're just friends."

Abe narrowed his eyes as though trying to decide if he was telling the truth or not. "I have lots of female friends, and I don't look at any of them the way you look at Lavender."

"Whatever," he muttered. He didn't look at Lavender any differently than he did any of his other friends.

"Look, man, I get you're trying to keep it quiet because you wanted in on this mission to rescue your girl, but you're here, we're here, we'll get her home, you don't have to keep your relationship a secret."

"We don't have a relationship. We are just friends," he said firmly.

Abe shrugged. "If you say so. Word of advice?"

"I don't need advice, but sure, say what you want to say."

"She's just been through a horrific ordeal, be straight with her, support her, give her what she needs. And most importantly don't mess this up." Abe shot him a steady look before nodding his head once and walking off to check in with the rest of his team.

Night watched the man walk away, he knew about the mess Abe had caused in his then fairly new relationship with his now-wife, Alabama. He'd said something hurtful, something that had cut Alabama deeply, and he'd almost lost her because of it.

But that situation was completely different than his with Lavender.

He and Lavender weren't a couple, they were just friends, he'd never thought of her as anything else.

Lavender reappeared from around the side of the rock, Benny approached her, put a hand on her shoulder, and said something that made her laugh, and Night felt a flash of jealousy spark inside him. Lavender wasn't his, he'd just explained that to Abe—although he was pretty sure the other man didn't believe him—and yet the sight of another man, even if he was married, touching her had his blood boiling.

Which was stupid.

He was acting like some sort of possessive caveman.

Forcing himself to relax, he cracked his knuckles and saw Abe watching him with a bemused expression. Irritated to be caught out watching Lavender talk to Benny and that he was so obvious in his dislike of it, he glowered at Abe then stalked over to Wolf.

"We should get going, we still have a lot of ground to cover, and Lavender will need to rest again soon or she's going to crash," he said.

Wolf nodded, and everyone prepared to move out. Lavender immediately hurried over to his side, smiling up at him as she stopped next to him. Stupidly pleased that she had chosen to come and walk with him, it was like being the person the puppy chose to come and curl up with, he held out a hand to her.

"Come on, let's get you out of here," he said.

Lavender smiled and put her hand in his, curling her mittened fingers around his.

"You tell me when you need a break, when your leg has had enough. It's broken, Lavender, there's no need to be a hero. I'll get you out of here, okay?" It suddenly seemed vitally important that she know that he would do whatever it took to get her back home.

Carefully balancing on the tiptoes of her good leg, she reached up and kissed his cheek. "I never doubted it for a moment."

As they both started walking, him trying to take some of her weight, Night found himself warmed more thoroughly by her words and the kiss than he would have if he'd curled up in his bed in his place with a fire burning in the fireplace.

And he absolutely didn't imagine Lavender there with him, naked and tangled in his arms.

~

2:23 P.M.

"All right, honey, time for us to hunker down for a while."

The words slowly seeped into her mind, and she lifted her weary head from Eric's shoulder.

Lavender had been able to walk for quite a while because the guys had kept the pace fairly slow as they made their way up the side of the mountain. But when they'd started back down the other side, her bad leg had trembled with exhaustion, her mind had started to get hazy, making her stumble more regularly, her face ached, her chest burned, and she'd been ready to check out.

Eric had been there, ready and willing to carry her on his broad shoulders, and with his hard body beneath her, she'd felt safe enough to drift into a kind of half-sleep. Not awake, but not really out either, she'd just rested, tried to recoup some strength because she knew that at any second they could come under fire again and she would have to be ready to pull her weight.

Eric carried her into a quiet, dark cave and set her down on the hard ground. She immediately missed contact with him, but they were in the middle of a dangerous ordeal, and she could hardly cling to him and beg him to stay.

Instead, she took the water he offered and drank a little before sinking down against the cave's floor.

"Hold on, let's get you some more heat packs," Eric said. He'd taken the other ones from her hours ago, and while she hadn't really thought about it—exhaustion had pretty much wiped her brain into an empty slate—now that he mentioned it she realized she was shaking from the cold.

"I didn't even realize I was cold," she murmured through chattering teeth.

Eric smiled as he pulled off one of her mittens. "You were too tired, but you haven't been moving much because I've been carrying you and your body temperature has dropped. We need to get it back up because as soon as it gets dark we're going to be on the home stretch."

"Really?" she asked as he put the mitten back on her hand. She hadn't been paying much attention to the guys' plan, knowing they would tell her what she needed to know when and if she needed to know it. They were the experts, not her, and she was well and truly prepared to do anything they asked her to. She had hardly dared to hope that everything was continuing with the plan, she'd thought that when she was rescued that would be it, she would just go home, she hadn't expected to be dodging bullets, sleeping in caves, and falling off mountains, or the walking, *so* much walking.

"Really. We will get you out of here, Lavender, keep believing that. Even if you have to repeat it like a mantra in your head, don't ever forget it. We're not out of the woods yet, we won't be until we're on that helo heading home, so cling to those words." He pulled off her other mitten to tuck another heat back against her palm.

Lavender considered his words and the truth behind them. When she had been abducted a few years ago the only thing that had kept her going was her hope that someone would come, that she would be rescued. She wasn't one to discount the importance of keeping hope alive.

Eric unzipped her jacket and touched the back of his fingers to her neck. "Your skin is a little warmer under here," he said softly. His fingers lingered against her skin and she felt something zing between them. They were friends, she'd never looked at him lustfully, but lying here, gazing up at his ripped body all decked out in his BDUs he looked like a warrior.

Her warrior.

With his sweet nature, his eyes that glowed like silver orbs, his brown hair that all she could currently think about was running her fingers through as she drew his mouth down to hers ...

"Everything okay?" he asked, concern shining clearly from those pretty eyes of his.

She gave him a tired smile. "As long as you're here then everything is fine."

He tucked a couple more heat packs in under her sweater before zipping her back up, rearranging her scarf, and then letting his fingertips trail across her cheek. "Sleep now, we're watching over you."

"You need sleep too," she reminded him. She was pretty sure that while she had crashed last night in the cave, he had stayed awake to keep watch over her.

"The guys and I will take turns sleeping," he assured her. "Don't worry about us, sweetheart, we're old pros at this."

"I do worry," she said seriously. Then fighting off a yawn as she lost the fight to keep her eyes open, she mumbled, "Don't want anyone to die for me."

Lips feathered across her forehead and the last words she heard before she drifted off were, "I'd rather die than see you hurt."

Her sleep was dreamless.

Empty.

Deep.

And then the next she knew, she was being yanked out of it by the sound of gunshots and a hand roughly shaking her.

"Lavender, we need to move. Now," Benny said, already pulling her up.

"What is it? What's happening?" she asked, trying to shake off sleep quickly but finding it difficult. When she'd dozed off it had been light out, everything had been calm, and she'd felt safe enough to be able to rest. Now it was dark, and she could hear the wind howling and gunshots ripped through the night. She must have been asleep for hours. What had happened during that time to change their situation so dramatically?

"We're taking fire," Benny said shortly, taking her arm and dragging her along with him toward the entrance of the cave.

The weather had taken a turn for the worse, gone was the mild temperature and lightly cloudy sky, in its place was a biting wind and swirling snow. Lavender scanned the area, she could barely see a couple of yards in front of her, but she needed to know where Eric was.

"Where's Eric?" she asked when she couldn't see him.

"He's further down the mountain, scouting a safe route and making sure the Taliban aren't in front of us. For now you're with me, sweetheart. Sorry," Benny added, his chocolate brown eyes sympathetic. "I know you want your guy, but you're stuck with me until we get down to join him."

"He's not my guy," Lavender protested automatically, even though the safety she had felt when she lay down to sleep was gone. Replaced with an uncertainty that left her with that same feeling plummeting off the mountain had.

Benny kept hold of her as he guided her into a crouch and led her from the cave.

Part of her wanted to resist, stay hiding in here away from the snow and the bullets, but the other part knew that staying there was signing her own death warrant and that of the guys who wouldn't leave without her.

Taking a fortifying breath, she let Benny's steadying hand keep her on her feet as she moved as quickly after him as she could. They headed for a large rock and hunkered down behind it for a moment. Lavender hated that her broken leg was going to slow them down, without having to lug her around, the guys would already be down the mountain.

Vowing that she would not let her leg get anyone killed, she straightened when Benny pointed at the path he wanted her to take and clamped her teeth together against the pain.

She could do this.

She *would* do this.

Visibility was appalling, and if it wasn't for Benny's hand that never left her arm she knew she would have taken another disastrous tumble over the edge.

As it was, she kept stumbling every few steps, and she was sure Benny was tired of having to hold her up and support her weight as well as his own and the heavy pack that he carried.

All of a sudden they stopped, and Benny yanked her up against him, shoving her up so her back was against the side of the mountain and covering her with his own body.

"What?" she asked, panicked, struggling to suck in air to her heaving lungs and rub out the stitch in her side.

"Night says there are four guys between us and his position," he whispered against her ear. "They're heading our way."

"What do you want me to do?"

Benny gave her a proud smile, she could see it because his face was only inches in front of her own, and it reassured her a little to know that she was at least making the guys happy by being willing to do whatever they asked without complaint. "About twenty yards up ahead is another cave. All you have to do is run toward it as fast as you can and not stop until you're inside." His hand grasped her chin, making sure he had her full attention. "I mean it, Lavender, you don't stop for anything, you hear someone scream you keep running, me or one of the guys get shot, you keep running. You don't stop for anything," he repeated. "You get into that cave, and you hide yourself in the darkest corner you can find, these guys don't have night-vision goggles, so if you get far enough back they might not see you."

She was shaking badly, but she nodded her understanding. "What if ... if you guys ... what if no one comes?" she asked hesitantly. She didn't want to even give voice to the idea, but she had to know the plan in case the worst happened.

"You stay there, another team will come in to extract you."

Lavender nodded again.

"You go on three, okay? One, two, three."

On three Lavender took off as fast as she could. Gunfire erupted, she could feel the bullets whizzing past her, feel the spray of rock and dirt as bullets hit. Once she tripped and fell, landing hard on her hands and knees.

Pain was a constant, but she staggered back to her feet and kept running, determined to fulfill her promise to run to the cave and hide.

When she reached it, she dove inside and put her hands on the wall, using it to guide her to the furthest corner she could find, where she sank to the floor, dragged her knees to her chest, and curled into a ball as she waited to see if the guys survived.

8:27 P.M.

His heart jumped into his throat when Lavender fell.

Had she been shot?

Frantically, Night searched for signs of blood, but through the dark and the snow, and the fact that he was a further fifty feet down the mountain, perched on a rock under the cover of a scrubby bush meant it was hard for him to tell.

Then she moved.

Relief knocked the breath out of him.

She was alive.

He watched as she staggered to her feet and continued running toward the safety of the cave that would shelter her until they eliminated the threat. Her leg had to be killing her, but she didn't let it slow her down, and he was in awe of her strength and fortitude.

Movement caught his attention and he adjusted his position. It was one of the Taliban terrorists who had participated in Lavender's abduction and who had been stalking them through the mountains.

He stared down the sight of his rifle, made adjustments for the wind and the snow, and then pulled the trigger.

The last of the tangos dropped.

Night was up and scrambling carefully up the mountain immediately, he had to get to Lavender.

She'd slept like a rock for hours after they'd got her into the cave, through the brewing storm, through him and the guys planning out their next move, through their update from his team—the news of which he wasn't sharing with her until they got her somewhere safe—and through him leaving to go and scout out a safe way down the mountain and to the exfil point.

That was when everything had gone to Hell.

Stuck further down the mountain, it wasn't being alone that had him terrified, he could do his job just fine on his own, it was knowing that he couldn't be there for Lavender.

She'd be terrified, being woken up to find it storming and people shooting at them.

Again.

He really hated the sight of bullets flying in her direction.

He'd been forced to listen helplessly as Wolf's team provided cover for Benny to get Lavender out of the way of the action. He'd thought she was finally in the clear when he'd spotted four men between him and the others, right in the middle of the path that Benny would take.

Never in his life had he been so afraid as when Benny gave Lavender the instruction to run to safety while the two of them provided cover.

But she'd done it, she'd run, they'd wiped out the extremists hunting them, and now he had to get to her, hold her, reassure her, and then get her to the helicopter.

It should be flying in within the next couple of hours—weather permitting—but they still had to get down the opposite side of the mountain, and then would come the really difficult part, they would have to cross the plains to get to the helo. Away from the safety the rocks, and shrubs, and caves afforded.

Although he'd been about double the distance away from Lavender as Benny was, they reached the mouth of the cave at the same time. Benny nodded at him and took up position watching for threats as the rest of his team worked their way down to meet up with them.

Not wanting to startle Lavender and scare her more than she already was, Night slowly entered the cave. Scanning the large area, he spotted her right at the back, she was curled in on herself, legs drawn up to her chest, her face buried against her knees, and she didn't give any indication that she knew he was there.

Since there could be more terrorists out there, he crept quietly to her then moved in a smooth motion, clamping one hand over her mouth as he pulled her up and into his arms.

"It's only me," he whispered into her ear as she startled and began to struggle.

At his words, she sagged in his hold, and when he removed his hand she wriggled in his grip until she was facing him and threw her arms around his neck. She was shuddering in his arms, and he tightened his hold, stroking his hand down her long red hair.

"It's okay, sweetheart, we're almost there, the finish line is in sight."

"Are you okay? Are you hurt? I was so scared that they might shoot you," she said, hands on his biceps as she leaned back and attempted to look at him in the dark.

"You were worried about me?" Night knew that Lavender had guilt issues that she felt stemmed from her lack of care and consideration for the people in her life, mainly her sister, but from where he was standing, she cared way more about others than herself.

"Yes, and you didn't answer. Are you hurt?"

"No, babe, I'm fine. What about you, you fell. Did you hurt yourself?" Not bothering to wait for her to answer, he started running his hands over her body. She winced when he probed her ribs, but that was probably from her earlier tumble, and other than that the only time she cried out was when he touched her hands.

"I landed on them hard when I tripped."

"Broken?" he asked, watching her face to check the truthfulness of her answer.

"No, just sore, at least I had the mittens on or they would have been all scraped up."

Deciding she was telling him the truth, Night nodded then hooked an arm around her waist and led her to the mouth of the cave. "From now on, we'll be keeping on the move. We have a couple of miles to go to get down to the bottom of the mountain, then after that we need to get across an open area to the helicopter. We can't afford to have you walking on your own, sorry, honey. You've done amazing so far, done everything we've asked without complaint, but you're injured, tired, and we have a dangerous hike ahead of us, especially now with the changes in the weather."

"I feel bad you guys have to carry me, but I won't argue with you, Eric. I trust you, and I trust Wolf and his team to get me home safely."

"We won't fail you." Night leaned down and kissed her forehead before grabbing hold of her wrist and draping her over his shoulders. "We're good to go," he told the team as he stepped out into the cold night. He wished he had something more than the emergency blanket from his pack to use to protect Lavender from the elements, but until they got to the helo they were all stuck out in the storm.

"We swap out carrying Lavender every fifteen minutes," Wolf said, "terrorists are swarming all over the mountain, and with the storm and low visibility it's not going to be an easy hike down."

With that, they all started walking. Night did his best to make sure he kept things as smooth as he could for Lavender. He walked cautiously, knowing that one slip and they would both take a tumble they might not survive.

The hike down the mountain was thankfully uneventful, and about two hours later they tucked themselves into a hiding spot behind a few rocks to wait for the helo's arrival. Night set Lavender gently down, propping her up against his knee. Her eyes were half-closed, and she appeared dazed and half asleep.

"Lavender, you need to drink some water for me," he said, unscrewing the cap from his canteen and holding it to her lips.

"Eric?" she asked sleepily.

"Yeah, honey, drink for me."

She obediently sipped a few mouthfuls of water. "C-cold," she whispered.

"I know, hon." He briskly rubbed her arms, she needed proper rest, fluids, and to be out of the snow. Since she hadn't been walking on her own, her body temperature had dropped again and he was worried about hypothermia. Sitting down, he dragged her onto his lap and closed his arms around her, trying to cover as much of her body as he could to try to impart some of his body heat to her.

"How is she?" Cookie asked, crouching beside them.

"Hypothermic, dehydrated, in need of morphine and proper rest," he replied.

"She'll get it soon, ETA is ten minutes."

"You hear that, Lavender?" he asked.

"Yeah, ten minutes till we can get out of here," she murmured, snuggling closer.

"You stay with me till them, okay?" he ordered.

"Mmhmm," she said.

"I mean it, Lavender. You don't check out when we're this close, okay?"

She tilted her head up and brushed her lips against his jaw. "I won't."

Night sat and clutched her to his chest as they waited out the last ten minutes, which seemed to pass in extreme slow motion, but eventually he heard the sound he had been praying for.

"Time to go, sweetheart," he said, standing with her in his arms and then setting her on her feet.

Just as he was about to prep Lavender to move, gunshots echoed through the mountains.

Really?

They were this close and yet they still weren't safe.

Frustrated, he shoved Lavender behind him as the helicopter approached. "You are going to make a run for it. As soon as the helo touches down you go for it, you don't stop for anything, you don't look back, you just run like the wind. Got it?"

"G-got it," Lavender said, fear evident in her voice and her stiff posture.

"The guys and I will provide cover, the guys in the helo will too, so all you have to focus on is yourself."

"I don't want you to get hurt," she said, clinging to him now.

"I won't," he assured her, knowing that he would rather die and make sure she survived, but not game to tell her that when he needed her to focus.

While Wolf's team returned fire at the terrorists shooting at them, Night kept his attention on the approaching helo. When it was time, he gave Lavender a small shove.

"Go," he ordered.

She hesitated, clearly worried about whether he was going to be following her, and he grabbed her arm, dragged her against him, and kissed her hard on the mouth, then he gave her another shove in the direction of the helo.

"Go," he said again.

This time, with one last look, she turned and ran.

Focusing his attention on the enemy, Night started shooting. It was like a never-ending parade, no matter how many of them they managed to hit more came up to take their place.

"Got her," a voice in his ear said, and Night let out a relieved breath.

Lavender was safe.

Now it was their turn.

He, Abe, and Cookie turned and ran, trusting the rest of the team and the guys on the helo to protect their backs as they crossed the open expanse between them and safety. When they reached the helo they dropped to their knees and provided cover for the rest of the team as they came running in hot.

This was his mission, and he was the last one to climb on board. As soon as he did, Lavender launched herself at him, clinging to him as she wept, and he dragged her in close, buried his face against her neck, and clung to her every bit as tightly as she was clinging to him.

CHAPTER 3

December 23<sup>rd</sup>
8:40 A.M.

Never again would Lavender take for granted the simple pleasures of life like being warm, dry, full, and out of pain.

She was in the small bathroom attached to her room, but she'd spent most of the last several hours tucked into her hospital bed. Doctors had checked her out, they'd given her painkillers, x-rayed her leg to determine that while it was broken, it wasn't too bad, and had fitted her with a moon boot. They'd given her an IV with fluids and something to eat, covered her with warm blankets, and once she was comfortable she'd immediately dropped off to sleep.

Lavender had thought that as soon as she had a pillow under her head, she would be out and stay that way for a long time, but not long after she'd fallen asleep the nightmares had come for her.

She wasn't a stranger to nightmares, she'd had them after

her last ordeal where she had been abducted by a madman, kept in a cage, then on a boat, she'd been raped and beaten, and adjusting to life after she and her twin sister were rescued was hard.

So hard she had fled to the other side of the country and started thinking about what she could do to regain her self-respect.

Unfortunately, her solution to making up for a lifetime of thinking only about herself and her own needs had ended in an unmitigated disaster.

But she was safe now, and she knew in time the nightmares would fade. She'd dozed off and on, every time she opened her eyes she wanted to see Eric, but so far she hadn't seen him since she'd gone to sleep that first time. He'd stayed with her through treatment in the emergency room, and while she got settled into a room, but then he'd disappeared and she wanted to know why but hadn't yet asked.

She hadn't been alone, each time she had tossed and turned and woken in a panic, believing she was back in that well, or dodging bullets, one of the other SEALs had been in the room with her. Their presence made her feel safe, but it didn't provide the same comfort that having Eric there would.

Lavender ran a comb through her long, unruly red curls and examined herself in the mirror. There was a huge black and blue bruise on her right cheek. The doctors had been concerned she'd broken a bone, but the x-rays showed just bruising. There were bruises all along her right side as well from landing on that rock when she had fallen, she'd cracked two ribs, but at least she was alive.

Alive.

She had to keep repeating that to herself because she had been so sure she wasn't going to make it.

Ignoring the dark circles under her eyes and the tight

lines around her mouth, she knew they were just from stress, the outward sign of her inner turmoil, but they would fade like the bruises.

Not completely though.

Never completely.

There would be scars that would last as long as she lived.

"How was the shower?" Dude asked as she stepped back into the room. He was lounging on a chair by the window but stood and walked over to her, plucking her up and carrying her the rest of the distance to the bed where he set her down and tucked her in with surprising gentleness.

"It was magic," she said as she settled back against the pillow.

"I'm glad, you deserve it."

"What about you guys? Did you get to shower and eat and sleep?"

Dude shrugged as he resumed his spot in the chair where he could watch over her. "We're all fine. Priority right now is getting you back home."

Lavender took that to mean that the guys had been too busy debriefing and organizing transport back to the US to worry about things like food and sleep like she—a mere mortal—had needed.

She studied him closely, trying to read in his too serene expression what was really going on. All of a sudden a horrible thought occurred to her. Had Eric gone back out there to help his team get the rest of the hostages out? Was he still in danger?

"What's wrong, sweetheart?" Dude asked, leaning forward in his chair to prop his elbows on his knees.

"Where's Eric?" She straightened up and gave him her best glower. "And don't lie to me, Dude, don't pacify me, don't patronize me, don't pat me on the head, and give me some line that you guys worked out so I won't worry.

Because I am worrying. Where is he? Is he okay? Did he go back out there?" Did ..."

"Woah, sweetheart, calm down." Dude moved so he was perched on the edge of her bed. "Night is here in the hospital."

Relief had her sagging back, but then disappointment hit hard. Now that he knew she was safe he had obviously lost interest in her.

"Hey, now, don't go getting all ... female," Dude said.

"All female?"

"Emotional, reading more into something than there is, worrying over something that isn't happening. Night wants to be the one to tell you, so relax, close those pretty eyes of yours, get some more sleep, because we're going to be moving out at lunchtime, and you haven't gotten enough rest yet."

Only marginally mollified, Lavender did lay down and close her eyes. Dude tucked the blanket around her again then she heard him drop down into the chair.

The next thing she knew, hushed voices woke her.

"Hey, honey, how you doing?" Eric pasted on a smile when he saw her awake and came over to kiss her cheek. He wasn't fooling her though, she could see in his eyes that something was wrong.

"I'm okay. What's wrong?" She struggled to drag her exhausted body into a sitting position, and winced as the movement aggravated her cracked ribs. Eric immediately slipped an arm around her shoulders, taking her weight while he piled up the pillows before easing her to rest against them. She met his gaze squarely when she knew he would have looked away and brushed off her question.

"You get right to the point, don't you?" He tenderly brushed a lock of hair off her cheek, his fingers stroked across her cheek before dropping to his side.

The door opened, and she saw Dude sneak out before she returned her gaze to Eric's, silently waiting for him to tell her what was going on.

Finally he sighed, then sat on the bed beside her and took her hands. "I can't give you details because it's classified, but extracting the other aid workers didn't go to plan. Our source was compromised, and unfortunately, the other three aid workers taken with you were all killed, and a couple of my team were injured."

Lavender gasped, tears blurred her vision and the world seemed to tilt beneath her.

Dead.

The others were gone.

And some of Eric's team had been hurt.

"Who?" she asked, voice tight with emotion.

"Spider was shot, just a flesh wound," Eric added quickly when he saw the look of horror on her face. "And Chaos has a concussion."

For a moment it felt like the world was closing in on her. Teddy, a sixty-year-old pastor, and Helen, his fifty-five-year-old wife, were dead. The couple had taken her under their wing, looked out for her, been more like a mother and father to her over the four months she had known them than her own parents had been. And Jan Watkins, a forty-eight-year-old who had dedicated decades of her life to helping those in need, had been so much fun, she'd eased the fear that Lavender had felt being alone in an unknown and dangerous country.

Now they were gone.

Murdered.

And she couldn't help but think that it would have been better if it was her.

They had all given their lives to helping others, they were selfless people, while she had been selfish and self-centered her whole life. She'd signed up to the aid organization to try to assuage her guilt and make herself feel better, but that had majorly backfired.

And her friends, Chaos and Spider were hurt. How was she going to look Abigail in the eye again knowing that her husband had been injured trying to rescue her?

"None of this is your fault, honey," Eric said, dragging her into his arms. "This is our job, we've all been hurt before, and we'll all be hurt again. None of the injuries are serious, everyone will be discharged at the same time as you, and we'll all be flying out together so you'll be able to see for yourself. And the other aid workers are dead because of the Taliban, that is nothing to do with you, it's not your fault. Are you hearing me? None of this is your fault."

Everything hit her all in one go, the abduction, the pain, the fear, the bullets, the deaths, the injuries, and a sob came bursting out. Then she buried her face against Eric's chest and sobbed as he held her tightly, rubbed her back, and whispered a string of nonsense in her ear.

She cried until exhaustion hit, and she cried herself to sleep.

# CHAPTER 4

December 24<sup>th</sup>
5:13 P.M.

Lavender yawned in the passenger seat of his car as Night drove her home. It had been a long twenty-four hours on top of an even longer couple of weeks for her, and she would need time to rest and recover.

Being debriefed and made to go over and over everything that she had lived through couldn't have been easy, and ever since she'd come out of the interview room she'd been pale and withdrawn. She'd clung to him at the hospital, needing reassurance, but now she seemed to have shut down. He'd waited for her, there was no one waiting for him at home, and he wasn't leaving Lavender to take a cab home, not after everything she had been through, so he'd hung around after the rest of his team had headed off.

Besides Spider who was heading home to his pregnant wife, no doubt to spend the rest of the day assuring her that his bullet wound was nothing more than a flesh wound and wasn't anything she should worry about, the rest of them would be heading home alone. Spider was the only one married, Fox had loved and lost—twice—and while there was a time when he himself had gone home to a woman after a mission, he had never been in love.

Which was kind of depressing.

He was thirty-one years old and yet he had never fallen in love. Part of that was because of one woman, a woman he had let down in the worst possible way, and his reluctance to go down the same path again, and partly because he had just never met a woman who got him.

There were plenty of women who wanted sex from him, not really from *him* but because he was a SEAL, but none of those women really cared about him or even wanted to know him. He wanted what his best friend and his little sister had, and as ashamed as he was that he had stood in their way, he was relieved that all of that was behind them. He loved how happy they were together, how Abby's eyes lit up when she saw Spider, how Spider couldn't wait to get home from a mission to see his woman, but he was … jealous.

Night hated admitting it because Spider and Abby had both been through so much and they deserved all the happiness in the world, but he wanted that.

Shaking off melancholy and the actions from his past he wished he possessed the ability to change, Night focused instead on the small woman curled against the window.

Reaching over, he put his hand on her thigh. "You doing okay, honey?"

Lavender shrugged. "Just tired."

"You want to stop off, grab some take out on the way to your place?"

"Not hungry."

"You need to eat, Lavender, your body needs the calories."

Another shrug and she hadn't turned from what he was sure was a sightless stare out the window. He wasn't sure what to do or say to pull her out of the fog she seemed stuck in. She'd held it together through flying bullets and snow-storms and falling off a cliff, but now it seemed like she had reached her limit.

It was understandable, he certainly didn't hold it against her, everyone had a limit, and he knew there had been times when he felt like he had reached his only to have to dig deep and find the strength to keep going.

His team had always had his back, and knowing that had provided him the strength he sought. Lavender didn't have a big support system, her closest friend was probably Abigail, but she was no doubt preoccupied with Spider and his injury, and Lavender wouldn't encroach on their time together, she'd rather sit alone than get in anyone's way.

Only he wasn't going to leave her sitting alone.

He pulled into a parking spot outside her apartment building. Lavender had intended to spend twelve months in Afghanistan, so he doubted she had any food in her place. He'd walk her up and then go and pick up a few necessities— and a few luxuries—at the grocery store for her, and then he'd try to get her talking, find out what she needed from him.

Because despite what she thought, she wasn't alone. She had him, she had Abigail and Spider, she had the rest of the team, they were all here, they all had her back, and they would all help her through this.

"Hey, hon, we're here," he told her when she didn't seem to realize they'd reached her building.

"Oh," she said in a small voice. "Thanks for the ride." She unclicked her seatbelt, opened her door, got out, and was hobbling toward the building's front door before he could say anything else.

Night was out of the car and scooping her up into his arms before she reached the door. "Honey, if you're under the impression that you're going up there alone, that I'm just dropping you off and turning around and leaving you here, then you are badly mistaken."

Her forehead furrowed. "You're coming up with me?"

"Yep, and I'm staying for as long as you need me."

"Really?" She sounded confused. "Don't you want to go home to your place, see your sister, do whatever it is you usually do when you get back from a mission?"

"This wasn't just a mission, Lavender, you have to know that. My place is just an apartment, it's nothing fancy and I'm not all that eager to go see it. My sister has her hands full with Spider, believe me," he said and made a face, he might be supportive of his sister and best friend being a couple but the idea of them doing … stuff made him uncomfortable. "And all I usually do after a mission is kick back, eat spaghetti, or fire up the BBQ, and chill, I can chill just as well at your place as I can at mine." It was true, he was in his thirties now, no longer obsessed with heading straight to a bar to drink and pick up women when he got home. He was ready for more out of life.

"Are you sure?" Lavender asked, her gray eyes studying him like she suspected he was merely pitying her.

"Positive."

She studied him a moment longer before relaxing in his arms. Was that what she had been afraid of? That she had to come home alone and face the horrors she'd endured without anyone there to catch her when the inevitable fallout hit her?

"I can walk you know," she said, making a half-hearted attempt to get him to set her down.

"Oh, honey, I know you can, you did amazing out there, you know that?"

Lavender blushed but looked pleased with his compliment, and now that they had established he was coming up with her he got them into the building and up to her apartment. He'd been there several times before so he knew where he was going, and when he opened her front door—Lavender's things, including purse, passport, keys etc had all been given to them by the aid organization and had been waiting for her when she returned to the country—he couldn't help but smile.

The apartment was one big living area with a bedroom—with its own bathroom—on either side of the main space. Lavender loved the color lavender, her walls were painted in the shade, and there were throw pillows on her white couch of the same shade. Lavender colored curtains hung at her windows, and even though she had been out of the country for five months there was still the faint fragrance of the flowers she was named after. It was a pretty, feminine apartment, and it suited Lavender's personality perfectly.

Setting her down on her feet, while she limped over to throw the curtains open to get the last of the evening light, Night went to the kitchen to see whether she had anything he could use to cook them both dinner. He was spending the night with her in her spare bedroom, then tomorrow they could talk properly when Lavender wasn't exhausted and figure out what she needed going forward, but for tonight he was all hers.

Finding a box of pasta in her pantry, Night was turning around to ask her if that was okay for dinner but found her standing right behind him. She had a funny look on her face, and when he opened his mouth to ask if she was okay before he could get a word out, she had curled her arms around his neck and was kissing him.

Her sweet mouth tasted like sugar, and almost immediately he was addicted. His arms moved around her waist, drawing her closer, and he kissed her back.

It wasn't until she moaned against his lips that he started thinking with the right head.

What was he doing?

Kissing Lavender had mistake written all over it.

She was vulnerable, and the last time he had taken advantage of a vulnerable woman he had lived to regret it.

That wasn't happening this time.

Breathing hard, he gently grasped her wrists and unhooked them from around his neck then looked down into her lust-filled gray eyes as he took a step back.

Confusion warred with hurt in her face, along with a healthy dose of need, and Night knew then and there that he was a goner.

~

6:09 P.M.

"What are we doing, sweetheart?"

The words cleared the desire-filled haze that had descended on her when she turned from the window to see Eric standing in her kitchen, looking sexier than any man should in worn jeans and a black shirt with the sleeves rolled up to his elbows.

"I can tell you what we're not doing, we're not kissing," she said, her breathing heavy from the kiss that had been the best one of her life. She'd kissed plenty of guys, slept with plenty too. Her twin sister had always joked that Lavender had a guy in every city she had ever lived in and Marigold wasn't wrong, but this felt different.

It was different.

Because this was Eric.

A man who had sat and talked with her for hours, sharing his deepest, darkest secrets with her and listening to hers in return. A man who had risked his life to save hers. A man who instead of heading home after a mission, had hung around while she'd been debriefed just so he could take her home. A man who hadn't even stopped there but had offered to stay with her so she wouldn't have to be alone.

Eric smiled down at her, his silvery gray eyes so warm it made her own eyes burn with tears. He released his hold on her wrists and smoothed a lock of hair that had fallen out of her ponytail off her cheek. "We're friends, Lavender, we shouldn't be kissing."

"Are you saying you didn't like it?" she demanded, perhaps a hair too shrilly, but the idea that he hadn't felt that same pull she had when their lips touched hurt.

"No, I'm not saying I didn't like it, I'm saying that this is the only way I should kiss you." He leaned down and touched his lips to her forehead. "Or like this." His lips moved to her cheek.

"Or like this," she said breathily, turning her face so his lips touched the corner of her mouth.

"Lavender, you've just been through Hell, I don't want to take advantage."

Her heart swelled, she knew that Eric still felt guilty for what he felt was taking advantage of a woman in the past, and she loved that he cared more about her and her feelings and how she would look at him afterward than he did about his own needs. And she could feel those needs pressed against her belly. "I'm the one doing the asking," she reminded him.

"But you're vulnerable right now, and you think that sex

is going to take away all the pain and terror that you lived through, but it won't, honey, it'll just be a temporary fix."

Lavender shook her head. "It's not about just sex. If that was all I was after I could go down to the bar, pick up some random guy." The darkening of Eric's gaze didn't go unnoticed, and she realized he didn't like the idea of another man touching her. "This is about me, Eric, I want to celebrate life, freedom, the future. Twice now I've survived what was supposed to kill me, I want to feel a connection to another person. I want *you*, Eric. I-I need you."

He was wavering, she could tell by the way he looked at her, the way his thumb was absently tracing across the sensitive skin of the wrist he still held.

Silence dragged out between them, and just when she was sure he was going to turn her down—something which hurt more than it should considering they were friends and not lovers—he slipped an arm beneath her bottom, lifting her feet off the floor. With the moon boot on her broken leg, it was too hard to wrap her legs around Eric's waist, but the awkwardness was quickly forgotten when his mouth closed over hers, and he was kissing her with the same flaming need that she felt.

Eric carried her through to her bedroom and laid her down on her king-size antique canopy bed with ruffly lavender net curtains tied to the four posts, but when she went to grab the hem of his t-shirt to pull it over his head, he grasped her hands and stopped her.

"Uh-uh, if we're doing this then we're doing it properly. You need me, baby, then you're going to get the royal treatment," he said, leaning down to feather a trail of kisses down her neck.

She moaned at the feel of his lips on her skin, but it was a delighted moan, she loved foreplay, loved spending time with her partner, exploring one another's bodies, making each other feel good, it always made the sex—when they finally got around to it—so much better.

Not wanting to just sit back, Lavender slipped her hands under Eric's shirt and let her fingertips trail across his abs. She'd seen him topless before, but there was a difference between seeing his eight pack and feeling it.

"You're so sexy," she murmured, shivering as Eric began to play with her nipples through her sweater. She'd always been attracted to Eric, any woman with eyes would be, but she'd never felt this before. This deep-seated need to touch him, to have him touch her.

"You're pretty hot yourself," he said, and then he was shoving her sweater up so that he bared her breasts.

Whatever she was going to say in response died in her throat as his mouth closed over one of her nipples making her arch off the bed, silently begging him for more. He kissed, licked, nipped, and suckled first one breast and then the other until her entire body buzzed with pleasure.

Never in her life had she been so close to coming just from a guy playing with her breasts.

"I want to touch you," she said, her hands fumbling with his zipper.

"No way, honey, this is all for you." Eric grabbed her wrists with one of his hands and stretched them up above her head, holding them in place while he kissed and licked his way down her stomach, pausing when he got to the waistband of her sweatpants. "You smell so sweet, just like your name," he murmured as his free hand pushed her pants and panties down. "Keep your hands up there," he warned as he carefully removed her moon boot before tossing aside her pants.

She almost exploded when his mouth closed over her needy little bud, and her hands came to curl into Eric's hair of their own volition.

"What did I say?" he asked, stopping his delicious assault on her throbbing center to grab her hands and put them back above her head. "You keep them there or I'll make this take all night."

"You wouldn't."

"Oh, yeah, I would." His eyes glittered with amusement, and she knew without a doubt that he would indeed tease her all night before he let her come.

Forcing her hands to stay where they were, she focused on the sensations Eric was painting on her body. His fingertips stroked her inner thigh, getting closer and closer to her entrance as his mouth continued to work its magic.

When he finally slipped a finger inside her hot center, she very nearly came apart on the spot. The combination of his mouth and his fingers stroking deep inside her had her body trembling, her eyes falling closed, as she squirmed and moaned, and then he curled his fingers around so they touched that hidden spot inside her and her brain short-circuited as she came in an explosion of ecstasy that stole her breath and her ability to think.

By the time she was capable of cognizant thought again, Eric had stripped off, found the box of condoms she kept in her bathroom cabinet, and was about to slide one on.

"Let me," she said, reaching out to take it.

With a grin, he handed it over and then sucked in a breath as she ran a finger down his hard length. He was so big, and she was already nearly drooling thinking about how it would feel to have him buried deep inside her.

As slowly as she could, she inched the condom over his erection and then pushed on his shoulders so he lay down beside her. Straddling him, she positioned herself above him and took just the tip of him inside her.

"Honey, you take too long and I'm not going to be responsible for my actions," he said with a grimace.

"You got to take your time," she shot back and lowered herself down another inch.

With a wink, Eric reached out and took one of her breasts in his hand, rolling her nipple between his nimble fingers, and Lavender moaned her pleasure and sank down, taking another inch of his impressive length inside her.

"You feel so good, so hot, so tight," he murmured as he played with her nipple and then kneaded her breast.

"You feel pretty good too," she said, slowly sinking another inch. She began to rock her hips, enjoying the feel of a man inside her. It had been a long time since she'd had sex, not since before her abduction four years ago. As part of her whole re-evaluate her life and make changes plan, she had given up sex with guys she didn't care about. She wanted to save herself for a man she might actually have a future with.

Could Eric actually be that man?

She'd never thought of him as anything but a friend before, but now …

A moan was dragged from her lips as Eric's hands curled around her hips and he pulled her down until he was buried deep inside her. He flipped them over until she was on her back and then he began to thrust, slowly at first and then faster and harder as his fingers played her sensitive little bud like a fiddle, and moments later a second climax came rushing to claim her.

Eric found his own release a moment later, and as he continued to move, dragging out every last drop of pleasure that he could for both of them, she felt a special sort of warmth flush through her.

She felt special, she felt sexy, she felt cared about, and Eric had made her feel all of those things.

"Thank you," she whispered, caressing his cheek.

"No need to thank me, babe," he said and kissed her on the mouth.

Then he pulled out of her, disposed of the condom, and returned with a warm cloth and proceeded to clean her up before he pulled the blankets out from underneath them, pulled her sweater over her head, and let it join the rest of their clothes on the floor, then lay down with her in his arms and tucked them in.

"Sleep now, honey," he said, spooning her from behind. "Merry Christmas, Lavender."

With everything that had happened these last couple of weeks, she'd lost track of the date, but he was right, it was Christmas Eve. There wasn't a gift she could be given that was better than the one she had been given this year. She was alive, and Eric had just given her the best sex of her life. Content, she closed her eyes, snuggled into Eric's hold, and let herself sleep.

# CHAPTER 5

December 25<sup>th</sup>
8:34 A.M.

She hadn't stirred since she'd fallen asleep in his arms after mind-blowing sex.

Night had dozed off and on throughout the night, spending way more time watching her sleep than he probably should have considering what they had done last night was a one-time thing.

Lavender was sweet and beautiful, but she was dealing with some insanely heavy stuff, and despite the fact that sex had been her idea, he was having some trouble believing he hadn't taken advantage of her. It wasn't why he had waited for her or driven her home and intended to stay in her spare room, he'd just wanted to be here for her, hadn't wanted her to be alone, and maybe …

Maybe he hadn't wanted to go home alone either.

This mission had been different than any others because Lavender was at the heart of it, and he had needed the reassurance of having her just down the hall where he could check on her when he needed to.

The problem now was where did they go from here?

His plan had been to stay with Lavender for as long as she felt like she needed the support, had that been just for the night or until his team was sent back out, but now he felt awkward here. He didn't want to ruin his friendship with Lavender, he didn't want to lead her on, and yet he didn't want to walk away.

He wasn't sure what he was feeling, but something had shifted between them when their bodies had joined together. Part of him had wanted to get out of the bed and as far away from her as possible before he found a way to mess things up, and the other part couldn't tear himself from her side.

The doorbell rang, and Lavender startled, bolting upright, a scream falling from her lips as she looked around to find the source of the noise.

Not sure that she was fully awake yet, Night sat and carefully grasped her shoulders. "It's okay, honey, it's just the door," he said, keeping his tone soothing.

She turned wide eyes on him then he saw her visibly relax. "Eric."

"The one and only." He gave her a smile to help reassure her.

Then her brow furrowed and she looked over his shoulder toward the door. "Who would be ringing my doorbell on Christmas morning?"

"My guess is that my sister and Spider decided to come over so you weren't alone."

"Oh, that's so sweet." She looked down at her naked body. "I guess I better go get dressed and let them in."

"Grab a shower and take your time, I'll let them in," he said, kissing her forehead before releasing her and climbing out of bed.

"Thanks, Eric, tell them I won't be long."

While Lavender hobbled into the bathroom, Night threw on the same jeans and shirt he'd worn the day before, and then hurried through the living room to the door. The buzzer went again just as he reached the panel and he spied his sister and best friend standing with their arms wrapped around each other at the building's front door. He pressed the button that would unlock the front door and then watched as Spider guided Abigail inside, those two always had their hands on each other, and he had to admit it creeped him out in a no man should touch his baby sister kind of way.

As he waited, he looked around Lavender's apartment. Since she hadn't been planning on being home for Christmas there was no tree, no decorations, no stack of gifts, or turkey roasting in the oven, and he wondered how he was going to make today special for her. His sister no doubt had something up her sleeve for a present for Lavender, and he'd be surprised if they'd come empty-handed. Abigail was five months pregnant and craving pretty much every food on the planet, so he was sure she had something in mind for a Christmas lunch.

"Lavender, I was so …" Abigail trailed off as she burst into the apartment to see him standing there instead of her friend. Her eyes—one silvery gray the other golden brown—narrowed like there was some nefarious reason for his presence. "What are you doing here?"

"Happy to see you too, sis," he said with a grin, walking over and kissing her cheek. "Merry Christmas. Hey, Spider, how's the leg?"

Abigail's eyes grew watery as she wrapped an arm around her husband's waist and rested her cheek against his chest, and Night felt bad for trying to divert attention away from him and his reason for being here by asking about Spider's injury.

"It's fine, man," Spider replied, then to Abby who looked ready to cry, "really, babe, it's okay, you know this, you spent an hour checking it out last night."

"Not an hour." She sniffed.

"Pregnancy hormones," Spider mouthed to him over Abigail's head.

"You better not have just told my brother what I think you just told him," Abigail warned.

Night laughed, the two of them were pretty cute even when they bickered. "You know it takes more than a bullet grazing our legs to take down SEALs. Your guy is fine, stop fussing over him," he said to his sister.

Turning back to face him, Abigail repeated her earlier question, "What are you doing here?"

"I didn't want Lavender to come home alone after everything she went through," he said. It wasn't really a lie, it *was* why he had come. It had just turned into something different. Something personal, between him and Lavender, and they hadn't even had a chance to talk about it yet so he certainly wasn't going to go blabbing to the lovebirds.

"Oh, you stayed here last night, that's so sweet," Abby softened, her suspicions gone, and walked over to wrap her arms around him, hugging him tightly.

"Same way we didn't want you alone after what you went through." He hugged her back, glad that they had found a way to move forward and find a closeness they hadn't shared when they were kids.

"You guys just look big and tough, but inside you're such

teddy bears," she said affectionately, half turning to hold out a hand to her husband.

"Sweetheart, I love you, but I am not hugging your brother," Spider told her with a grin, making them all laugh.

"What are you guys laughing about?" Lavender asked as she came to join them. The hot shower in her bathroom had done her a world of good. She had some color back, and she'd obviously applied makeup because the bruising on her cheek was barely visible. She was wearing a simple pair of black jeans paired with a gray sweater, and he had never seen her look so beautiful.

It was her strength.

It shone through in the fact that her hair was piled into some fancy-looking bun thing on top of her head, her simple makeup, the moon boot on her broken leg, the fire in her eyes that said she might be battered, but she wasn't broken.

Lavender was a warrior.

A survivor.

Night knew about her previous experience with a deranged killer and how she had worked hard to put the pieces of her life back together and knew that she would do it again.

"Nothing important," Abigail said, rushing over to her friend. "Let me look at you. You look tired but so beautiful. I want you to know that you're not alone, Ryder and I are here for you whatever you need."

Lavender returned Abigail's hug. "I appreciate that, I really do, especially knowing you went through something kind of similar. Maybe it will help to talk about it, if you don't mind of course."

Abigail waved that off. "Course I don't mind. And take it from someone who learned the hard way, don't try to bottle that stuff up, it has a way of exploding out when you least expect it. Most important thing to remember is that you're not alone."

"Oh, I know I'm not," Lavender said, smiling over at him. She crossed over to him, her arm out, and he knew that she was going to thank him, going to tell the others how he'd helped her not feel alone last night, but he wasn't ready for Abigail and Spider to know what he'd done.

Quickly, he stepped away from her, ignoring the look of confusion on her face, as he hurried to the kitchen to put the kettle on. "I told Spider and Abby how I stayed here so you wouldn't be alone last night," he said, preempting whatever she might have said.

She stopped, her arms hanging limply by her sides, hurt mixed with the confusion now as she obviously wondered why he was acting so weirdly. "Yeah, it was nice of Eric to think of me."

It wasn't her words so much as her tone that cut through him, made him realize what a jerk he was being, brushing her off as though what happened between them meant nothing.

But the problem was it had meant *too* much.

The last time he'd taken advantage of a vulnerable woman he'd wound up relieved that his unborn baby had died, and that was a time in his life he wasn't ready to revisit.

Or recreate.

Lavender turned to Spider and hobbled over to him, throwing her arms around him. "How's your leg? I'm so sorry that you got hurt rescuing me. I don't know how I can ever thank you."

Spider hugged her back. "It's fine, and you thanked me already, several times."

"I'm glad we all got home in time for Christmas," Lavender said.

"Best Christmas present I ever got when Ryder walked

through the door on Christmas Eve," Abigail agreed. "We didn't know Eric was here, and we didn't want you to be alone on Christmas, so Ryder and I come bearing gifts and a whole Christmas dinner. It's in the car, I wanted to carry it in but Ryder was worried about me walking on the wet ground in my condition," Abigail said with an eye roll. "He thinks pregnant is the same thing as helpless."

"Hey, nothing is more important than my girls, or my girl and my little guy." Spider stepped up behind Abigail, put his arms around her, and drew her back to rest against his chest, his hands spanning her swollen stomach. The expression on his face was pure unadulterated love and adoration, the same expression mirrored on Abigail's face as she tilted it up to kiss Spider's jaw.

Night watched them with an ache in his chest. So many things he'd do differently if only it was possible, so many wrongs he would right, starting with an apology to the mother of his dead child.

Lavender was watching them with a funny expression on her face, and he couldn't help wonder if it was because of what they had shared last night, and what her hopes had been for this morning.

Had he dashed them?

Had she wanted more?

Or was she relieved he was sweeping it under the rug and pretending it hadn't happened?

He wasn't sure which option terrified him the most.

"Now that you're settled up here I'll go start bringing things up," Spider said.

"I'll help," Night added quickly.

Anything to get away from Lavender's hurt eyes.

Anything to get away from those sexy lips he wanted to kiss but knew he shouldn't.

Anything to get away from his guilt.

≈

9:11 A.M.

Eric was acting weird.

It was like the amazing experience they had shared last night had never happened, and he really had just spent the night in her guest bedroom instead of in her bed holding her in his arms.

Is that what he wanted?

To pretend that they hadn't had sex?

Uncertain as to their relationship's current status, but hoping hard that Eric was just embarrassed to have his sister and best friend come just after they'd slept together, especially given what she'd just lived through, Lavender watched him hurry out the door after Spider. She hoped he wasn't about to hurry out of her life the same way.

She needed him.

Needed him in a way she hadn't even known you could need someone.

Part of it was no doubt because he had been the one to come down into that hole and get her out. He'd stayed with her, risked his life for her, kept her safe, in short he was her hero, and that made it hard not to put him up on a pedestal and feel safe around him. But it went deeper than that, he made her feel something she'd never experienced before. He made her feel warm from the inside out no matter how cold the outside world was.

"You doing okay?" Abigail asked, lightly touching her arm as though she knew that Lavender might not be in a place where she was comfortable being touched yet.

Lavender appreciated that and was comforted to know that whether Eric was bailing or not, she wasn't alone. She had Abigail, and Abby actually completely understood what she was going through. Their situations were different and yet also kind of the same.

"Yeah, just overwhelmed," she said, offering up a tired smile. Although she'd slept well in Eric's arms, she was still exhausted.

"Let's sit." Abigail led her over to the sitting area, and they both dropped down into the soft leather cushions. "You know I'm here if you need someone to talk to. It's been six months since Ryder found me and rescued me and I'm still overwhelmed, so please I want you to reach out to me whenever you want because ... maybe I need someone to talk to too, someone who understands. Ryder is always there for me, whatever I need, but he doesn't *get* it, you know?"

"I know, I'm sorry I wasn't a better friend for you. I'm sorry I left just after you got home." She had contemplated postponing going to Afghanistan after Abigail was found, but she hadn't wanted to leave them shorthanded.

"I'm glad you went." Abigail smiled reassuringly. "It was what you needed, and I hope before everything went bad that you were able to get out of it what you wanted."

"I think I was starting to, but I can't go back." She shuddered at the thought, there were too many bad memories for her there. Right now she wasn't sure what her future looked like. Before she could contemplate it the guys came back into the apartment, arms filled with containers of food.

"Are you inviting the entire team over today?" Eric asked his sister as he set a stack of six Tupperware containers on the counter. "You have enough food to feed a dozen people here, and you thought you were only feeding three people."

"It's Christmas Day. What would Christmas be without a feast? Besides, Lavender needs cheering up, and what better way to do that than with lots and lots of comfort food. And we brought gifts," Abigail said with a grin.

"You brought a gift for me?" Lavender asked, confused. She'd only arrived back in the country the day before so they couldn't have had time to shop. "You sent me makeup already. I'm not overly patient, and I opened it the day it arrived," she admitted sheepishly.

Abigail laughed. "That's fine, you could open it whenever you wanted, it's your gift, but yeah, we have something for you today."

"I don't have anything for you guys," she said, feeling embarrassed.

"We got the gifts you posted, we were going to open them today anyway, but when we found out you would be here we thought we'd wait to open them here with you. Ryder, can you put the turkey and the roast vegetables into the oven? And the …"

"Relax, babe, I do know how to cook. Sit, put your feet up, and relax," Spider said with an affectionate smile.

Lavender sneaked a look at Eric to see what he was doing, he appeared to be busy loading the food onto oven trays and putting them into the oven, but she saw that he was sneaking looks at her too.

Apparently, she wasn't the only one who noticed.

"Is there something going on between you and my brother?" Abigail asked, looking from her to Eric and back again.

"Umm … why would you ask that?" Lavender knew she sounded lame, and she could feel her cheeks had heated so she was pretty sure Abigail wouldn't be buying it.

"Umm … maybe because of the way you're looking at him. Do you like my brother?"

"Of course I do, he's my friend, and he saved my life."

Abigail rolled her eyes. "I mean do you *like* like him?"

"I don't know, I'm so confused right now."

"Of course you're confused, you've just lived through Hell, been injured, scared you were going to die. But you're safe at home now, and you have time to figure everything else out. And if you do like my brother, your secret is safe with me until you're ready to do something about it," Abigail whispered conspiratorially.

"What secret?" Spider asked as he sat down beside his wife and pulled her into his arms.

"What part of the word secret don't you get?" Abigail teased Spider before kissing him. "Okay, let's do gifts. We don't have yours, Eric, because we didn't know you were here and were going to go see you for dinner."

Eric took a seat on the other couch since the three of them had taken up all the space on this one, and Lavender couldn't help but be disappointed with the distance between them. It wasn't the five feet between the two sofas that worried her, but the emotional distance she could feel growing between her and Eric. Just hours ago his body had been joined with hers, and she'd felt like that connection had run deeper than just sex, but maybe she was wrong.

"We can exchange gifts later," Eric told Abigail.

Abigail got up and grabbed a small silver box tied with green ribbon from the counter where the guys had left it when they'd carried everything up. "This is from Ryder and me."

Lavender took the box and untied the ribbon. Inside was a single piece of paper which she pulled out, unfolded, and read. Her eyes went wide, and she looked up at Abigail, touched that her friend had been so thoughtful.

"I remember how much it helped me when Ryder had a security system installed,

Abigail explained. "I felt unsafe all the time, even at home, and knowing that someone was watching over me even when I was alone at home helped so much. And Tex is going to set it all up so that he can monitor it, so you don't ever have to feel even a little bit unsafe here."

"I'd say you don't know how much this is going to help, but I know you really do." She had been afraid about the possibility of being alone, which was why Eric waiting for her and bringing her home and staying with her had meant so much, and this security system was one small step toward letting go of that fear.

"There's one condition on the gift," Abigail told her. "The company can't come and install it until January because of Christmas and New Year and all, so Ryder and I want you to come and stay with us until then."

She immediately looked at Eric, wondering if he had an opinion on the matter. He'd told her that he would stay with her as long as she needed him to, but then things had changed, and this morning he'd been acting distant. Did he still want to stay with her?

"I think it's a good idea," Eric said as though reading her mind. "Spider and I could get called away again at any time. Staying with Abby means even if we do you won't be alone."

He had said the words gently, as though taking great care not to hurt her feelings, and Lavender tried not to be disappointed. It wasn't like she had been planning marriage and a future with Eric, she hadn't really thought any further ahead than the moment last night, but knowing Eric had already discounted anything else being between them did hurt.

Pasting on a smile, she looked back at Abigail. "I would love to stay with you guys until the security system is installed."

Abigail beamed. "Great. We'll have lots of fun, and even after the system is up and running if you need to stay with us you can, for as long as you want."

Things might be odd with Eric—and in hindsight, she probably should have expected that they would be, sex couldn't not change things—but she had amazing friends, she was alive and relatively unscathed from her ordeal, and she had the rest of her life to figure out how to become the person that she wanted to see looking back at her when she looked in the mirror.

# CHAPTER 6

December 31ˢᵗ
9:50 P.M.

She was going to be here tonight.

After spending most of the last week painfully hard, his body aching for Lavender even as his brain tried to tell it that touching her again was a bad idea, Night wasn't sure he would be able to control himself.

And by control himself, he meant not grab her, shove her up against a wall, and kiss her until that haunted look left her gray eyes.

The haunted look was killing him.

Was it all just because of what had happened to her in Afghanistan, or was part of it because after sleeping with her, he had all but avoided her for the last week?

How egocentric was that?

She'd been abducted at gunpoint, watched over a dozen people—people she knew and had lived with for five months

—be gunned down in front of her, terrorized, threatened, injured, and shot at. After all of that, what was being avoided by a guy you had sex with in comparison?

Or was that just his guilt speaking?

Night knew he had hurt her, knew it each time they unavoidably ended up at the same place at the same time, saw it in the way she snuck what she thought were covert glances at him, in the way she started to come up to him—no doubt to ask him what was going on—but then seemed to think better of it and withdrew.

Fair or not, he blamed Abigail and Spider for this mess.

If they hadn't shown up on Christmas morning, catching him unaware and making him feel uncomfortable about what he'd done, then he and Lavender would have had a chance to sit down and talk about it. If they'd been able to talk then he'd know where her head was at and whether she regretted what they'd done, and blamed him for taking advantage of her vulnerable state.

Every time he thought about her, he saw Jackie's face the morning after they'd had sex.

Her words echoed in his head, telling him she shouldn't have slept with him.

As clear as it was on the day it had happened, he could see Jackie holding up the pregnancy test, announcing he was about to become a father.

He saw the words on the screen informing him of the miscarriage flash through his mind.

The relief he'd felt.

The deep shame following close on its heels.

How could he have been glad, relieved, that his child was gone?

What kind of man was he?

After what his parents had done to Abigail, making her think they didn't love her or respect her, all but ignored her for most of her life, and then the way he had treated Jackie and his unborn baby, he had to wonder if maybe some people just shouldn't have kids. Not Abigail though, she had gotten all the warm, caring genes in the McNamara family. She was going to be an amazing mother.

He was so proud of her, his little sister was the strongest person he knew, and he knew a lot of strong people. But she had survived hell, and while he knew she was far from healed from her ordeal, she had the man she loved standing behind her and a baby on the way, she finally had the family she had longed for all her life, and he was grateful that she was forgiving enough to let him share in her happiness.

Abigail wasn't the only one he was proud of, Lavender too had held up throughout a horrific ordeal proving she was one strong woman.

Then, as though she stepped out of his mind there she came, walking out of the spare bedroom at Abigail and Spider's place.

Looking like a goddess.

She didn't seem to notice, but the eyes of every single man in the place followed her as she walked through the living room and over to the kitchen to grab herself a drink.

Night groaned as he watched the gentle sway of her hips. Lavender wore a lavender-colored dress that clung to every inch of her perfectly curved body, it had a halter neck and just enough of a plunging neckline to show a little bit of cleavage without giving anything away. Her goldish red hair hung in a braid down her back, and the makeup she wore highlighted her large eyes and plump lips making it hard not to think about kissing her. The dress hung to mid-thigh showing off her shapely legs, and even with the bulky moon boot on her broken leg, she looked like a sex goddess who had just stepped out of the pages of a magazine.

"Doesn't Lavender look stunning," Abigail gushed, appearing at his elbow, a glass of orange juice in her hand.

"Not as stunning as you," Spider said, slipping an arm around his wife's waist, letting his hand rest on her swollen belly.

"As if," Abby shot back. "I'm stuck in this, too big for my regular clothes but not really big enough for maternity clothes. This dress was the only one I own that I could fit into," she said, indicating the loose flowing white dress she was wearing. "And high heels, I had to give those up, they just make my ankles swell so much more."

"Lavender isn't wearing heels either," Night muttered, unable to take his eyes off her as she stopped to greet some of the guys. He just wanted to be left alone to dwell on how badly he had messed things up with the most beautiful woman he had ever seen, not have how happy and in love his sister and best friend were rubbed in his face.

"Heels or not, you are the most gorgeous creature on the planet," Spider told Abigail, turning her in his arms and tilting her backward, supporting her weight with one arm while he kissed her deeply.

"Do you two always have to be kissing and touching each other?" Night snapped, regretting the words the moment they were out of his mouth. It wasn't either of their faults that he was in a bad mood. They weren't the ones who had gotten drunk and slept with a woman who had just found out her fiancé had been cheating on her the day before the wedding. They weren't the ones who had slept with her knowing she was vulnerable and that it was a bad idea. They weren't the ones who got her pregnant. They weren't the ones who had proposed to her out of a sense of obligation, then dumped her as soon as she miscarried the baby.

That was all on him.

And as much as he had messed up with Jackie, he felt

worse about what he'd done to Lavender. Finding out your fiancé was cheating, and being abducted and held hostage were too completely different things. Besides, he hadn't felt anything for Jackie, she'd been hot and needy, and he'd been drunk and horny, that was all that had ever been between them, but his feelings for Lavender were ...

He didn't even know, but they were more than he had ever felt for any other woman.

"Eric?" Abigail tentatively laid a hand on his forearm. "What's going on? You don't usually snap at us like that."

"Not cool, man." Spider frowned at him, protectiveness for his wife rolling off him. He wouldn't stand for anyone— even her brother—upsetting Abigail.

"I'm sorry," he said, pulling his sister in for a hug. "I'm just a little on edge."

"We got that," Spider muttered.

Abigail swatted at her husband then hugged him hard. "It's okay, apology accepted. I don't know what's going on with you, Eric, but stop shutting Lavender out, she needs all the support she can get these days."

He knew that.

He drilled either Abby or Spider every day to find out how she was doing. Was she sleeping, was she eating, was she having nightmares, any signs of PTSD developing.

It was complicated, but he didn't want to discuss it with his sister or anyone else, especially not here at what was supposed to be a fun New Year's Eve party, the last that Abigail and Spider would ever have without kids.

"I'm not shutting her out, just trying to give her space," he said, which was half the truth. The other half was he was afraid to see the pain and hurt in her eyes when she told him that he had taken advantage of her. He may not have loved Jackie, but that look she had given him when he'd told her that since the baby was gone there was no need for them to

101

stay married had never left him. He was trying not to make the same mistakes with Lavender. They needed some time and space, and then they could sit down and sort out what had happened with them.

At least this time he had used protection.

There would be no surprise baby, and that was a blessing he couldn't ignore.

"I don't think she needs space, Eric, she needs support," Abigail said, and the look in her eyes said she was saying this from personal experience.

"All right, sis." He leaned down, kissed her forehead, and then took a fortifying breath. He could do this. He could go and talk to Lavender, find out how she was doing. They were in a crowded room filled with their friends so it wasn't like she would go off on him now.

Feeling more anxious than he would have facing a dozen armed terrorists alone, Night forced his feet to move and started walking toward Lavender.

10:27 P.M.

He was coming toward her.

Lavender had to force herself not to outwardly react when she noticed Eric and that he was walking in her direction.

Well, if she was being honest, she had noticed him the second she walked out of her room. She hadn't known whether he was going to come and say hi, it had been six days since Christmas Day, and while he'd stopped by his sister's house at least three of those days, he made sure not to end up alone with her. It wasn't that she wanted to believe he was avoiding her on purpose except ... he was.

"Earth to Lavender." A hand waved in front of her face, and she started and realized she'd been in the middle of a conversation with Fox.

"Oh, sorry, Fox," she said, her cheeks flaming red.

He looked over his shoulder, saw who was coming toward them, shot her a grin that said he knew exactly why she'd stopped listening to him, and patted her on the shoulder. "No worries, go talk to your guy."

"He's not my guy," she said automatically. She had no idea what Eric was these days. Were they even still friends? Why was he shutting her out? It wasn't like she had made any demands, she hadn't asked him for a ring and a commitment, she hadn't even asked him for another night of mind-blowing sex. Was he acting all weird because of Jackie and everything that had happened with her? She had no idea because Eric wouldn't sit down with her and talk.

"You two could have fooled me. If you're not dancing around each other then you're doing the best impression of angsty, tortured lovers I've ever seen," Fox said with a grin before standing up and walking off to chat with one of the other guys.

"Hey," she said when Eric reached her. He stood far enough away that she couldn't touch him if she reached out to him, and she *did* want to reach out to him. Both Abigail and Spider had gone out of their way to make sure she was comfortable in their home, that she felt safe, that she knew she could talk if she needed to or have space, but it wasn't the same.

She missed Eric.

She missed the way he made her feel safe, like sooner or later the sun would come shining through the fog that engulfed her because right now, she didn't see an ending in sight.

"Hey," he said, shoving his hands into his pockets, and she wondered if it was an attempt not to touch her.

For the first time ever she felt awkward around Eric. They'd always had such an easy-going relationship. It wasn't like they had jumped straight into sharing their deepest, darkest secrets, they'd started off with the small stuff, but right from the beginning she'd felt comfortable around him.

Now she could barely look him in the eye.

Was sleeping with her such a mistake that he couldn't even stand to be around her anymore?

It wasn't like he could be comparing what they'd done with Jackie. He had to know what they'd done was nothing like that. She'd needed comfort, and a connection, and Eric had been there for her. What they'd shared meant something to her, she'd hoped it might mean something to him too. Even if it didn't, Eric had to know that this time there wasn't going to be a baby he didn't want.

"How're you doing?" he asked.

Lavender shrugged. "Okay, I guess. I'm home, and I'm alive, and that's what matters. The others weren't so lucky." Somehow that haunted her almost more than anything else she had endured. They'd been good people, dedicated their lives to helping others, they didn't deserve what had happened to them.

"You know we would have saved them if we could," Eric said.

"I know," Lavender said emphatically. "Spider and Chaos were hurt trying to save their lives. I know your team is amazing, you're all heroes, but that doesn't make you super-human, you can't save everyone. I just wish that things had been different, that none of it had happened." While that was mostly true, she was selfish enough to not want to take back making love to Eric even if it was the only time they did it.

"Yeah, I wish things had gone differently too," Eric said. Did he mean her abduction or the two of them sleeping together?

Lavender wished she knew the answer to that, but it was hardly like she could come right out and ask.

Right?

Or could she?

She had no claim on Eric, wasn't even sure she wanted one. While she might feel like the seeds of a wonderful relationship might have been planted that night, she wasn't sure she had it in her right now to water it, tend to it, and help it grow, especially if it wasn't what Eric wanted.

Yet, at the same time, she wasn't sure she wanted to throw away what could be something special.

She'd never felt anything beyond friendship and a shared sense of fun with any of the other men she'd been with, but she and Eric had a bond, built on years of friendship, solidified during their fight for survival, and that seemed like something she shouldn't walk away from without a fight.

Maybe there was a way to kind of hedge her bets, put out some feelers, see where Eric's head was at without outright asking him if he regretted what they'd done.

"So, hard to believe another year is over, huh?" she asked, twisting her hands together as nervous butterflies danced in her stomach.

"Yeah, it certainly turned out to be a crazy year. Finding Abby and finally bringing her home, her marrying my best friend, a baby on the way, and then you going to Afghanistan and the kind of dramatic way you came back." Eric shot her a teasing smile, and for a moment, things felt normal between them. She so badly wanted that.

"It's not the first time I've been accused of being dramatic," she agreed with a giggle. Growing up, she'd certainly had a flair for all things theatrical. She'd been loud and full of energy, she'd had a huge posse of friends, and had loved to party. "This year certainly hasn't ended the way I thought it would. I thought I would be out in the middle of Afghanistan, away from my family and friends, I didn't think I would be having a Christmas celebration or a New Year's one. Yet here I am, all dressed up, surrounded by people I love, warm and safe, and ready to count down to a new—and hopefully better—year. Well, almost ready."

Eric arched a brow, and for a moment all she could think about was how he had looked at her when he'd been lying above her in bed. She shivered as she remembered just how wonderful he had made her feel.

She wanted to carry that same feeling with her into the new year.

Her entire future was up in the air. She didn't have a job, she didn't have a purpose, she wasn't sure what she would do next, but she knew she wanted to find a way to the redemption she felt she needed.

May as well just spit it out and get it over with. "Do you want to kiss me as the ball drops?" Lavender blurted out.

Heat flared in Eric's silver eyes, so she knew for sure that he was attracted to her, but he quickly shut it down, and then his face turned gentle. Only this time his gentleness didn't soothe, didn't calm, didn't reassure, all it did was irritate her. "I don't think that's a good idea, honey."

It wasn't until he shot her down that she realized just how badly she had wanted to kiss him.

But his rejection gave her the answer she needed.

Eric might have enjoyed it, but he regretted that they'd had sex, he saw her as another vulnerable woman he had taken advantage of, and he was going to let that color how he saw her. While she couldn't stop thinking about him, about them, all he had been thinking about was how to let her down gently.

Well, he'd done it now.

Not wanting to embarrass herself by begging, or even worse by crying and let him know how much his rejection had hurt her, Lavender nodded once, then turned her back on him and walked away. The loss weighed down on her, she hadn't just lost a potential boyfriend but her very best friend. She had never felt so alone in her entire life—not as a child unwanted by her parents, not when she'd been kidnapped and kept in a cage, not when she had been abducted by terrorists and left for them to reclaim later and use for their pleasure—as she did in this moment when she had to face the gaping black hole that was her future without anyone to watch her back and catch her if she fell.

# CHAPTER 7

January 3<sup>rd</sup>
10:24 P.M.

"Show me the money."

Night glared at the grinning Chaos as he pulled another twenty from his pocket. "Aren't you supposed to be recovering from a concussion?" he grumbled.

Chaos took the bill and kissed it before folding it with exaggerated carefulness and sticking it in his jeans pocket. "Pfft, that was ten days ago, I was over that nine days ago."

"Whatever, man," he said, giving up on darts for the night. He knew the problem wasn't really Chaos and his super-human dart skills, it was Lavender and the fact that it didn't matter what he was doing or where he was, all he could do was think about her.

"Hey, it's not my fault you suck tonight," Chaos told him.

"I don't suck," Night muttered.

"The fact that I just won fifty dollars says otherwise," Chaos taunted.

"You're really annoying, you know that?" Night asked his friend.

"I know," Chaos agreed cheerfully, already collecting the darts from the dartboard and looking around for his next victim.

He and his team were out tonight, hanging in one of their favorite bars, but his heart wasn't in it. Usually, he had a great time when he hung with his friends, especially after a long day of PT, it was nice to chill and unwind, but today he would rather have gone home and moped.

Yep, mope.

Mope because he'd been stupid enough to be manipulated into meddling in Abigail and Spider's relationship. Mope because he'd taken out his guilt by getting drunk and taking advantage of a vulnerable woman. Mope because he'd rejoiced that the unborn baby tying him to a woman he didn't love had been gone. And mope because he wanted Lavender but couldn't have her.

"You're just a bag of fun to be around tonight, aren't you," Fox said, lounging in his chair, a drink in his hand.

Since he couldn't argue with that, he simply shrugged and joined his friend at the table. Chaos was talking Shark into playing darts with him. King was on the dance floor, a woman in his arms, their bodies grinding against each other, nothing new there. King picked up women whenever they went out. The man looked like he could be a model with jet black hair and bright green eyes. He had dimples and could charm anyone into doing what he wanted. Women fell at his feet all but begging him to take them to bed.

There was a time when Night would have picked up a woman tonight, taken her back to her place, made sure they both got what they needed, then headed home to his place to crash. After he'd gotten Jackie pregnant five years ago he'd cut right back on the sleeping around, he didn't want to wind up with another kid with a woman he wasn't in love with. If he was going to become a father, he wanted the whole thing, wife, dog, and white picket fence.

"Would you just talk to Lavender," Fox said.

"And say what?" he demanded.

"I don't know because I don't know exactly what happened between you two. But given that Lavender is just sitting around Abby and Spider's place moping, and all you do is sit around your place and mope, it doesn't take a genius to figure out that neither of you are happy. Who knows, maybe actually *talking* to each other might help," Fox said with exaggerated patience like he was speaking to a child who refused to learn a lesson.

"I don't know what to say to her," he admitted. Everything was so messed up, he didn't know where her head was at, he wasn't even sure where his head was at.

"Wing it."

"Wing it?" he repeated.

Fox shrugged. "Why not? Lavender is a great woman, sweet and strong, but less secure than she likes people to believe she is. Trust the guy who has loved and lost twice that sometimes you just have to take that chance."

"Do you regret it?"

"No. Julie was the love of my life, and Evie ... Evie was my heart. I regret lying to her, I regret hurting her, I regret a lot of things that happened between us, but I will never regret loving her." From the tender smile on his face and the faraway look in his eyes, Night could tell that Fox meant every word he had just said.

"I'll think about it."

"Don't wait too long. Sometimes you get to thinking that you have all the time in the world, but life can change in a second, and then it's too late. You should know that better than most, our jobs are dangerous, we all know that there is a bullet or an IED out there somewhere with our names on it. Life is finite, I believe our time to die is already written in stone. Live your life like you know the exact date that you're going to leave this place."

"That's really profound, man," Night said, staring at his friend in surprise.

"I have my moments." Fox shot him a smile, but there was sadness etched into his features and Night knew he would never completely get over the loss of either woman he had loved. Fox might have lost them in very different ways, but he had grieved both equally.

"Hey, guys, I'm going to call it a night," Spider announced as he left the pool table and joined them. "Abby will be waiting up for me." Spider wriggled his eyebrows making Night wince.

"I do not want to hear about your sexual escapades with my sister," he told his best friend.

Spider just laughed and slapped him on the back. "You ready to leave?"

They'd come together but Night wasn't ready to head home yet. He needed time to clear his head a little first. "I'll catch a cab."

"I'm ready to get out of here," Fox said, setting his glass down and pushing away from the table. "Chaos, Shark, you guys ready to go?"

"Nah, we're hanging for a while longer," Chaos replied. "I reckon I can get more cash out of the Shark man."

Shark rolled his eyes, but from the glower he shot Chaos it was clear that he'd already lost to him several times. Nobody bothered asking King if he was ready to go, he wasn't leaving until he decided which lady he was spending the night with.

Night waved to his friends, and then as they headed out the door he headed to the dance floor. He didn't really like dancing, but his body needed to move and he needed to let his mind shut down for a moment. He'd been obsessing over the whole him and Lavender thing for over a week now and hadn't been able to figure out his next move, maybe it was time to take a break, let the answer just come to him instead of trying to force it.

It didn't take long for one of the many single women who hung out here primarily to find themselves a SEAL to take to bed to latch onto him. Her slim arms wrapped around his waist, her hands resting low on his abdomen, as she ground into him from behind.

He gently grasped her wrists and turned around to find a stunning blonde with huge breasts, big brown doe eyes, and a pouty smile looking up at him. She was dressed in a neon pink dress that barely covered her, and with her heels, she was only a couple of inches smaller than him.

"Hi," she said. Her voice was sexy, and he couldn't deny that she was exactly what he was looking for when he needed the release that only sex could bring.

But now when he looked at her, all he saw was Lavender's sweet face, her long red locks, her soulful gray eyes, and the smattering of freckles that made her look like even the sun couldn't resist kissing her.

There was only one woman he wanted to have sex with.

The revelation hit him like a ton of bricks, but he quickly realized it was true.

Gorgeous as this woman was, she didn't turn him on. "Sorry, beautiful, it's not going to happen. I'm not looking to hook up tonight."

"You married?" she asked, looking annoyed to have been turned down.

"Nope."

"Involved?"

"Nope."

"Then why can't we hook up?" She stuck her bottom lip out, ran the tip of her tongue across it, then because he still held her wrists in a loose hold she pressed her body up against his.

Was she really that desperate to hook a SEAL that she couldn't take no for an answer? "We're not hooking up because I'm not interested, it's not why I came here tonight. Good luck though." With that, he released his hold on her and turned and walked away, feeling her angry gaze following him as he headed out into the night.

He didn't want sex with random women, he wanted something more, something deeper. He wanted a connection. Now he knew what he wanted, he had to find a way to figure out what Lavender wanted.

## CHAPTER 8

January 4<sup>th</sup>
6:47 P.M.

Her stomach was in knots, and Lavender had no idea how she was going to eat.

She should have said no to dinner tonight.

She probably would have, but Abigail and Spider had been so good to her these last two weeks, and she hadn't had the heart to say no when Abby had organized for everyone to get together for a night out at the restaurant where Lavender used to work, which had been where she'd first met them.

So here she was.

It would be the first time she had seen Eric since the New Year's Eve party where he had turned her down flat when she'd asked him if he wanted to kiss her at the end of the countdown to the new year. Lavender had managed to avoid him for the rest of the party, and the last two times he had dropped by to see his sister and friend. She'd also ignored his calls last night, she felt mean doing it, but there was only so much rejection she could handle.

Especially right now when everything she had survived was still so raw.

Of course she would make time to sit down with him at some point, and they would talk things through, she didn't want to lose him as a friend, and he would always be her hero. While their friendship could never go back to the way it had been, they could still hang out together with the rest of their friends.

"I have bad news," Abby announced, setting her phone down on the table.

Given her recent history, Lavender's mind jumped to all sorts of horrific scenarios. Gunshots, bombs, blood, and death all flew through her mind in the second or so that it took for Abby to continue speaking.

"The guys are running late, they think they'll be able to make it, but Ryder said they might be another hour."

Relief literally stole her breath for a moment, and she quickly tried to cover it with a cough not wanting to worry Abby or let her realize just how terrified she had been for a moment there.

Her relief quickly morphed from being glad the guys were all okay and no one had been hurt, to being glad that they were coming late.

She wasn't ready to see Eric.

Maybe she should just leave.

Tonight after dinner she'd be going back to her apartment. The security system was installed and all setup, so there was no reason for her to stay with Abby and Spider anymore. Lavender wasn't lying to herself. She was going to miss their company and the sense of safety that came with knowing Spider was sleeping just across the hall, and that he was armed and able to protect her from any threats. She was also going to miss their company, it was hard knowing she was going home alone, but it was time to start moving on with her life. She'd already told her sister that there was no need for her to come out for a visit. Marigold was busy with her husband and her two sweet babies, and besides, Lavender felt like this was something she had to learn to deal with on her own.

It wasn't going away.

It was a part of her now the same way what had happened to her with Cage Anderson was a part of her.

She'd never forget.

The pain, the fear, they were etched into her soul now, but she knew she could find a way to live with them. The nightmares would fade, the paranoia that someone would jump out and hurt her would fade, the constant checking over her shoulder, that would fade too. One day all of this would be a distant memory, which was something she had to keep reminding herself of.

"Nothing lasts forever," she whispered under her breath. After her assault four years ago, she'd repeated that like a mantra as she struggled to deal with the overwhelming emotions being kidnapped, raped, and nearly killed brought forth.

"Did you say something, Lavender?" Abby asked, watching her with thinly veiled concern.

Embarrassed to see that now their friends were looking at her, it was the pity in their eyes that hit her hard. She hated that look. She knew that they meant well, that they were worried because they cared, but it made her feel about two inches tall like she was incapable of looking after herself or doing much of anything, like she needed to be coddled and patted on the head and fed a million platitudes.

"No, just talking to myself," she said, trying to smile to alleviate everyone's concerns. While it was nice to have people who cared about her, she had to remind herself that she was on her own from here on out.

"Sorry if I upset you, maybe my wording wasn't the best, I was just annoyed because I wanted us all to be here tonight for you. This is a dinner to celebrate you being home, and even though I'm used to PT getting in the way of things, I wanted everyone here. I'm sorry though, I shouldn't have phrased it like that, I worried you. Eric is okay," Abby added. Her unusual eyes—one a silvery gray the other a golden brown—were watching her closely, and her face was a mask of dismay.

Forcing herself to relax, she reached out and squeezed Abby's hand. "It's fine, really, I guess my mind is kind of pre-programmed to jump to worst-case scenario at the moment."

"I should have known that," Abigail said, her tone full of self-recrimination.

"Don't worry about it, Abs, really, I overreacted, and that's not even really what I was upset about."

"You're nervous about seeing my brother," Abigail said.

Lavender thought about lying but rejected the idea. Abby already knew there was something between her and Eric, and the others at the table had gone back to chattering amongst themselves. "It's just kind of weird between us at the moment."

"Well, my brother can be a jerk," Abby said, a conspiratorial smile on her pretty face.

"Nah, he's a great guy." Lavender considered that and how he had so easily avoided her for almost the last two weeks. "Well, maybe sometimes," she amended.

"He shouldn't be making things harder for you right now, he should be trying to make things better."

"It's not just him, it's me too. I don't want to talk about it, it's just weird, and I don't have the energy to deal with it on top of everything else."

"Of course you don't," Abigail agreed.

"I'm going to go get a little fresh air," Lavender said, pushing back her chair and standing up.

"Want me to come with you?" Abigail asked.

"Thanks, but I just need a moment." Snatching up her purse, she hurried past the tables and the area where they had live music and dancing, she bypassed the bar, and instead of going out the back door to the parking lot, she headed through the staff-only door. She might not work here anymore, but she didn't think anyone was going to stop her as she headed for the stairs that led up to the roof.

After being locked in a cage for over a week she'd found herself sometimes in need of being in large open spaces where she didn't feel like the world was closing in on her. Working long hours as a waitress, she'd started taking her breaks up on the roof. She had liked lying up there, staring at the sky, the clouds, or the stars, letting her mind wander to nothing in particular. Despite the hustle and bustle of the city, up there on the roof it was like another world. This was where she had found the peace and tranquility she had so desperately needed.

That she desperately needed now.

This was where she had first properly met Eric besides just making small talk while she took their orders. She'd been up there one night, a dropped glass jug and the water that had splashed out of it had triggered a flashback to nearly drowning, and she'd fled up there where she'd let her tears flow freely, thinking she was alone. It wasn't until strong arms drew her into a warm embrace that she realized she wasn't.

And so their friendship was born.

As she wandered across the roof to stand at the edge, she tilted her face up and drank in the sight of the stars. It was a cold night, and she'd forgotten her coat, but the gentle breeze and the expanse of sparkling diamonds above had her anxiety fading away.

Worrying over things with Eric was silly. They'd had one night of sex, okay the best sex of her life, and that had stirred some indescribable feelings in her, but it was time to let it go. When it boiled down to it, it wasn't anything that was worth losing her friend over. Whatever it took to get through the awkwardness so things could go back to the way they used to be, she would do.

~

8:03 P.M.

He had been looking forward to this all day.

Since Lavender hadn't returned his calls, Night had been relying on the fact that she would be there tonight to give him the chance to finally sit down with her and talk. He wasn't sure exactly what it was he wanted, and he had no idea where Lavender's head was at. She'd just lived through a major trauma so it was perfectly reasonable if she wasn't thinking about him—or them—at all, although asking kissing him on New Year's Eve was an indication that she was indeed thinking about them, but regardless, they needed to talk.

Night was just sorry he had put it off this long. He'd let the past and what had happened with Jackie and his determination not to repeat mistakes that he still hated himself for committing cloud his judgment.

But no more.

If he could walk into a warzone outmanned and outgunned, then he could certainly have *the talk*.

If Lavender turned him down flat then at least he'd know.

It wasn't until a rush of disappointment washed over him at the thought, that he realized he might actually be falling for his pretty red-headed friend. He'd always thought her beautiful. He'd been pleased to see her outgoing and carefree side coming out as she worked to put the ordeal she'd suffered behind her and figure out who she was now, and longed to help her get back the woman she'd been before. He had always admired her strength and her courage, he'd trusted her enough to share not just the disaster of what happened with Jackie but the shame of being relieved his child was gone.

Maybe there had always been more between them than friendship, and they'd both just been too busy with life to see it.

A tragedy had a way of cutting away all the excess so you focused on what was important.

And what was most important to him right now was Lavender and figuring out where they stood with each other.

As they stepped into the restaurant, Night's gaze searched the room for that fiery hair he loved so much. He didn't spot her, but he saw his sister and some of their friends, and he and the guys headed over toward them.

"Hey, sweetheart." Spider greeted his wife and immediately drew her into his arms.

"Hey," she said, but it was clear not just from the tone of her voice but the worried look in her eyes that something was wrong.

Protectiveness wasn't something you could turn off and on, it was just a part of who you were, and he noted the immediate change in himself and the rest of his team as they scanned the crowded restaurant in search of whatever threat had upset the woman they all considered a little sister.

"What's wrong, honey?" Spider asked. Bending his knees so he could look Abigail in the face, he cupped her chin in his hands, his fingers caressing her skin in an attempt to soothe her.

"I said something stupid and upset Lavender," she said, her eyes teary.

"Oh, I'm sure she knows you didn't mean it," Spider said, pulling her into a hug.

While the rest of the guys relaxed now that they knew no one had done anything to hurt either Abigail or any of their other friends, Night found himself standing straighter, the tension still coiled tightly in his gut. "What did you say to her?" he asked, trying to sound casual, but pretty sure it sounded like he was about to full-on interrogate his sister.

Spider glared at him. Night still wasn't quite used to this side of his best friend. He and Spider were more brothers than friends and had known each other since they were ten, they'd always been close, but now that Spider had Abby back, he wouldn't stand for anything or anyone causing her pain. Not even him.

Forcing his voice to come out calmer this time, he said, "I'm not angry with you, Abs, just worried about Lavender. Can you tell me what happened?"

Abigail nodded, sniffed, then wiped at her eyes and looked up at him. "Ryder called to say you guys were going to be late, and when I went to tell the others I said I had bad news. I didn't think that anyone would take it the wrong way, but Lavender went really pale, and I realized that I'd worried her and she'd thought the worst, like one of you guys had been shot or something. I explained and apologized, and she said she was just overreacting. I think once her panic passed, she was more worried about seeing you, Eric, than anything else. She said things were weird between you two, and I said you were a jerk because well, you can be, then she said she needed fresh air and disappeared. That was half an hour ago, and she hasn't come back. I didn't mean to upset her."

The sight of tears in his baby sister's eyes twisted something inside him. Abigail wasn't a crier, but pregnancy hormones had definitely changed that. She'd forgiven him for doing the unforgivable, and he was trying hard to be a better brother to her, yet couldn't help but feel that once again he'd failed, upsetting her over something that was his fault, not hers.

"Come here." He tugged her out of Spider's arms and pulled her into his, hugging her tightly before kissing the top of her head. "It's not your fault, honey, it's mine. You're right, I can be a jerk, and I was one with Lavender."

"You'll sort things out with her?" Abigail said, and he thought it was as much a statement as it was a question.

"Absolutely." He was pretty sure where Lavender would be, and he was going to go there right now and sit her down and talk.

"Good. And sorry about the tears, I just can't seem to stop them lately," Abigail said as she wiped at her eyes again.

"You're pregnant, honey, it goes with the territory," Spider reminded her as he placed one of his hands on her little baby bump.

Leaving the others to sit down and order their dinner, Night headed to the back of the restaurant, through the staff-only door, where he took the stairs two at a time up to the roof. He remembered the day he'd found Lavender up there. His team had just come back from a mission that they nearly hadn't survived. Needing some fresh air, he'd come up there, not long later he'd heard the sound of crying and found the pretty red-headed waitress sobbing her heart out.

He hadn't hesitated, he'd just gone to her, embraced her, then the two of them had started talking. It hadn't taken long for this to become their place, he'd often find her up there, and he'd come to join her, and before he knew it they were sharing their darkest secrets.

He should have known from the moment his heart had cracked at the sound of her tears that something was bound to happen between them.

"Lavender?" he called out as he stepped out onto the roof.

Silence met him.

When he looked around he didn't see her anywhere.

He'd been so sure she would be there, but if she wasn't then where was she?

Panic would have engulfed him, but there was no reason to believe that Lavender was in any sort of trouble. She probably wanted to go for a walk. Sometimes she found it hard to be still, he understood given that she'd been held captive in a cage, those memories no doubt exacerbated by being held in an old well when she'd been taken hostage.

Ready to spend the night searching for her since he was pretty sure she would ignore his phone calls, when he walked back into the restaurant, one look at his friends' faces told him that wouldn't be happening.

"What is it?" he asked.

"We've been called out," Chaos replied.

He couldn't help but mutter a curse. It was the nature of the job, but this time the timing couldn't be worse. It meant having to hold off on talking to Lavender until they returned, but that could be in days, weeks, or months from now. The longer he put off talking with her, the harder it would be, but this wasn't the kind of thing they could hash out in an email so it wasn't like he was being given a choice.

"Be safe," Abigail said, holding tightly to Spider.

"You know I'll always do everything in my power to come home to you and our little one." Spider knelt and kissed her stomach and then stood and pressed his lips to Abigail's.

"You be safe too." Abby stood on her tiptoes to kiss his cheek.

"Always, sis," he assured her.

"You all better come home in one piece, this baby wants to meet all his or her uncles," Abigail warned as she made the rounds hugging Fox, King, Chaos, and Shark before giving her husband another hard hug.

The love on his sister's face as she watched the man she loved walk away tugged on his heart. He wanted a woman who looked at him the way Abigail looked at Spider.

Could that woman be Lavender?

# CHAPTER 9

January 18<sup>th</sup>
9:36 A.M.

Lavender wandered aimlessly around her apartment.

She felt like she'd been tossed overboard and left floating in the ocean, unsure which direction to take to find land. She'd been home for over three weeks now, and yet she was still uncertain what her future held.

Go back to the aid organization?

Find a new job?

Waitress or something new?

All she knew was she couldn't keep sitting around in her apartment day after day, staring at the walls, trying to read or watch TV, but not having the concentration to focus, and barely sleeping for fear of nightmares. There was a limit to how long she could expect to keep going like this before she set herself up for the breakdown she was terrified of having.

A plan.

She needed a plan.

Focusing on something would help her spend her time doing something productive instead of dwelling on what had happened and what could have been but wasn't going to be.

Her phone rang, and of course that sent her mind running straight to thoughts of Eric. She had to stop doing that, he had made his position clear when he decided not to tell her that he and his team were heading off on a mission. He always told her. Always. It didn't matter if she was in the middle of a shift at the restaurant, or it was the middle of the night. If he got called away he let her know.

Except this time he hadn't.

Leaving her to conclude that things between them were permanently changed and it was time to move on with her life.

The sudden silence drew her out of her thoughts, and she realized that whoever had been calling had either given up or the phone had sent them to voicemail.

Just as she walked over to retrieve her cell phone from the kitchen counter it began to ring again. This time she picked up her cell and pressed answer, ruthlessly shoving away the hurt and confusion she'd felt when she returned from her walk to the restaurant and learned that the guys were gone and Eric hadn't said goodbye.

"Hey, Abby," she said, having seen her friend's number and face on the screen before answering.

"Hey, yourself. How are you doing?"

It had been a couple of days since they had last caught up, and while Abby checked in every day with at least a text, Lavender always felt uncomfortable because she wanted to ask if Abby had heard anything about Eric, Spider, and the guys, but didn't want to outright ask. Asking went against her leave the past in the past and look to the future plan.

"I'm doing okay," she replied.

"So, I have something to ask you. Have you contacted the aid organization to ask them to place you somewhere new?"

"No."

"Are you going to?"

"I'm ..." Lavender let the thought trail off. She didn't want to, she wasn't sure she could go off somewhere dangerous ever again, but at the same time that job had been about giving up her old more selfish ways and putting others first for a change. No more spending her life hopping from country to country, party to party, man to man, all but ignoring the only family she had. If she gave up on that job, it felt like giving up on earning her self-respect back. She'd been having this argument with herself for days, her brain said one thing, her heart another.

"You don't owe anyone anything, Lavender, not even yourself."

"I can't go back," she admitted before she could talk herself out of it.

"I knew that, but I'm glad you finally accepted it and stopped beating yourself up over it. Since you won't be leaving again I have a job offer."

Abigail sounded excited, but Lavender was confused. Her friend was a ballet dancer who thanks to an injury had given up a professional career and instead turned to teaching. Lavender couldn't dance, well she could sway to the music, her body pressed up against some hot guy, but she certainly couldn't teach ballet. "A job?"

"Yep. Our receptionist retired, so we're looking for someone and I thought of you. I know you liked waitressing, but this could be fun and something different. You'd be answering phones, scheduling private lessons, organizing competition entrance fees, and music and travel. You'd be dealing lots with the kids and their parents, so nothing at all like the restaurant, but you love kids, and I thought this might be something you'd enjoy."

Lavender could certainly feel her friend's enthusiasm coming down the line. The job sounded like it could be fun. She'd dropped out of college when she got into traveling the globe housesitting, what was being stuck in a classroom compared with making new friends and experiencing new cities. Now she wasn't really qualified to do much, and as much as she enjoyed waitressing this did sound like something new and fun.

"When do you need an answer?" she asked. There were specifics she would need to know before she made up her mind either way.

"Mrs. Alistaire will be leaving in the middle of next month, so you have time to decide. Why don't you come over for dinner tonight, I'm having my friends from the dance studio over, and you can come and meet everyone and find out more about the job. Plus, I'm making my famous fried chicken and homemade curly fries."

Nausea immediately churned in her stomach at the thought of chicken, which was odd because she usually loved chicken, especially Abby's who had her secret blend of spices and herbs that she refused to share with anyone else.

But today the very thought of it made her feel ill.

So sick she had to press a hand to her mouth as her stomach revolted. "Abs, I'm going to have to go, I'm not feeling too well. I'll pass on dinner, but I'm definitely interested in finding out more about the job. I'll call you, okay?"

"Okay, let me know if you need anything," Abigail said, sounding concerned.

"Will do. Bye," she said quickly, disconnecting and all but throwing the phone onto the counter as she made a dash for the bathroom.

Lavender barely made it to her knees in front of the toilet

before she threw up. It took several minutes before her stomach settled enough that she could crawl over to the vanity and use it to leverage herself up. She grabbed a face washer, ran it under cold water, then sank to the floor again as she blotted at her face.

She might have to make an appointment to see her doctor. This was the fifth time in the last two weeks she'd been sick, although it was the first time that the thought of food had set it off. She'd been tired too, although she had assumed that had to do with her ordeal and fear of nightmares which had her sleeping less, and not that she was ill. She'd been peeing a lot too, running to the bathroom what felt like every hour. And ...

Lavender gasped, the washcloth falling from her hands.

No.

It couldn't be.

It was impossible.

And yet ...

She was late.

*The* late.

The one women dreaded unless they were married and planning for it.

But she couldn't be pregnant.

Could she?

The only man she had been with was Eric, and they'd used a condom. She'd been abducted of course, but none of the men had touched her, well they'd groped her, but they hadn't raped her, and she hadn't been knocked unconscious or drugged so she would have remembered it happening.

Except condoms were only like 98% effective which meant that it was a possibility.

Panicking now, Lavender leaped to her feet and scrambled through her cabinet in search of pregnancy tests. She had some left over from a scare she'd had about two years ago. Since moving to California she'd only been with three men, one of whom she'd started getting serious with until they thought she might be pregnant, and he had panicked and all but run out the door.

Thankfully, she hadn't been pregnant then, but was she going to be that lucky this time?

Finding the test, she shoved her leggings down and squatted over the toilet, peeing on the stick.

Then came the hard part.

The waiting.

Lavender set the test on the counter, washed her hands, and then paced around the bathroom, struggling not to hyperventilate.

This couldn't be happening.

Not now.

Didn't she have enough to deal with?

And Eric, he would be horrified if she was pregnant. He'd already gotten a woman he didn't love pregnant once, and he still hated himself for being relieved when she had miscarried.

What would he say if she did wind up pregnant?

Would he blame her?

Would he think she had somehow done something on purpose to trick him into being with her?

Would he support her?

Yes, she knew he would because he had with Jackie, but he would hate every second of being with her and the baby. He wanted a child with a woman he loved, not one he had sex with once and regretted it.

Maybe she was panicking about nothing. She might not be pregnant, and condoms worked the vast majority of the time so the chances of her being one of the unlucky 2% were minuscule.

With shaking hands, she picked up the stick, and her stomach dropped.

Pregnant.

She was pregnant.

Pregnant and alone.

# CHAPTER 10

January 20<sup>th</sup>
12:12 P.M.

Two days.

For forty-eight hours, she had known that she was going to have a baby, and it still didn't feel real.

Lavender felt like she was living in a dream world, too much had happened too close together, and she definitely felt like she was suffering from emotional overload.

It sucked going through this alone.

And yet, as hard as it was to deal with this by herself, part of her was grateful Eric wasn't here. She hadn't heard from him since he'd left on his last mission, and while it wasn't uncommon for him not to be able to get in touch while he was working, sometimes it could even be months before he sent an email or called, this time felt different.

Abigail had told her that Eric had been looking for her

right before his team got called out, but if that was true, why hadn't he sent her a text?

Just one word even, something to let her know that everything would be okay between them, even a single emoji would have been better than nothing, although there probably wasn't much chance of Eric sending her any emoji. For some reason he really didn't like them, and she'd always made a point of including at least one in any texts she sent just to tease him. Sometimes she'd even send a text made entirely of emoji just for the fun of seeing the annoyance in his gray eyes.

Lavender smiled despite her down mood.

When the doorbell rang a second later, she debated ignoring it. She wasn't in the mood to see anyone right now, but it was probably Abby, and since she'd been dodging her friend's calls ever since she took the pregnancy test, she couldn't ignore her now.

Dragging herself off the couch and over to the door, when she saw her friend standing outside, arms wrapped around her growing stomach bouncing from foot to foot in the cold, she buzzed her into the building. It wasn't Abigail's fault that her brother wasn't into her the way she was into him.

Taking the chain off her apartment door, she left it slightly open and went to the kitchen to get them drinks and snacks.

She picked up the coffee and then stopped. Could she still drink coffee?

There was so much to learn about being pregnant. She had a two-and-a-half-year-old nephew and a nine-month-old niece, but she hadn't been around while her twin was pregnant, and most of Abby's pregnancy she'd been in Afghanistan.

Researching pregnancy jumped to the top of her to-do list.

"I have to go to the bathroom," Abigail announced as she came all but running into the apartment. "This little one is tap dancing on my bladder this morning."

So Abigail had been bouncing from foot to foot because she needed the toilet not because she was cold. It wasn't until the bathroom door clicked closed that Lavender realized what was going to happen.

And that there was no way to stop it.

"Lavender Vaile, we are going to talk as soon as I get out there," Abigail screeched through the closed door.

Busted.

Unable to throw away the pregnancy test—or any of the dozen others she'd taken in an attempt to prove she wasn't in fact pregnant—they were all lined up on the bathroom vanity.

She should have told Abigail she couldn't use the bathroom, only she knew that she would never have said that, just like she would never have turned her friend away. From the second Abigail had decided to come over here today this moment had been inevitable.

The toilet flushed, the tap turned on, and Lavender braced herself.

"You're pregnant," Abigail said as she threw open the bathroom door.

Denying it would be futile. "Yep."

"Eric is the father, right?"

Again denying it would be futile. "Yep."

"I knew something weird was going on between you two. Christmas Eve?"

"Yes."

"Well, you're full of information," Abigail said with a

scowl before she broke out into a grin. "You and my brother, this is so cool, we'll be sisters."

Lavender hated to burst her bubble. "Abby, we're not together. That's why it's weird between us."

"Not together?" Abigail's brow scrunched.

"Nope. We slept together on Christmas Eve. He was so sweet, brought me back here, and was looking after me, I just needed to feel alive, connected to someone, feel something good instead of pain and terror, and it was ... Eric. We made love, slept in each other's arms, then you two showed up before we got a chance to talk. After that, it was like Eric could hardly stand to be around me. He told me to stay with you and Spider even though he had offered to stay with me here, and then he avoided me. It's been weird and awkward between us ever since. Then when he left, he didn't even say goodbye."

"The guys had to leave in a hurry, and he had been looking for you before that, don't discount things just because he was acting weird before that," Abigail said earnestly. "And when he finds out about the baby, he won't turn his back on you."

Exactly.

That was the problem.

She knew for a fact that if he knew about the baby he would step up and be there for both of them. He would offer to marry her, and even if she turned him down, he would be a terrific father to their baby.

But his heart wouldn't be in it.

He didn't want another baby with a woman that he wasn't in love with, and the simple fact was that he wasn't in love with her, and the baby wasn't going to change that.

"I'm not going to tell him about the baby," she said.

Abigail's eyes bulged. "You're not going to tell him?"

"Well, not right away. I need some time, Abby, please try

to understand that. I just had to fight for my life, I thought I was going to die out there, and then I was safe, and then I was home, and then Eric was there, and now I'm pregnant, and I'm just …"

"Overwhelmed," Abigail finished for her, enfolding her into a hug.

"Yeah, overwhelmed," she agreed, returning the hug. "I'm thinking I might move back to the east coast to be closer to my sister."

"You're leaving?" Abigail pulled back, her hands on Lavender's shoulders.

"I've been thinking about it ever since I took the test, and yeah, I think for now it's what makes the most sense."

"So you're just going to leave and not tell Eric that you're carrying his baby?"

Lavender flinched because that was exactly what she wanted to do. She didn't want to put him in the same position he'd found himself in once before. She didn't want to make him feel like he had to step up for her like he had for Jackie. Maybe him never knowing about the baby was what was best for all of them.

"I can't lie to my brother about this, Lavender. I'm sorry, I love you, but Eric is my brother, and I won't keep my little niece or nephew from its father."

"I would never ask you to, I just need some time, please."

Abigail looked uncertain, but then finally she nodded. "If you haven't told him by the time the baby is born then I'm telling him. I know when you conceived so I know when you're due. I mean it, Lavender, if you haven't told him by then, then I will."

From the look on her friend's face, Lavender knew Abigail meant it. "Deal, and thank you, I really appreciate you understanding. I just have to get a handle on this, figure things out in my head before I can deal with telling him and his emotions about it."

If she was lucky, Eric would be away for weeks or even months, and maybe by then she would feel more in control of the situation. Because whether she told Eric or not, she was going to be a mother, she would have a little person to provide for, not just provide financially but emotionally as well, and to do that she had to deal with everything her ordeal put her through. If she could show Eric that she could take care of their baby on her own then maybe he wouldn't feel like he had to propose. He would want to be a part of the baby's life, and she wouldn't prevent that from happening, they would find a way to make it work so they both got to be a part of their child's life, but she didn't want to marry for any other reason than love.

She'd always dated casually, believing that when the right man came along she would know it, and they would fall in love and have a family. Now she was falling in love with a man who didn't love her back, and although they were having a family they weren't really a family. They could both love this baby, both be an active part of its life, but they wouldn't be doing it together.

## CHAPTER 11

January 24<sup>th</sup>
5:20 P.M.

He should have gotten her flowers.

He should have dressed up a little, not just thrown on the jeans and shirt he had in his go-bag.

He should have called first to let her know he was coming.

Night found himself uncharacteristically nervous as he parked his car outside Lavender's building.

This was it.

He was here to finally have the talk he should have made sure he and Lavender had as soon as they had sex. It had been naïve to think that it wouldn't change anything between them, and while he regretted letting his hang-ups come between them, he was here now to fix that.

There was a chance of course that Lavender would turn him down flat, tell him that she wasn't interested in him, or that his behavior after they had sex had turned her off, ruined any chance of what could have been, but it was a risk he was willing to take.

Bottom line was he couldn't stop thinking about her. He felt something for her, something that might grow into love, and the whole time he'd been away on this mission Lavender had been hovering at the back of his mind. He couldn't get the feel of her off his skin, the taste of her off his lips, and he didn't want to.

Had it really been only a month today that he'd brought her home and they'd made love?

It felt like he'd shared his body with her for a lifetime.

Night wasn't presuming that given the way he'd treated her they'd fall into bed again tonight, and he was surprised to find that he didn't even care. This was Lavender, she deserved the best, she deserved candlelit dinners and romantic dates, she deserved flowers and chocolates and anything else that would make her happy.

Turning off the engine, he got out of his car, locked it, and then headed over to the building. As he pressed the buzzer for Lavender's apartment, he realized his hands were sweating, and he hastily wiped them on his jeans.

When had he ever in his life been this nervous to talk to a woman?

Then again, when had a woman ever meant something to him beyond a good time?

Lavender meant a lot to him, and he was regretting letting this much time pass before he got his head on straight. But now he had, and he was determined to make things right no matter what it took.

His nerves got worse when he waited a full minute without Lavender buzzing him in, or using the intercom to turn him away. Night pressed the buzzer again and waited.

Still nothing.

Nerves morphed into concern, had something happened to her?

A couple came through the door, and he quickly grabbed the door before it could close and headed inside, ignoring the wary look they shot him.

Bypassing the lift, he took the stairs up to Lavender's floor and hammered on her door.

"Lavender? It's Eric. Are you in there?" He was no doubt overreacting, she was probably just out for the evening, or maybe she'd gotten a new job. It had been three weeks since he'd last seen her, and their mission had occupied all of his time, and he hadn't had a chance to check in with her.

When he didn't get any response, he pulled out his keys. Since he and Lavender were friends she'd given him a spare key when she'd left to do aid work so he could check in on her place from time to time. If she was in there and ignoring him, she wasn't going to be pleased to see him break-in, but he couldn't fix this problem he had created if he couldn't talk to her.

Unlocking her door, he opened it, stepped inside, and gasped.

Lavender was gone.

Her furniture remained, but there were boxes stacked in neat piles, clearly labeled with a room. Bathroom, kitchen, living room, bedroom, her whole life had been packed up into boxes.

She was moving.

The thought hit him hard.

She was gone.

Lavender had gone.

Without telling him.

Okay, he knew he had only himself to blame, he was the one who had panicked because of what happened with Jackie and feeling like he had taken advantage of Lavender, but he hadn't thought that she would just pack up her life and leave.

With trembling hands, he pulled his cell phone from his pocket and called his sister. If anyone knew where Lavender had gone and how to reach her it was Abigail. It wasn't until he had already pressed call that he realized his sister and Spider were probably busy in bed right now. Not that he cared about interrupting them, Spider could make out with his wife any time he wanted, but Lavender could be gone forever if he didn't act quickly enough.

"Eric, what's wrong?" Abigail asked in his ear.

"Where is she?" he demanded.

Abigail sighed. "Are you at her place? Is that how you know she's gone?"

"I came straight here to talk to her."

"I'm on my way," she said. In the background he could hear Spider grumbling, but Abigail added, "We'll be there in ten. I've got Lavender's keys so I can let us in."

How had things gotten this bad this quickly?

Sure, he knew he'd messed up and hurt Lavender by pulling away right when she needed the most support, but he hadn't thought she would just pack up and leave. Where had she gone? Had she decided to go back to live closer to her sister? Had she already left California? Was she staying in a hotel? If she'd already gone then the chances of him convincing her to move back here to give them a chance were virtually nonexistent, and he couldn't leave, his job tied him here, which meant that they were over before they had ever even begun.

Dropping down onto one of the sofas, he propped his elbows on his knees and rested his head in his hands. The only time he had felt worse about himself than he did in this moment was when he realized he was relieved his unborn baby had died, and he was free of his commitment to Jackie.

"Hey."

The softly spoken word and the gentle hand on his shoulder jerked him out of his head, and he realized Abby and Spider had arrived.

"Where is she?"

"She left, Eric. I'm sorry," Abby said, sympathy in her unusual eyes as she sat beside him.

"She just … *left*?" As much as he knew he had hurt her it seemed extreme that she would pack up her entire life and move.

"Yeah, she did."

"Has she already left the state?"

"She just left this morning. I'm sorry, Eric," she said again.

This morning.

So he had missed her by just hours.

While he and his team had been debriefing, Lavender had probably been at the airport getting on her flight.

"Did she go back to be closer to her sister?" he asked. It was the only thing he thought she would do, but he also knew that Lavender sometimes withdrew from everyone who loved her to tough it out on her own when she felt overwhelmed. It was what had led her to California in the first place.

"Yeah, she did," Abby replied.

"I have to call her." Standing, he went in search of his cell phone and found he'd left it on the kitchen counter.

"I don't think that's a good idea," Abigail said, following him. "She left because she needed space, time to think."

"I came here to talk to her, Abby, to fix the mess I made."

Tentatively, she rested a hand on his forearm. "I'm not sure you can."

No.

He wouldn't accept that.

Lavender knew about Jackie. He could explain to her how

he'd felt like he was taking advantage of her the same way he had with Jackie, he would explain how that had made him panic, she would get that. If there was anyone in the entire world that would get it, it was Lavender.

"Give her some time, Eric," Abigail said.

"Listen to her, man," Spider said, stepping up behind his wife.

"Like you walked away from Abby, no way," he said adamantly. Night knew it was a low blow because he had played a huge part in keeping his sister and best friend apart, something he would never completely forgive himself for, but there was no way he was walking in Spider's footsteps on this one.

Spider said nothing, but his lips pressed into a thin line and his expression went hard.

"The situations aren't the same," Abby said softly. "She left because she needed space. I suggest that if you want a chance with her, you give it to her."

A chance with Lavender?

She now lived on the opposite side of the country to him, and he could hardly go AWOL to go running after her.

Which meant that any chance he had with Lavender was gone.

Knowing that left him feeling completely empty inside.

The worst part was he knew he had no one to blame but himself.

# CHAPTER 12

January 25<sup>th</sup>
8:44 A.M.

Lavender straightened her spine and prepared herself.

She could do this.

It was only knocking on her sister's front door for goodness sake, she shouldn't be standing in the street, bordering on a panic attack.

Abigail had wanted her to take her time in deciding to move, but Lavender was more of a make a decision and then jump in with both feet kind of person, and once she had decided to leave California and come back to New Jersey, she just wanted to get it done. So she'd packed up her apartment, paid rent through February, and then as soon as she found a place here she would hire movers to pick up her stuff and drive it across the country.

While she had arrived here yesterday afternoon, she'd chickened out on going straight to Marigold and Jonah's place and instead spent the night in a hotel, but she couldn't put this off forever so this morning she was determined to catch a cab and come straight here.

With one last fortifying breath, Lavender walked across the street and knocked on Marigold's front door. Her twin and Jonah had bought this cute little house not long after they'd gotten married, it had been a fixer-upper, and they'd done a great job turning it into a family home.

Her hand went to her stomach when she heard the sounds of multiple sets of footsteps inside. This house was a family home, but would she ever be able to give this baby the same kind of life that Marigold had given her children?

"Lavender?" Marigold said, her gray eyes wide with surprise when she opened the front door.

"Surprise," she said, trying to smile but knowing it didn't make it to her eyes.

Marigold grabbed her and dragged her into a hard hug. "I wish you'd let us fly over to see you. I was so scared when we got the call you had been taken hostage. Are you okay? How's your leg? I wish you'd come sooner," Marigold babbled as she cried and held onto her.

Right now as she stood in her sister's arms, she couldn't remember why it was she had insisted that there was no need for Marigold to disrupt her family's life to come to see her when she was okay. "I'm sorry, I thought I was okay, but I'm not," she admitted, crying freely onto her sister's shoulder.

"Mama, hungry," said a firm little toddler voice, and Marigold pulled back to look down at her son.

"JJ, say hi to Aunt Lavender," she told the little boy who was like a mini version of his daddy.

"Hi, Aunt Lavender," JJ dutifully said.

"Hi, sweet boy," she said, bending down to hug him. She hadn't come out to visit many times since JJ and his baby sister were born, but she video chatted all the time with

Marigold and her family, and she loved her twin's children as if they were her own.

"Come in. I'll just get JJ a snack and put on one of his shows, and then we can talk. Lavender, I'm so glad you're here." Marigold pulled her in for another hug before leading her inside.

She'd been to her sister's place before so she followed her past the master bedroom on the left and a study on the right, down to the living area at the back. While Marigold got her son a snack and set him up on the floor in front of the TV, Lavender sunk into a chair at the kitchen table.

The house was bright, mostly clean with the mess that came from two little ones in the house. There were family photos on the walls and children's pictures on the fridge. There were toys scattered about and a stack of picture books on the counter beside a bowl full of fruit. This was how she had pictured her life when she'd thought of having a family. She'd thought that she would be married to the man she loved and have someone by her side as they navigated the winding and uneven roads of parenthood.

Instead, she'd be doing all of this alone.

"So, why didn't you call to say you were coming?" Marigold asked.

Because that would have led to questions she wanted to answer in person. "I wanted to surprise you."

"Well, you achieved that," Marigold said, dropping down into the chair opposite the one Lavender was sitting in. "You worried me too, I tried calling you several times yesterday, but it kept going straight to voicemail."

"I turned the phone off for the flight." And deliberately hadn't turned it back on because she didn't want to talk to anybody.

"Wait, the flight? You flew in yesterday? Then why are

you only stopping by this morning? Did you stay at a hotel last night instead of here?"

Ignoring the hurt look on her twin's face, she blurted out, "I'm pregnant."

Marigold's mouth dropped open in shock, but quickly horror filled her face. "Did they rape you?"

"What? No," she quickly assured her. "They were going to, but I was rescued before they got a chance."

"Then who's the father?"

"You remember Eric McNamara?"

"The sexy SEAL? Of course, who could forget that hot body? Although don't tell Jonah I said that," Marigold added with a grin.

"Your husband is pretty hot himself."

"That he is. So you and Eric are together? I didn't know that."

"We're not together, that's kind of why I'm here."

"Okay, I'm going to need details because if you're pregnant then you were definitely together at some point."

Lavender smiled sadly. "It was just one night. Christmas Eve. We had just flown into the country, and he waited while I was debriefed. He drove me home, he was being so sweet and protective, and he's such a good friend, and I just needed him, and he was there for me."

"Then I'm confused. Why aren't you together? Did he dump you when you found out you were pregnant?" Righteous indignation had Marigold's cheeks turning the same shade of red as the long hair that hung loosely around her shoulders.

"He doesn't know," Lavender explained. "I haven't told him. He's away on a mission, and I don't know when he'll be back."

With eyes narrowed suspiciously, Marigold asked, "But

you are *going* to tell him, right? You wouldn't keep the baby from him?"

Her sister didn't get it.

Eric wouldn't *want* the baby.

They might be friends, but that didn't mean he loved her, and since he didn't love her and didn't see a future for them, this baby represented only one thing.

An unwanted responsibility.

"Lavender?"

"I need time, it's not that simple. Eric has been in this position before, getting a woman pregnant, and he did the right thing, married her, but they lost the baby. This isn't what he wants."

"Well, it's what he got and he better man up and deal with it."

And Eric would.

But that wasn't what she wanted.

"I'm trying to do the right thing here, I really am," she told Marigold. "I don't want to keep this baby from its father, but I also don't want Eric to feel trapped. I don't want him with me because of the baby, I want him with me because it's where he wants to be."

"You love him," Marigold said.

Lavender nodded sadly. "Falling in love," she agreed. "Well, I was, I realized after we slept together that I had feelings for him, but he doesn't feel the same way. He's basically avoided me for the last month, he didn't even tell me when he got called out, and he *always* tells me. I don't want him to be obligated to me, to us," she amended, placing a hand on her stomach. It was so hard to believe that there was a baby growing inside of her. "I just need some time, okay? Time to figure things out and get used to the idea that I'm going to be a mother. Figure out what I want for the future and how I'm going to take care of this little one."

"Okay, I guess I can understand that," Marigold acknowledged. "You know that Jonah and I will be there for you, whatever you need."

"I know, that's why I came here."

"Are you here for good?" Marigold asked hopefully.

"Yes. At least I think so. As I said, I have a lot to figure out. I truly don't want to hurt Eric or the baby by keeping them apart, but I need him to know that he doesn't owe us anything. I can take care of this baby on my own, and I would rather he be a part of its life because he wants to be, not because he thinks he has to be."

It was all so complicated, this should be the happiest time of her life, but instead it was so confusing. She was trying so hard to do the best thing for all three of them, but she just didn't know what that was.

# CHAPTER 13

February 1st
1:18 P.M.

A month.

It had been basically a month since he'd last seen Lavender, and it felt like the hole in his heart from missing her got worse with each passing day, not better.

It was supposed to get better.

Easier.

It had to because he couldn't keep going on like this.

Night had tried calling her a dozen times, sent even more texts, but she hadn't replied to a single one, he didn't think she'd even gotten them. It looked like she had turned her phone off when she got onto that plane and never turned it back on.

It was like she had shut him out and everything to do with her life here and simply moved on.

He still didn't get why she was so angry with him. Okay,

he had been a jerk ignoring her, but it wasn't like they had made each other any promises or discussed the future. Again that was on him, she was the one who had been vulnerable that night, and he was the one who had taken advantage, but it was like she couldn't stand the very thought of him. Running from her problems was classic Lavender, but he'd thought that she would at least at some point call him or send a text or even an email, if for nothing else than to check he had returned safely from his mission.

But nothing.

She'd just vanished.

Night had decided to give her a month. One month to get her head on straight and then he was going to get her twin sister Marigold's number from Abigail, or he'd find it any way he could and call her, demand that she listen to him.

Well, not *demand*. The last thing he wanted was for her to start seeing him as some sort of unstable stalker.

*Yeah, that chance has been and gone, buddy.*

The number of times he'd called and texted pretty much had to convince her he was an unstable stalker, but he'd hoped it would show her that he cared. He cared enough to feel like he was losing his mind not seeing her and talking to her every day. Unless he was on a mission and unable to check-in, then they usually did at least text every day, and not having that just showed him how important she had become to him without him even realizing it.

"Is this all you're going to do now? Just sit around and mope?" Chaos asked as he dropped down into the chair beside the one Night was slouched in.

"I'm not moping," he said, but there was no strength to his words.

"Man, that's all you do, ever since we brought Lavender home," Chaos said. "Would you just hurry up and sort things out with her?"

"It's not that easy."

"Make it that easy."

"I can't force her to listen to me." If he could do that then he would have done it already, but if they had any chance at working things out then Lavender had to be prepared to meet him halfway. Not even halfway, he'd take it three quarters, eighty percent, ninety percent, all she needed to do was take one step toward him and he'd cover the rest of the distance himself.

"Then maybe it's time to move on," Chaos suggested gently.

Even the idea of that had his stomach revolting.

Lavender was special to him.

The first woman he'd ever even considered having a future with. Sure, he'd enjoyed sex when he was younger, slept with women without any talk of a commitment, but after Jackie had wound up pregnant he'd found it safer to take his needs into his own hands most of the time rather than risk another unwanted pregnancy.

But Lavender changed all of that.

She made him want things he had thought he would be content to live without.

He'd never really been into the whole marriage, kids, dog, and white picket fence ideal, but with Lavender he could see himself wanting the whole package. The cute little house near the beach, a front lawn to mow, a swing set in the backyard, bikes on the front porch, family dinners around the kitchen table ... yeah, he was already sucked into that world.

"That bad, huh?" Chaos asked.

"What?"

"You have it that bad for her. I can see it on your face, you can't imagine yourself with another woman because you're so hung up on Lavender. Dude, are you sure she feels the same way you do?"

Was he?

His brain said no. There was no way he could know what she was thinking or feeling because they hadn't yet sat down and talked about it, but his gut said yes.

She was into him, but something had her running scared.

"I'm pretty sure that she does, but I messed up, I waited too long to figure out how important she is to me. I'm afraid it's too late," he admitted. Talking about sex with his teammates was one thing, but talking about relationships had him shifting uncomfortably in his chair.

"Nah." Chaos waved a hand like the idea was preposterous. "It's never too late for love."

"You ever been in love, man?" Chaos was loud, full of life, the life of the party, he lived his life to the fullest, and that constant buzz of energy was what had earned him his nickname.

"Nah, don't ever see it happening either, but I believe in it. I believe in true love and soulmates and happy ever afters. I believe in it for you and your girl too. Lavender's real sweet, but she'd been through hell twice now, I don't think it's any wonder she feels like she needs some time and space to sort herself out before she can consider starting a relationship."

"Yeah? You think that's why she left? Why she hasn't gotten in contact with me?" Night heard the desperation in his voice, hated that he sounded like some whiney, needy high school cheerleader, but this was all new territory for him. He'd never been this hung up on a woman, and the distance between them—both physical and emotional—had him twisted up inside.

"I think that's why. Can you blame her? She selflessly goes to another country to help the people there and winds up a hostage. She knew what they were going to do to her, and given what happened to her before she moved out here, I don't think it's any wonder she needs some time to deal with it all."

"I wish she would come to me, let me help her."

"I know, man, but that's your ego talking. Trust her to know what's best for her right now, trust her to know what she needs, trust *her*. When she's ready she'll come to you. Question is, can you wait? Are you going to be there when she comes?"

"Yeah, I can wait. I can wait for her for as long as it takes." As he said the words, he realized that he meant them whole-heartedly. His best friend had grown to be something more, and there wasn't anything that he could envision coming between them and tearing them apart. Lavender needed time to process her ordeal and needed the support of her sister to do that, he could understand that, and when she was ready he would be there.

"Good." Chaos stood and slapped him on the shoulder. "So you think you're ready to come help the rest of us now?"

They were supposed to be helping Spider paint his and Abigail's new house, but he'd been sitting in their yard, staring at nothing pretty much since he arrived there this morning. "Yeah, I'm ready. Thanks, man, for talking, I didn't know you could have such a serious conversation," he said, only half-teasing. Chaos was the lighthearted one of their team, the funny one, the one always looking for fun and adventure. He'd have believed dark and broody Shark could have this conversation with him before Chaos.

"I'm a man of many surprises," Chaos said with a wink and a grin. "Hey, guys, I convinced Mr. Mopey here to finally come and pull his weight," he called out as he entered the house where the others were busy painting rooms so Abigail and Spider could be moved in and settled before the baby came.

"About time," King grumbled. "I gave up a day of sex with

the hottest woman you've ever seen to come paint walls pink, and this guy gets out of working by brooding."

"It's not pink, it's elusive mauve," Spider corrected.

"Dude, why do you know that?" King asked with a laugh.

"Because Abby and I went through every paint sample for every company that makes paint."

"And then she made all the decisions," Fox laughed. "I remember how it goes."

"Hey, man, she can make all the decisions she wants, a happy wife makes a ..."

"Happy life," King interrupted.

"Actually, I was going to say a happy wife makes a man happy in the bedroom," Spider corrected, winking.

"Eww, dude, that's my sister." Night made a face as he picked up a paint roller and began to put elusive mauve paint on the walls of what would be the master bedroom.

The guys laughed, and as they all started painting, Night felt a little of the tension roll off his shoulders. He could give Lavender the time she needed to get a handle on what she'd lived through, and then all bets were off, and he was claiming the woman as his.

# CHAPTER 14

February 4<sup>th</sup>
10:31 A.M.

Six weeks.

As of today, she was six weeks pregnant.

Lavender wasn't anymore used to the idea now than when she took that pregnancy test and found out she was carrying a baby. She was starting to wonder if it would ever feel real, she'd probably be sending her kid off to college still in shock about the fact that she had a kid.

"This feels wrong."

Lavender looked over at her sister. "What feels wrong?"

"This." Marigold waved her hands at the waiting room. "All of this. It's your first appointment and Eric should be here with you whether he wants to be or not."

They'd had this conversation several times over the last ten days she'd spent at her sister's house. Between lots of talking, spending as much time as she could with her niece and nephew, and attempting to make plans for the future, she and Marigold had discussed Eric several times.

But as many times as they'd talked about it, nothing could change the facts.

Eric didn't want her.

Eric didn't want another baby with a woman he didn't love.

She didn't want a man who was with her only because of her child.

That left them with not a lot of options.

"We've been over this," she said with exaggerated patience. If she wasn't getting this same conversation from her twin, she was getting it from Abigail who called nearly every day to check-in.

"I know, and I one hundred percent understand your need for space while you figure this out. Finding out you're having a baby is big. Jonah and I were married and trying, and even we took some time to adjust to the idea that I was pregnant and that hypothetical baby was now a reality. Given that you're alone and unsure of what role the father will play in your lives I get how much harder that makes all of this, then add in what you lived through just a couple of months ago, and I respect that you need time."

"But?"

"But ... you *are* going to tell Eric, aren't you? You're not thinking of keeping it from him. Even if he doesn't love you, I'm sure he'll want to be a part of the baby's life. And even if he doesn't, it should be his choice."

She had gone over and over this in her head ever since she'd taken that pregnancy test, but when it boiled down to it, Abigail's ultimatum gave her no choice.

"I've thought about keeping it from him," she admitted in a small voice, sure that made her a horrible mother even before the baby came into the world.

Marigold smiled sympathetically. "I don't think you'd be human if you didn't."

"It's just that I know for a fact that this isn't what Eric wants. It's not like I'm just basing this on my gut feeling or anything, I mean, he told me. After already getting a woman pregnant and marrying her out of a sense of obligation he was determined that the next time he fathered a child it would be with someone he loved and was committed to, and … well, that's not me."

"Are you sure about that? Like, absolutely positive that he doesn't want to be with you?"

"As sure as I can be," she said. "His sister Abigail knows about the baby. She found the positive pregnancy test when she came over to visit and went to the bathroom, she's not comfortable keeping this secret from her brother, and she said that if I don't tell him before the baby is born then she will."

"And if Abigail hadn't found out, would you have still told him?"

Lavender sighed.

So many reasons to keep this quiet, never let him know so that he could find someone, fall in love, and have the family he wanted.

And yet …

"Yeah, I would have told him. Guilt wouldn't have let me keep it a secret. It's just before he knows I have to have a plan in place. I have to have a place for me and the baby to live, and I have to have a job where I can support both of us. I have to show him that I can do this on my own so that if he decides he wants to be with us it's because he actually wants to be with us, and not just because he feels like he has to take care of us. And if he doesn't want to be with me, but he does want to be a part of the baby's life then we can figure something out, we'll share custody, fly the kid back and forth so spend time with both of us, we'll make it work as best as we can."

"What do *you* want?" Marigold asked softly. "We've talked so much about your need to prove to him you can do this on your own so if he's with you it's for the right reasons. And we've talked about how you would prefer to keep this from him. We've talked about a lot of stuff, but you haven't told me yet what you want in your heart."

"I'm trying to think with my head right now and not with my heart."

Marigold gave her a sad smile. "I know you are, but I'm your twin sister and I love you and want you to be happy. What do you want, Lavender?"

What did she want?

Wasn't that a loaded question?

There were so many things she wanted she didn't even know where to begin.

"I want to not feel guilty that I was such an awful sister to you, that I was never there for you, and that I left you to deal with all the stuff Mom and Dad didn't provide for us. I want to make it up to you somehow. I want to make up for being so selfish all my life, only caring about myself and what I wanted and not the people who mean everything to me. I want to be able to give this baby everything that it deserves, everything that we didn't have, everything that you've given JJ and Violet. I want someone who looks at me like I'm the only thing that matters in their world. I want a home and a family. I want Eric to care about me the way I care about him, I want him to fall in love with me like I'm falling in love with him. I want him to want to be with me and the baby because we're his whole world and not some unwanted responsibility. I want to be happy," she finished a little too loudly given where they were, and a few of the other expectant mothers and their partners looked over at her.

"Oh, Lavender." Marigold leaned sideways in her chair and pulled her into a hug.

Lavender hugged her back, holding on tightly. Marigold and her family might be the only family she ever had. She was pregnant, not a lot of guys would be willing to take on another man's child and raise it as their own, so she was facing the very real possibility of spending at least the next eighteen years of her life single.

She didn't want to be alone.

She didn't want to be facing all these challenges without someone by her side.

But life didn't always give you what you wanted.

"I wish I could give you everything that you want. I wish you could have with Eric what I have with Jonah. Don't ever feel alone though, me and Jonah, we're here for you. Morning sickness, cravings, labor, we'll be there through it all. Teething and sleepless nights, we'll help however we can. Your baby will always have two cousins as defacto siblings to love it and tease it. And you know what else?"

"What?"

"I can give you one thing that you want."

"Which one?"

"I can take away your guilt about me. I love you, you're my sister, the past is in the past, and I don't want you to lay that heavy burden on your shoulders. You loved me, that was what was important. And I love you so much. So please, no more guilt about that. I mean it, Lavender, let it go."

The earnestness in her twin's voice made her smile, but it also made her heart crack a little. "You were always the better half of us."

"I love you, you know that, right?"

"Of course I do. You've shown me that every day in so many ways since we were kids."

"Good. So no more guilt?"

It would be hard but she would work on letting it go, if for no other reason than to be the best mother she could to this little one growing inside her. "No more guilt."

"Lavender Vaile?" the doctor called out.

This was it.

It was time to go and take that first step toward becoming a mom. She'd learn about pregnancy, what she could do to help her little one grow big and strong, and whatever the doctor told her to do she'd do.

She might not have been a great sister, and she wasn't very good at the relationship thing, but she could be the mom this baby deserved.

# CHAPTER 15

February 8<sup>th</sup>
9:07 A.M.

"There, done," Spider said with satisfaction as they both took a step away from the newly assembled crib.

"Yay," Abigail said when she turned from the dresser. "Seeing the nursery come together makes it seem that much more real. We are really having a baby."

"I still can't believe you're more than six months along now," Night said as he looked at his sister's stomach. It seemed to grow bigger every time he saw her. He was excited about becoming an uncle, all the fun of baby cuddles without all the responsibility. He couldn't wait to take the baby out hiking and camping and all the other fun things he'd enjoyed doing with his parents when he was a kid.

"I know, just a couple more months and that crib you two so expertly put together will have an itty bitty baby sleeping in it," Abigail said, the dreamy smile on her face she always got when she talked about her baby.

"Sleepless nights, spitting up, dirty diapers, crying, lucky us," Spider said as he made a face.

Night laughed at his best friend. He knew how excited Spider was about becoming a dad, he was going to love every second of those sleepless nights, spitting up, dirty diapers, and tears. "You can't fool us, Spider, I know you're itching to hold that little one in your hands and see it looking up at you, hear it call you daddy for the first time, the hugs and kisses."

"Well, when you put it that way it certainly does sound like fun." Spider grinned.

"You two are so silly." Abigail shook her head at both of them. "Can you hang the mobile above the crib, Ryder?"

"Sure thing, babe." Spider gave Abigail a quick kiss on the lips before leaving the room to retrieve the other boxes of things for the nursery.

"I love the yellow you chose for the walls," Night told his sister. The house was now freshly painted, and Abby and Spider had moved in. While most of the other rooms were more stacks of boxes than livable spaces, she had wanted to get the nursery set up first so he was here to help out however he could.

"It's called butter ridge," Abigail said as she resumed folding tiny baby clothes and putting them in draws in the dresser. "I chose it because it'll be nice whether we have a boy or a girl, speaking of which, whatever we don't have we can give those clothes to Lavender which will be one less thing she has to buy."

"So you're still on the waiting till the baby is born before …" Night trailed off as he realized what she'd just said.

No.

She couldn't have said that.

But as he turned around and took one look at his sister's stricken face, he realized that she had indeed said it.

Lavender was pregnant.

"What did you just say?" he demanded, taking a step toward Abigail.

"I ... umm ... it was ..."

"Repeat it," he growled.

"What's going on?" Spider asked as he entered the room and took in his terrified-looking wife and the angry snarl on Night's face.

"Abigail just told me that Lavender is pregnant."

Spider's gaze darted to Abby, and from the look on his face, it was clear this wasn't news to him.

"You knew as well. Is it my baby?" he demanded, knowing it was the only thing that made sense.

"Yes." Abigail nodded sadly, tears welling up in her eyes. "It was conceived Christmas Eve when you two ... well, you know."

The room didn't seem to have any oxygen left in it.

His heart thundered in his chest as he attempted to draw a breath.

Lavender was having a baby.

*His* baby.

That was why she'd left the state.

And his sister and best friend knew about it and didn't tell him.

"How long have you known?" he asked, voice cold.

"I found out by accident while you guys were on your last mission."

"That's why she left?"

"Yes."

"Was she going to tell me or keep my child from me?" How could this be happening to him again? Another baby after taking advantage of a vulnerable woman. Only this time he had been careful, they used a condom … which wasn't one hundred percent effective.

"No, she said she just needed time to process everything," Abby told him.

"What about you?" he demanded, taking a step toward her. "Were you going to keep my child from me?"

Spider crossed the room in two strides, putting himself in between Night and Abigail. "Ease off, man," he warned.

"She lied to me, Spider, kept it a secret that Lavender is having my baby," he roared. Never in his life had Night felt this level of rage. The people who were supposed to care about him the most had conspired to keep a huge secret from him.

"I didn't want to lie, Eric, I swear I didn't," Abigail begged as she tried to move around Spider who kept himself firmly planted between the siblings.

"But you did. I've been home from that mission for two weeks now, and you never said a word. Was this some kind of payback for my part in keeping you and Spider apart? Is that why you kept my child a secret, Abigail?"

"What? No!" She looked horrified by the possibility that he could think that about her, but right now he didn't know what to think. All he knew was that a woman was carrying his child and he had been kept in the dark. "I told Lavender that she had to tell you," Abigail said, crying now, "I told her that if she hadn't told you before the baby was born that I would. I would never keep you from your child, Eric. You know that. You know I wouldn't."

She managed to dart around Spider and grabbed onto his arm, but he didn't want to be touched right now, especially not by someone who had betrayed him.

"I'm out of here." He shook her off, stormed for the door, doing his best to ignore the sound of her sobbing, but then her cries changed, became ones of pain.

"Abby?" Spider asked.

"Ryder, something's wrong," she said, fear evident in her tone.

Night stopped, turned around, and saw Abby's hands pressed to her stomach, her face contorted in pain. Spider had his arms around her, panic on his usually calm face.

"I think I'm having contractions," Abigail said, her breathing accelerating as her fear grew. "Ryder, it's too soon, I'm only twenty-seven weeks. Make it stop, please," she begged. "Please, make it stop. I don't want to lose my baby."

"It's okay, sweetheart, it's going to be okay, you just stay calm, focus on your breathing," Spider said, his voice strained as he tried to calm his near-hysterical wife. Anger sparked in his blue eyes when he turned to Night. "I need you to drive us to the hospital, it will be quicker than waiting for an ambulance, and I need to try to keep her calm."

It was clear from Spider's expression who he thought was to blame for Abigail having contractions almost three months early.

Obviously, it hadn't been his goal to upset his sister to the point where she had gone into labor. He'd just been hurt and angry about their lies and lashed out.

"Yeah, man, of course. Do you need help with her?" Night asked, already pulling out his keys.

"No, I got her. You go get the car ready." Spider was already lifting Abigail into his arms, whispering soothingly in her ear as he walked with her.

Night ran through the house to get the car, the fear on both his sister and her husband's face making him think of Jackie. He might not have wanted that baby, but she had and was devastated when she miscarried. While he had been relieved to be off the hook for the marriage of obligation, she had been grieving the loss of her baby.

Alone.

Because he certainly hadn't been there for her.

He'd been too selfish and self-absorbed, too happy to have an out for a situation he hadn't wanted to be in.

Abby and Spider were already in love with their unborn baby, and they would never get over losing it. That's how a parent should feel about their child from the moment it was conceived.

How would he feel if something happened to Lavender and their baby?

She might have kept their child a secret, but once the hurt and anger started to dial down he had to realize that she hadn't known he was coming back from that mission to sort things out with her, all she had known was the story of Jackie. She had no doubt assumed he would feel the same way about her and her baby that he had about Jackie. No wonder Lavender had packed up and moved back to be closer to her sister. She was having a child, and right on the back of a traumatic ordeal, she needed stability, she needed someone she could count on to be there to support her and her baby no matter what.

Unfortunately, that hadn't been him.

Night knew he had a lot of apologizing to do, a lot to make right, but first he had to get his sister to the hospital so she didn't lose her child.

~

2:45 P.M.

Night sat with his head in his hands, waiting for news.

It had been hours since they'd arrived at the hospital. Abigail had been whisked away, Spider had refused to leave her side, and not wanting to leave until he knew both his sister and her baby were going to be okay, Night had hung around the waiting room.

As soon as he knew that Abby was going to be okay he was going to go and see Jackie, there was no way he could even hope to build a future until he let go of the past, and the only way to do that was to apologize to the woman he had hurt several times over.

"You're still here," Spider growled.

Night looked up to see his friend standing beside him. "How is she?"

"How is she?" Spider repeated incredulously. "Dude, she struggled for weeks keeping that secret, talking to Lavender nearly daily to try to convince her to call you only Lavender has it in her head that you won't be pleased to have another baby with someone you don't love, which I can only assume has something to do with that chick Jackie you were briefly married to a few years back. Then she accidentally lets Lavender's pregnancy slip, and you accuse her of trying to get payback on you by keeping your child from you. Man, if you really think Abby would do that then you don't know her at all."

"I know she wouldn't, I shouldn't have said it," Night agreed. He'd let his anger take over, and he'd hurt the baby sister he had vowed to never hurt again.

"A little late for that given that my wife is sitting in a hospital bed right now."

"I know, I'm sorry, Spider, that's all I can say. I shouldn't have yelled at her, and I shouldn't have said that to her. I know Abby is too sweet for her own good, her heart is too big, and she was trying to do what was best for everyone. Are she and the baby okay?" If anything happened to either his sister or her child he would never forgive himself.

Spider ran his hands over his face then gave a small smile. "Yeah, they're okay. They gave Abby steroids to speed up the baby's lung development and drugs to stop the labor, they seem to be working, but she's going to be here for probably a couple of days, and then they'll see what happens next. Best case scenario, she has no more contractions and carries to term, worst case we take it week by week and each week that passes the baby's chances of survival and no complications increases."

Night ran his hands over his face and then stood. "I'm so sorry, man. This is all on me. I'm so, so sorry."

"I get it, where you were coming from, you just learned that you were having a baby and that people had been keeping it from you, so I understand that. But if you ever speak to my wife that way again, best friend or not, teammate or not, it's over, our friendship, your relationship with Abby, you will be out of our lives for good. I forgave you for messing with our relationship because you were trying to keep a promise to your dying father, and I can forgive you for this because I know how I would feel if you didn't tell me about my kid, but three strikes, man."

"Understood." Spider had been more than generous with the forgiveness, especially considering what was at stake this time, and Night completely understood that there couldn't be another time.

Not that he wanted there to be.

He had to get his stuff together.

No more stupid mistakes.

No more immaturity.

No more lashing out in anger.

He was going to be a father, and he wanted to be someone his kid could look up to and respect.

"Tell Abby I'm sorry and that I love her, and I'll be back to check on her and apologize in person later tonight."

"Where are you going?"

"I have something I have to go and do, something that I

should have done a long time ago. Text me if anything changes with her condition and I'll be right back. Do you need me to text the rest of the team, let them know what's going on?"

"Yeah, actually that would be great, thanks, Night."

"Least I can do for causing this mess."

Night was just turning around to leave when strong arms pulled him in for a quick hug. "Just because I don't like you taking your anger out on Abby, doesn't mean we aren't brothers and that we won't always be brothers."

"You're a better friend than I deserve, Spider."

"Yeah, you're right." Spider shot him a grin then turned and headed back down to Abigail's room.

Typing out a quick text to the team he let them know what had happened, that Abby would be in the hospital for at least a day or two, and that Spider could do with some company and some food, he then checked his phone for the address he needed and headed to his car.

Pumping in the details to his GPS, he started driving. As much as he knew this was something he needed to do, something he should have done long before now, it didn't mean he wasn't nervous as he drove across town.

He'd gotten her new address from the divorce papers, but he'd never been to Jackie's new place, hadn't kept tabs on her life after they separated, they'd shared nothing more than a single night of pleasure that had resulted in a baby neither of them was ready for. He hadn't seen her since the day he came back from the mission, told her that he was leaving, and packed up his stuff. The divorce had gone through easily, they had only been married a month and hadn't had any joint bank accounts or property.

When he parked in front of her place he saw it was a nice townhouse in a nice part of town. There were two cars in the driveway so she was probably involved with someone, and in this moment he wished he had taken the effort to at least remain friends, after all this woman had been pregnant with his child.

His knock on the door was answered almost immediately by a pretty woman with blonde hair brushing her shoulders, wide blue eyes, and a small baby cradled in her arms. Her eyes grew wide when she recognized him. "Eric McNamara."

"Hi, Jackie, may I come on?"

"Umm, yes, of course." Clearly confused, she stepped back and allowed him to come in before closing the door and leading him through to the living area where a man with salt and pepper hair held another small baby.

"Twins?" he asked.

"Yes, they're four months old. We also have a two-year-old," Jackie answered.

"You have your hands full," he quipped.

"Sure do. And you are?" the man asked, coming forward and holding out his hand.

"I'm Eric, an old friend of Jackie's. I just wanted to talk to her for a bit if it's not a bad time."

"It's fine. Dave, could you put them down for me?" Jackie asked her husband, passing him the baby she'd been holding.

"Sure thing, nice to meet you, Eric."

"Likewise."

Once Dave was gone, Jackie looked him straight in the eye. "Why are you here?"

"To apologize," he said simply.

"Apologize?"

"For the way I treated you. You deserved better. I knew you were vulnerable that night, and I shouldn't have had sex with you. Or at the very least I shouldn't have been so drunk that I forgot a condom."

"We were both drunk and upset that night," Jackie

reminded him, taking a seat on a sofa filled with stuffed animals.

"No excuse on my part, I was the guy it was my job to remember the condom. I'm sorry for asking you to marry me just because of the baby, but most of all I'm sorry for what I did after you lost it. I was ... relieved to have an out of a relationship I didn't want. The way I left you, that was unforgivable. You wanted that baby, and you were grieving, I should have at least remained with you through the worst of that." There, he'd said what he came for, now all he could do was hope for a miracle.

"Come, sit." Jackie patted the cushion beside her. When he sat, she took his hands in hers. "I was angry at you for a long time, Eric. It was all I could think about, how you were my husband, the baby's father, and you could just move on so easily. But then I realized that in being angry with you I was hurting myself. I was as much to blame for the unplanned pregnancy as you were, it's not just the guy's job," she said with a smile. "And I accepted your proposal, knowing you didn't love me, and I shouldn't have done that. Maybe if I had been strong enough to say no you wouldn't have felt like it was such a burden. So really we were both to blame for what happened."

"How can you be so forgiving?" he asked. It really was his lucky day, he'd been a jerk, more times than he cared to admit, and yet people were forgiving him left, right, and center.

"Because everything worked out the way it should. Will I always miss that baby? Yes, of course. Will I always wish that you hadn't dumped me as soon as the baby was gone? Sure. But if you had stayed just because you thought you should I would never have met Dave. I love him, Eric, the way you're supposed to love someone when you marry them and have a baby with them. Dave and I are so happy, and we have three beautiful children who I adore. I love my life. What about you? Are you happy? Married?" She looked down at his hand, noticed there was no ring, and then looked sad. "You're still single."

"Yes."

"Because of me and the baby?"

"In part. I won't ever completely forgive myself for my relief at our baby being gone, and for leaving you when you needed me. I'm ashamed of my behavior. With you and my sister."

"That's why you were drunk that night?"

"Yeah, I guess you could say that making decisions I'm ashamed of is my MO."

"Was."

"Was what?"

"*Was* your MO, but you came here today to apologize to me, that says you're ready to change the self-destructive behavior. Right?"

Was she right?

Was that what this sudden need to come here was about?

Looking at his past bad behavior, he could see it as self-destructive. Maybe knowing what he had put his sister and best friend through, he'd felt the need to punish himself. Not allowing himself to get attached to his baby because he didn't think he deserved it, running from Jackie the second the baby was gone, running from Lavender when he realized he had feelings for her. He felt the need to continue to punish himself for that one bad decision he had made without having all the information.

If he'd known the reason why his father had wanted to keep them apart he would never have gone along with it. But he had gone along with it, and he'd nearly destroyed two people he loved. It was time to start forgiving himself for that, he could regret it without beating himself up. It was time to stop punishing himself by continuing to make bad decisions that gave him another and another reason to hate himself.

"You're right. I hadn't thought it through like that, but I do want to stop being self-destructive, I want to be a better man."

"You *are* a good man, Eric." Jackie took his hand and squeezed it. "You're a man who has made mistakes, who hasn't always done the right thing, even done some things you're ashamed of, but in the end you are a good man. Remember that and move forward, don't forget that if there are parts of yourself you don't like, you can change them. Become better, do better, expect better of yourself. Be the person you want to see looking back at you in the mirror. That's what my mom told me when we got divorced. She told me to look inside myself, find all the parts I didn't like, and make a conscious decision to work on them."

"Your mom sounds like a smart lady, and you obviously take after her."

"Make sure you tell Dave that before you leave," she said with a wink.

Eric laughed and it felt good. It felt like shedding some of the weight he had piled high on his shoulders. He had to be a better man, for Lavender, for himself, and for that baby growing inside her. He wanted his son or daughter to respect him as well as love him, and if he wanted that he had a lot of work to do on himself first.

# CHAPTER 16

February 9th
8:30 A.M.

Lavender looked up from the floor where she and Violet were building with blocks when the phone rang. The nine-month-old grabbed a block and threw it at the tower, distracting Lavender, and she laughed and began to rebuild.

"You think you're so funny, don't you, Vi?" she said, tickling the baby's chubby little tummy.

Whenever she'd come to visit Marigold and her family before, she'd played with the kids, but she'd never really helped with anything else. This time, knowing that in just a few short months she would be a mother herself, she'd been helping with everything. Changing diapers, feeding, bathing, putting to bed, she'd even been helping with potty training JJ. Being able to get hands-on experience with some of the things she'd soon be doing with her own baby made her a little less nervous about becoming a mom.

A little bit.

"It's for you."

"Huh?" she said, looking up at her sister, the next block in her hand ready to be placed on top of the three others already stacked. "For me? Is it Abby?" Abigail had been continuing to call every day, but she usually called later in the day, maybe early afternoon.

"No."

The look on her twin's face put her on edge, and she passed the block to Violet and stood up, barely noticing the baby throw the block at the little tower, knocking it down. "Who is it?"

"It's Eric."

"Eric?" Panic had her heart rate picking up and her breath catching. Why was he calling? Did he know? "What does he want?"

"To talk to you."

"Oh, my gosh," she said breathily, struggling not to hyper-ventilate.

This couldn't be happening.

If he had found out about the baby then he was going to be so angry with her.

"I'm not ready," she told Marigold.

"Ready or not, honey, it looks like you don't have a choice." Marigold shot her a sympathetic smile and held out the phone. "Go and take it in the office so you can have some privacy, and I'll try to keep the kids quiet."

With a nod, she took the phone because she knew there was nothing else she could do, no way to wiggle out of it, and dragged her heavy feet through to the office. Curling up in the large rocking chair by the window, she tucked her legs underneath her and tried to get herself under control.

She could do this.

"H-hello?" she said when she thought she could speak without breaking into a cold sweat.

"Lavender," Eric said, his voice hard, almost cold. If she'd doubted that he knew about the baby then that doubt was now gone, the tone of his voice clearly communicated that he was angry with her, and there was only one reason for him to be angry with her.

The baby.

Their baby.

Not knowing what to say, she just sat there. She would give Eric a chance to vent, he deserved it after all. She had fled to the other side of the country with his baby and kept it a secret from him. He had every right to be angry with her, and she would sit here and take anything he wanted to dish out.

"Is it true?" Eric asked.

She could pretend that she didn't know what he was talking about, but that seemed like an insult to both of them. "Yes."

"You're pregnant."

"Yes," she said again even though it had sounded like a statement, not a question.

"And it's mine?"

Anger sparked inside her at the insinuation that she slept around. Okay, maybe when she'd been younger and traveling the globe housesitting she'd slept with more than her share of guys, but that had all changed when Cage had kidnapped and held her captive, raping her and her sister before almost killing them.

Did Eric really think she had come back from an ordeal that had nearly broken her and proceeded to have sex with a bunch of guys?

If he thought that, then he didn't know her very well.

"Of course it's yours. How could you ask me that?"

Lavender hated that her voice wavered, but his words had hurt her. Maybe she and Eric didn't really know each other as well as she'd thought because her friend Eric who had sat on the restaurant roof and talked with her for hours would never insinuate she was a slut.

On the other end of the line, Eric sighed, and she could hear regret in his voice when he spoke, "You're right, I shouldn't have asked you that. I'm sorry. Were you going to tell me or were you going to keep my baby from me?" he demanded.

The ice in his voice hurt more than it should because she *did* want to keep the baby from him. Well, not keep it from him, she just wanted to do the right thing, and she still believed that not putting Eric back in the position where he had to accept responsibility for a baby he didn't want was the right thing to do. Lavender believed that the baby was both their responsibility, but she didn't want her child to grow up feeling that was all it was. She wanted it to know it was loved and wanted, not just an obligation. But in the end, no matter what she'd thought, she couldn't have kept him from his child even if Abigail hadn't issued her ultimatum.

"I would have told you before the baby was born even if Abigail hadn't made me promise to do it or she would," she said, injecting as much confidence into her voice as she could so he would know she was telling the truth.

Eric didn't say anything, and the silence stretched between them. She didn't know what he was thinking or what he was feeling besides being angry and no doubt wishing he had never said yes to sleeping with her that night.

She tried to wait him out, but when he didn't say anything she started babbling. "I thought it was the right thing to do, Eric. I didn't want to put you in the same situation you were in with Jackie. You could barely stand to look at me or be in the same room as me, it was pretty clear that you weren't feeling what I was feeling after we had sex, and I didn't want you to feel trapped. I care too much about you to make you responsible for a baby you don't want. I know your dream, you want a child with a woman you love, who you have a future with. I know that's not me, and if you don't want to be a part of the baby's life that's okay. I don't want you to propose, I can take care of this baby on my own, so you do whatever you want to do. Don't feel obligated. Please."

Eric was still silent, and she actually pulled the phone away from her ear to see if the call was still connected.

It was.

But he still didn't say anything.

Well, she guessed that told her all she needed to know.

Eric didn't love her.

He didn't love this baby.

He didn't want to be a part of either of their lives.

"I'm sorry it had to end this way. Goodbye, Eric." She was just moving the phone from her ear again to end the call when she heard him call out her name.

"Lavender, wait."

She held onto the phone, but this time she was the one who didn't speak. She honestly didn't know what else there was to say.

"I'm flying out there, I have a flight booked for late tonight. I'll be there in the early hours of the morning. I'll be staying at a hotel near the airport, and then I'll drive into the city to see you. There's a park close to your sister's house, I'll meet you there at nine o'clock. That gives me plenty of time to get settled and grab a few hours' sleep."

Lavender knew the park, she and Marigold had taken the kids there several times already to play at the playground and kick a ball around on the open grassy space. It was a neutral location, and she guessed if she had to see Eric face to face, then that was the place to do it.

"Okay. I'll see you at the park at nine," she said.

"See you then."

The line went dead, and Lavender sat for a good two minutes just listening to the empty dial tone. What was she going to do? Could she face Eric tomorrow? Just talking to him on the phone was bad enough. How was she supposed to look at him, see the anger burning in his eyes, hear him talk to her in that cold tone?

She couldn't do it, but what choice did she have?

How could she get out of it?

Feeling like the future she had been starting to piece together had been ripped out from underneath her, Lavender covered her face with her hands and cried.

# CHAPTER 17

February 10<sup>th</sup>
8:42 A.M.

He was early, but he hadn't been able to wait any longer.

As it was, Night had struggled to make it through the night in his hotel room without jumping in a cab and going straight to Marigold's house. It was only the fact that Lavender's twin had two young children in the house that needed their rest that kept him from storming the place at two in the morning. So he'd been a good boy, gone to the hotel, showered, eaten, even got into bed and dozed for a couple of hours, but he'd been up and ready since six, and he hadn't been able to hang around the hotel room a second longer.

So here he was.

Pacing the park, probably looking like some sort of creep to the few parents here with their little ones this early in the morning. He checked his watch religiously, all but counting down the seconds until nine o'clock.

Lavender hated to be late so chances were she would show up early, probably within the next eight minutes or so.

Eight minutes felt like an eternity.

Hearing her confirm that she was pregnant yesterday had whipped up a hurricane of emotions inside him. He'd been angry of course that she'd kept it from him and left the state without informing him. He'd been scared, and nervous, and apprehensive at the idea that he was going to be a father. And there was also ... excitement.

Something he hadn't felt when Jackie called to tell him she was pregnant.

Then, all he had felt was a sense of being trapped, like the walls of the world were closing in on him. He wasn't proud to admit it, but sex with Jackie had been nothing but a drunken mistake, and while he would forever regret his relief at the loss of the pregnancy he was glad that he hadn't ended up in a loveless marriage.

Did that mean he was in love with Lavender?

No.

That was his immediate reaction.

It was too soon for them to be talking the L word, but he definitely had feelings for her. And as angry as he was with her for trying to keep their baby a secret, he could see things from her point of view. She knew the Jackie story. She knew that when he had a kid he wanted it with someone he was committed to.

What she didn't know was that he had been ready to make a commitment to her.

A commitment that had nothing to do with the baby.

He'd been ready to tell her he cared for her and that he wanted them to try dating before he found out that Lavender was pregnant.

Speaking of Lavender, he'd thought she'd be here by now. It was nearing nine, and he couldn't see her anywhere.

Standing from the bench where he'd been sitting staring out at the pond and waiting for Lavender to show up, he did a closer sweep of the park. There were four adults and nine children at the playground, a group of five plus their trainer doing a workout session, and another two people out jogging.

No sign of Lavender.

The first inclining of doubt started to creep into his mind.

Had she blown him off?

Surely she'd know that was pointless because he had her sister's address. All he had to do was drive to Marigold's house and hang around there until she showed up.

Unless...

No.

She wouldn't do that.

On the phone, Lavender had told him that she had planned to tell him about the baby but wanted to prove to him first that she was capable of providing for it on her own so that he wouldn't feel obligated to propose. She wouldn't have told him that and then ghosted him this morning.

Except if she'd been lying on the phone.

Maybe she'd never intended to come this morning. Maybe as soon as she hung up with him yesterday, she'd packed up and taken off somewhere, intending to hide from him, keep their baby all to herself.

Anger at being kept from his child swept through him.

Yes, this wasn't ideal, if he and Lavender had a kid together he would have preferred they dated for a while first, got to know each other as boyfriend and girlfriend instead of as just friends, then once they found out if they worked as a couple he'd propose, and then once they were married they could plan for kids. Even though this wasn't ideal, he cared enough about Lavender and thought they shared something special, that he didn't care that it wasn't the way he'd always planned this happening. He just wanted a chance with the woman who was very quickly worming her way into his heart.

Lavender better not be getting any ideas of disappearing.

There was no way he was walking away from his kid or letting anyone keep it from him. He'd find a lawyer, track her down, get a DNA test done, then petition for custody.

Joint custody.

Because even if Lavender was planning on keeping the baby from him, he wouldn't stoop to that same level. That child deserved to have both its mother and father in its life so he could never cut Lavender out. His belief that both parents should be a part of the baby's life was why he had proposed to Jackie, it might not have been what he wanted, but he would *never* abandon his own flesh and blood.

Since it was now after nine and she hadn't shown, Night decided he had given her enough time and began to walk through the park. He'd said to meet at the park, and he'd chosen a spot fairly close to the parking lot so that she would see him when she arrived, but now he wondered whether maybe she had come in from the other direction and was actually waiting for him around the other side of the pond.

It took only a few minutes to debunk that theory.

She wasn't there.

She hadn't come.

That hurt more than he'd thought it would. The betrayal was like a knife through his heart. He had thought he knew Lavender, she'd been his friend, and then she'd become more, now she was carrying his baby inside her, and yet she cared so little about him that she was willfully going to keep him from his child.

Yanking out his phone, he called the same number he had yesterday. If Lavender was going to cut off contact, he would do this through her sister.

"Hello?" Marigold Vaile said when she answered.

"Did you help her?" he growled.

"Who is this?" Marigold asked.

"It's Eric McNamara. So did you?"

"Oh, Eric, right. Help who do what?"

"Help Lavender disappear."

"What do you mean help her disappear? Isn't she there with you now?" There was a slight pause before she added, "It's after nine. I assumed you two were talking things through."

"She never showed up," he said. If Lavender had decided to pull a disappearing act, he was positive that her twin had helped her. He wouldn't hold it against Marigold, Lavender was her twin sister, and she'd never even met him. It didn't take a genius to figure out who she would side with.

"What? She's not there?" Marigold sounded worried, and that edged away some of his anger, replacing it with concern.

"No, she's not."

"You think she ran?"

"Hard to know what to think. We were meant to meet to discuss the baby and she doesn't show up. Tell me what I should think."

"She didn't run, I swear, Eric. She left here around half-past eight. It's only a five-minute drive, even if there was some traffic it shouldn't take her more than ten to get there. She was nervous about talking to you, but I think part of her was relieved that you knew, she wasn't trying to hurt you, just trying to do the right thing for all three of you."

"You sure she wouldn't have run and just not told you?"

"Positive. Lavender was scared to raise the baby on her own, but equally as determined that she wouldn't make you feel obligated to be with her. She wouldn't run and keep your child from you. If she didn't show up at the park then it's because something happened to prevent her from doing so."

The confidence mixed with fear in Marigold's voice convinced him.

"I'm on my way to your house now," he said, already striding towards his car.

"You think something happened to her?"

"It's either that or she did a runner."

"She wouldn't do that."

"Then yeah, something happened to her."

"I'll call Jonah, ask him to come home, he can call hospitals, make sure Lavender wasn't in an accident," Marigold said, and Night could tell she was a hairsbreadth away from panicking.

"Be there in five," he said before hanging up.

If something had happened to Lavender it wasn't just her life at risk, but his baby as well. He wasn't finished with Lavender, he still wanted a chance with her, his own words and past actions had contributed to her fear of telling him about the baby, and he had no intentions of holding it against her. And even if things between them didn't end up working out, then he was already starting to love that little baby.

They were his and no one messed with what was his.

He would get her back because nothing else was acceptable.

She'd fought near-certain death twice before and come out victorious. He prayed that her luck could hold for a third time.

9:35 A.M.

"Ugh," Lavender groaned.

Why did her head hurt?

And her stomach ... she was going to throw up.

Rolling onto her side, she threw up the meager contents of her stomach, retching over and over again until the nausea settled enough that she could sink back down.

Pain was ricocheting around inside her skull, and she whimpered as much from the pain as from unknowns.

Where was she?

What had happened to her?

Why did she hurt so badly?

She couldn't remember.

She couldn't remember anything.

Panic started to edge in, nudging aside the throbbing in her head. Why couldn't she remember?

Forcing herself to slow her breathing, still her erratically beating heart, calm herself enough to think, Lavender dragged in a deep breath, then another, and another.

Okay.

Calmer now, she focused her mind on the last thing she could recall. This morning ... well she thought it was this morning ... she had forced herself to eat a light breakfast before getting into her car to drive to the park for her meeting with Eric. She'd spent way too long choosing what to wear and doing her hair and makeup, and in the end hadn't really been happy with the final choice, but appearances aside, she'd been both nervous and excited to see Eric again. He was angry with her, she knew that, but he'd also tracked her down, and she had to believe that was because he cared about her, and to be honest, she had been relieved that he finally knew about the baby.

So she'd driven out to the park, she'd got out her phone to text Eric and ask where he was, there had been a bunch of messages from him, she'd started to read them, listen to the voicemails, and then ...

Nothing.

That was the last thing she remembered.

Her panic was creeping back in. Why couldn't she remember? Had she been in an accident maybe?

Hopefully.

Because the alternative was too terrifying to even consider.

Very carefully, Lavender cracked open her eyelids and took in her surroundings. She was lying on something hard, the floor she thought, until she saw that there was something on either side of her.

Walls.

Startled, she reached out her arms and was able to touch them, feel them, they were wood, like a box or something.

Her gaze flew straight up, and she saw that the same smooth wooden boards were there as well.

She was ...

She was boxed in.

Buried alive?

The horrific thought flew through her mind, any control she had snapped, and she began to beat her fists against the lid of the box, hammering at it as she screamed and howled and thrashed about as though she could batter her way out.

Pain jackknifed through her skull and when her vision started to go gray, Lavender didn't fight against it, instead she welcomed the blissful ignorance that would come with unconsciousness, and took its hand and allowed it to drag her away.

Sometime later, she slowly swam back to the surface.

Her stomach still churned, her head still ached, and awareness came quicker this time around.

She'd been kidnapped.

No use in denying it or pretending there was some alternative to what she saw when she looked around. She hadn't been injured in an accident and taken to the hospital.

She had been abducted and locked inside a large wooden box.

Before she could lose it again, Lavender made herself start taking in facts. Facts could be dealt with however unpleasant they were and were better than facing the wide unknown.

Fact; she had obviously been grabbed as she got out of her car near the park.

Fact; the person had hit her over the head to knock her out.

Fact; she had been put inside a wooden box that appeared to be around six feet long, by four feet wide, by two feet high.

Fact; whoever had put her in there had left some small light in there with her because she could see the blood and bruising on her hands from trying to break out of there before she passed out.

Fact; she could also see that ... oh no ... the control she had been clinging to, began to slip out of her grasp again.

She was naked.

Had she been ...

Lavender couldn't even make herself think the word, it was too horrific. She had survived that one already, spent two days preparing herself to face it again in Afghanistan, but now she was home, she was staying with her sister, expecting a baby, she was supposed to be safe.

Why was this happening to her?

She knew she hadn't been the best sister to Marigold, she'd been selfish and self-centered, but she'd never been cruel or malicious. She felt guilty for that and for being the trap that lured her twin into Cage's grasp, but she hadn't done it on purpose, she hadn't known her boyfriend had a history with her sister. She'd had selfish reasons for deciding to start working for an aid organization, but she still was there to help people. And she'd kept this baby from its father, but she had her reasons, and it wasn't for forever, just until she could prove to Eric that they didn't need him.

None of that meant she deserved this.

Right?

Now she wasn't so sure.

Her head hurt, and her hands burned, and it was hard to think.

Maybe she did deserve it.

Maybe she deserved to lie in this box until she suffocated or died of dehydration, or whatever it was her abductor intended to do with her.

Tears stung her eyes as she tried to concentrate enough to see if she hurt between her legs. She didn't feel any pain there, and when she carefully eased up onto one elbow so she could reach down, she didn't feel any blood or stickiness there either.

Thankful for small mercies, she drooped back down. The movement sent her head into a tailspin, and she spent the next several minutes just trying to lie still and breath through the sickening sensation before she could even form a coherent thought.

Once she no longer felt like the box she was trapped in was spinning in circles, Lavender tried to figure out what she should do. The pain in her hands was proof that she wasn't breaking her way out of there. So what other options did that leave her with?

Pretty much none.

She could attempt to talk her way out, try to form a bond with her abductor, get them to see her as a real person and not just an object, try to convince them to let her go. It probably wouldn't work, but she would definitely try it. She wasn't going to just lie there and wait to die.

Eric would have to know by now that something had happened to her, when she didn't show up he'd be worried, call Marigold, who would call her husband Jonah, who was a cop, and they would start looking for her.

Unless …

What if Eric thought she hadn't shown up on purpose?

What if he thought she had gotten off the phone with him the day before and promptly packed up her things and disappeared?

The very idea of Eric believing she had betrayed him had her struggling to breathe. He wouldn't think the worst of her, would he?

Of course he would.

Why wouldn't he?

That was exactly what she had done when she found out she was pregnant.

He had every right to think the worst of her, but if he did, then no one was looking for her. She was trapped, she was going to die, and worse, she would die with the man she loved thinking that she had betrayed him.

Lavender began to cry, huge wracking sobs that seemed to tear at every part of her body. The pain in her head became unbearable, and she cried and screamed and clawed at the wooden box again in the vain hope that maybe somehow she could get out of there.

If she could, she would throw herself at Eric's feet and beg for his forgiveness. She would do anything if only she could see him one more time, talk to him, touch him, kiss him, tell him how important he was to her.

She should have done that already.

She should have told him what she was feeling.

Instead, she'd been a coward. She'd been waiting for him to make the first move because he was the one who had pulled away after their wonderful night together.

She should have trusted her instincts. If she hadn't

thought that something real could develop between her and Eric, she never would have asked him to make love to her.

Now it was too late, she'd been so busy trying to do what she thought was the right thing for all involved that she'd chosen the wrong path, and now she wasn't going to get a chance to rectify that.

Her pain crescendoed, her sobs left her weak and shaky, and darkness crashed down upon her, washing her away into blessed unconsciousness.

∼

9:51 A.M.

"I was expecting you nearly thirty minutes ago. What happened? Did you find her? Did you find something that might tell us where she is? Did you ..."

"Whoa," Night said. He held up a hand as the door to Marigold's house was flung open as he stepped out of his car, and a redhead who looked exactly like Lavender came running toward him. He hadn't met Marigold before, when Lavender spent time with her twin she went to her not the other way around, but he had heard a lot about her. Right now the woman who was Lavender's exact double looked completely panicked. Her red hair was loose, flying around her shoulders, she had a baby on her hip, and her eyes were red-rimmed and puffy, a sure sign she had been crying.

"It's bad news, isn't it?" Marigold stopped in front of him, one hand pressed to her mouth as her fearful gray eyes latched onto his, begging him not to tell her that her sister was dead.

"I'm sorry," he said, then quickly continued when Marigold gasped, "I should have texted to tell you what I was doing. Before I left, I wanted to walk the entire park, make sure she didn't get waylaid. I checked the parking lot, but there was no sign of your car there."

"So she might not have made it there?"

"Right, something might have happened to her along the way."

"It's only a five-minute drive," Marigold protested, "how much could have happened to her along the way?"

"I don't know, but we'll figure it out," he promised, praying that he was right. With each second that passed, his anger was fading, replaced by fear.

Something was wrong.

He could feel it in his gut.

When you had the kind of job he did, you learned to trust your gut because if you didn't, you died.

Right now, his gut screamed that Lavender was in danger, but he couldn't just assume that, he had to approach it logically, the same way he would any mission his team undertook. Lavender was under a lot of stress, she had nearly died and then just weeks later learned she was pregnant. She was using his past as a reason to run from him, and since she had done that once already he had to believe she could do it again.

He had to play this with his head, not his heart.

Only problem was, neither of them were reliable when it came to Lavender.

She was special, strong, and sweet, and yet there was a sadness about her that called out to him. He wanted to make her world a better place, wanted to see her smile, hear her laugh. The joy he felt when he knew he was the cause of even a moment of her happiness was something he'd never experienced before.

That woman had the power to own him, heart, mind, and

soul, and he had no intention of allowing anyone to snatch that away from either of them.

"Come on, let's go inside and we can talk. I called my team, and they're all on their way out here to help us find Lavender," he informed Marigold as he led her back inside her home.

"Aren't you SEALs? You guys can't just drop everything to come and look for a missing person. And Lavender is an adult who's only been missing less than an hour. Even with my husband being a homicide detective we still can't list her as officially missing for another two days."

Marigold sounded just like Lavender, she looked just like her, and yet they *felt* like two completely different people. Which they were, of course, it was just that as much as it looked and sounded like he was talking with the woman he was falling for he felt the difference right down to his soul.

"My team got clearance from our commander to come and see if we can find her," he assured Marigold. "Have you been able to get through on her cell phone?" He had been calling Lavender's cell nearly non-stop but hadn't gotten any replies. His calls kept going straight to voicemail indicating that the phone was still turned off.

Or destroyed.

"No, I keep getting voicemail."

"She didn't get a new cell when she got here?"

"No, she kept her old cell turned off after she got off the plane, said she just needed space and time. Abigail was calling her on my phone, same as you did when you called yesterday. This morning she said that since you knew where she was and that you two were meeting and going to talk things through that she may as well go ahead and turn her phone back on. She took it with her this morning."

So they were going to have to contact her carrier and get permission to access her phone's GPS system. If it was still on her, they could use it to find her, and if not they could at least find out where she was when she was taken. The only problem was that it would take more time than Lavender might have to get the court orders.

"Can I go and check out the room Lavender is staying in?" He wanted to do something that would prove—not so much in his mind but for the cops and his team—that Lavender hadn't disappeared of her own free will.

"Sure, it's down the hall, last room on the right. I've got to get Violet a snack," Marigold said, setting the baby down and buckling her into her high chair.

Following Marigold's directions, Night walked down the hall and into the bedroom Lavender had been staying in. The room was simply decorated, nothing like Lavender's bedroom in her apartment back home. There was nothing in her favorite color, no paintings on the walls, no frilly pillows piled on the bed. He checked out the closet, found Lavender's suitcases sitting empty on the floor inside, her clothes hanging in the same orderly fashion he'd seen in her place. Likewise, the dresser was full of piles of neatly folded clothing, both of which indicated that Lavender hadn't been planning on running.

Feeling like he was intruding into her personal space, Night moved to the two nightstands, one on either side of the bed. The first was empty, but the second had an e-reader in the top drawer and a small notebook with a bouquet of lavender on the cover.

Without even thinking he picked the book up and opened it, finding Lavender's diary. He knew he should put it down, these were her private thoughts and feelings, but she was missing and … besides that, he needed to know what was really going on inside her head, and right now, this was the only way he could do that.

Flipping to the last entry, something fluttered down to

the floor at his feet. Night bent to pick it up and found himself grinning stupidly when he saw what it was.

It was a photo of himself and Lavender, taken the Christmas before last. They were sitting side by side on the couch at his place, his arm was around her shoulders, and she was leaning into him. He was smiling down at her, and the look on her face as she smiled back up at him said that what had been brewing between them had been coming for a long time now.

Lavender had printed this photo out—he could count on one hand the number of times he had gone to the trouble of getting a physical copy of a photograph—and kept it for the last year, tucked inside her diary. She'd brought it here with her even though she had left to get away from him and her fears that he didn't want her and wouldn't want their baby.

Needing reassurance that he wasn't seeing something that wasn't there, he looked down at Lavender's cursive script.

Eric knows the truth, and I'm kind of relieved. It's like I can breathe again. I'm not quite sure how he found out about the baby, but he knows, and he's coming here to see me. I hope it means he cares, but I'm afraid that he doesn't feel the same things for me that I feel for him. I'm so afraid he'll see me as Jackie and the baby as another responsibility he doesn't want. I want him to want it, I want him to want me, but I don't know if I want the impossible.

"No, baby, you don't want the impossible," he whispered, his fingers caressing the Lavender in the photo and wishing it was the real thing.

Relief unlike anything he had felt before calmed a part of his heart.

Lavender's words were like a balm, assuring him that they both wanted the same thing. Each other. They had a whole lot to sort out, lots to work through, lots to still learn about each other as lovers and not just friends, but they both wanted the same thing, and that was what was important. The rest could be dealt with.

When he got her back.

With renewed determination, he closed the diary, tucked the photo into his back pocket, and headed back through to the living area, ready to do whatever it took to find his girl.

*I'm coming, sweetheart, all you have to do is hold on until I find you.*

～

12:19 P.M.

Lavender lay in a kind of pain-filled haze, unsure if she was asleep or awake or stuck in some sort of in between land where nothing existed but fuzziness and pain and a horrible thirst that made it hard to think of anything else.

Her head buzzed with a constant pounding pain, and her hands ached from battering at her prison. She was sure she'd broken at least a couple of fingers, and she had definitely torn out a few of her fingernails trying to claw through the wood. It probably hadn't been her best move trying to batter her way out, but she'd slipped into hysterics and hadn't even known what she was doing until it was too late and the damage was already done.

Thirsty.

She was so thirsty.

It was almost worse than the pain.

Almost.

197

Since there was nothing else to do in there but try to lie as still as she could because any movement made her so dizzy she was sure she was going to throw up again, all she could do was think.

Or try to at least.

Between her pain and fear and thirst, plus the hysteria that still bubbled inside her and was only one moment of weakness away from swamping her, it was hard to focus her fuzzy mind enough to actually think, but one thought circled her mind in a never-ending loop.

Eric.

He must be so disappointed in her right now.

He was so strong. He had faced up to his mistakes, apologizing to Abigail and Spider for his part in keeping them apart. He fought terrorists protecting not just people from his own country but others as well. He was a good and honorable man, one who had made mistakes, done things he regretted, but what person hadn't?

Bottom line was, he might have avoided her after they slept together, but she had done the same thing. She'd been too scared of rejection that she had been a coward. She'd always thought there would be plenty of time, but now time was the one thing she didn't have much of.

Whoever had taken her would come for her sooner or later. He would rape her, beat her, torture her, whatever it was he had planned, and then he would kill her.

If she was lucky her body would be found, and her family would be able to get closure, maybe even use it to find out what had happened to her and bring her abductor to justice.

Yes.

The idea strengthened Lavender, helped her to push away the cobwebs a little. She wanted this man to be caught and punished for doing this to her and her unborn baby, and she was going to do everything she could to make sure it happened.

When he came for her, she would make sure she scratched him or bit him, anything that would ensure that a little of his DNA ended up on her. When her body was found and examined, that evidence could be used to throw this monster in prison.

Satisfied, she was able to smile through her suffering.

A purpose.

She had a purpose, and that seemed to help calm her a little. She couldn't give her baby life, but she could give it justice, and nothing would stop her from doing that.

Her death was inevitable, she had already accepted that, but she wasn't going down without a fight.

With that thought clutched firmly in the forefront of her mind, Lavender had nothing else to do but wait. She wanted to make Eric proud, she wanted him to know that she had fought with everything that she had, that she hadn't just laid down and died. And maybe he would find her diary and know that her dream had been the two of them falling in love and raising this baby together.

Unfortunately, dreams could disappear into a wisp of smoke in a second, and that was what had happened to hers.

Lavender froze, her thoughts scattering as she focused her attention on straining to hear past her ragged breathing.

She'd thought she'd heard footsteps.

Someone was coming.

This was it.

The only chance she might have.

Looking death in the face brought with it a certain measure of power. This man could do horrific things to her, hurt her in ways she couldn't even imagine, steal something that he had no right to, but he had no say over how she chose to respond.

And she was responding to his violence with a fight of her own.

The footsteps got louder, and she knew she hadn't imagined them.

All of a sudden she felt herself moving.

Not just her, but the box she had been locked in went moving sideways, smoothly like it was on wheels.

There was a small window right above her head, and as the box was moved, light suddenly shone through it, spearing through her eyes and making her wince as pain zinged inside her skull.

Shoving the pain away because she had no time for it right now, it was an obstacle she couldn't allow to get in the way of her achieving her goal. She squinted and looked through the little plastic space to see a face looking down at her.

A woman's face.

A cop?

That thought was quickly dashed when she realized the woman was smiling at her. It wasn't a don't worry you're safe now kind of smile, it was an insane smile, one that clearly said its owner was living in a universe all on her own.

Was this woman the one who kidnapped her?

Why?

It made no sense at all.

"You're awake," the woman said with a grin as she pushed the little plastic window up and held out a straw. "Thirsty?"

The angry part of her wanted to say no, not take anything this woman offered, after all this was the person who had knocked her unconscious and locked her up in here, but the sensible side of her knew she needed the water. Keeping up her strength was the most important thing in the world right now.

"Y-yes," she croaked weakly.

The straw was held to her lips, and she greedily sucked at it, savoring the cool water that slid down her parched throat.

Too soon the straw was pulled away, and she had to bite her tongue to keep her from begging for more.

"I'm sorry I had to leave you here," the woman was saying. Her green eyes shone brightly with a kind of insanity that Lavender had never witnessed before. "I had a few things to take care of, I needed to make sure that the kitchen is fully stocked, I'm not much of a cook, but I'll be making you homemade meals every day, I'm sure that's good for the baby."

Lavender's brows knit together.

The baby?

She was only seven weeks pregnant, not even close to showing yet. How could this woman know that she was pregnant?

Had she been stalking her?

Lavender had only been in the state for a few weeks, and other than her sister and Jonah and the kids, she hadn't seen or talked to anyone aside from polite and casual conversation with the checkout person at the supermarket and the pharmacy. The only other people she had spoken to were the nurses and doctor at the OB-GYN offices.

A horrible thought occurred to her.

Was this woman a patient as well? Had she lost her own baby and decided to steal someone else's?

"I want the baby to come out all big and healthy," the woman was saying. "I made your little space big enough for you to fit in as the baby grows, and big enough for you to deliver."

Deliver?

This woman was planning on keeping her here for the next seven months and then making her give birth in a locked box.

She was even crazier than Lavender had first thought.

"You were sick in there," the woman said, curling up her nose. "I'll bring you a wet towel, and you can clean it up."

"No, wait," Lavender called out. "Please, you have to let me out, I can't stay in here for seven months, and I can't have a baby here, alone. I need vitamins, and ultrasounds, and a doctor, and …"

"I can give you all of that. Well, not the doctor part," the woman said, then giggled like that was funny. "I'll take care of you, make sure you take your pregnancy vitamins, and eat healthily. I don't want to hurt you." The last she said like she was offended by the very notion.

"But you are hurting me if you keep me here. Hurting me and my baby."

The woman made a confused face. "That's my baby you're carrying, and I have every intention of making sure that nothing bad happens to it."

Just like this insane woman had every intention of making sure that once Lavender delivered the baby and outlived her sole purpose, she wouldn't be telling anyone what had happened to her.

As soon as her baby was born, this woman was going to steal it and kill her.

*Eric, where are you, I need you.*

∾

3:38 P.M.

*I need you.*

The words flew through Night's mind as clearly as if Lavender were standing beside them and uttered them herself.

*Hold on, baby, I'm doing everything I can to find you.*

A knock on the door had him looking up from the files he'd been pouring over. "That should be my team, I'll go let them in," he told Jonah Jagger who was sitting across the table from him.

"Sure," Jonah said shortly. He knew it wasn't that the guy didn't like him, from the moment Marigold had introduced them there had been mutual respect and a shared concern for Lavender. Both of them were feeling the pressure to find her, and that was all either of them could focus on.

Night walked through the house, opened the door, and met his team's worried faces looking back at him. That they had dropped everything to fly to the other side of the country to help him find Lavender meant everything to him. It was one thing to know they had his back on a mission, but this wasn't a mission, they weren't cops, they had no jurisdiction here—although having Jonah on board helped—and yet here they were, ready to do whatever it took to get his girl back alive.

"Appreciate you guys coming," he said as he led them inside.

Fox waved off his thanks. "Nowhere else we'd be, you know that. Lavender is a friend to all of us, and we all know she's more than that to you."

There was no point in denying it, and he didn't *want* to, it was true, Lavender was more than a friend to him ever since they'd spent Christmas Eve together, and it had nothing to do with her carrying his child.

His *child*.

If he lost Lavender, he didn't just lose the woman who had always been destined to be his other half, but a baby he already loved.

"This is Lavender's brother-in-law Jonah, he works homicide," Night said as they entered the living room. "Jonah, this is my team, Fox, Shark, Chaos, King, and Spider." That Spider had left his wife in the hospital to come and help made him feel so much worse for the way he'd lashed out at Abigail. He owed them both another apology.

With the introductions out of the way the men immediately took seats around the table and got straight down to work.

"We have any leads?" Fox asked.

"Not yet," Night replied. "All of her stuff is in her room, so she didn't pack up and disappear. I've read her diary—not proud of that, but under the circumstances, I couldn't not do it—and she said she was relieved that I knew and was hoping things worked out between us, so we can eliminate the possibility that she ran." He felt the need to start things off with that. It wasn't just that he didn't want to be wasting time working leads that weren't going to get them what they needed, he also didn't want anyone thinking badly of Lavender. His team was a big part of his life, and when he got her back Lavender would be too. He didn't want his team holding her rash decision to not immediately tell him about the baby against her.

"Understood, man," Fox said, and the look on his face said he got why Night felt the need to say that.

"What about this thing from a few years ago?" Shark asked.

"You mean Cage?" Jonah asked. Fire brimmed in his eyes as he no doubt remembered how Cage Anderson had tormented Marigold and nearly killed both sisters.

"Any chance he could be behind Lavender's disappearance?" Chaos asked.

"No. He's still in prison, he's never getting out," Jonah replied.

"Could he have connections on the outside he paid to target her?" Spider asked.

"Anything is possible I suppose, but I don't think so. His empire pretty much crumbled when he was arrested. Most of his men were arrested along with him, and when I checked, they're all still behind bars," Jonah informed them. "I couldn't find any of his old associates who were still free and were in the area."

"So we can rule out Cage Anderson," Fox said.

"I think so. To be honest, I don't think he'd go after her, if anything he'd target Marigold, not Lavender," Jonah said, although they could see it pained him to say those words.

"Any chance it could be a case of mistaken identity?" King asked. "How identical are the sisters?"

"Very," Night said. "You couldn't tell them apart if you didn't know them."

"They are complete clones of each other," Jonah agreed. "Physically anyway. If you didn't know them, you could be fooled and get them mixed up, but there are differences you notice if you know them. I know I would know my Marigold anywhere, and I'm sure Night feels the same about Lavender. Could this have anything to do with her being held hostage in Afghanistan?"

"The terrorists might have power over there, but I doubt they have the resources to pull off an abduction over here. And I don't think they'd get anything out of it anyway," Fox said.

"What about one of the families of the other hostages? A family member could be angry that Lavender survived the ordeal and their loved one didn't," Jonah suggested.

"We'll look into it, but I'm not sure that anyone would have cause to go after her because of that," Fox said.

"Anything else in Lavender's life that could put her on someone's radar?" Shark asked.

"You know her, man," Night said. "She's not into drugs or anything illegal."

"Not suggesting she was, brother," Shark said calmly. "What about guys who may have asked her out and she turned them down, someone who might be angry that she hooked up with you."

"Marigold and I went through that before she took the kids and headed out, and she said that Lavender never mentioned any guys who showed an interest in her. She never mentioned one to me either and we talked about pretty much everything," he said.

"Which leaves us with only one other possibility," Chaos said, and he didn't look happy about it.

"That this was a random abduction," King said the words they were all thinking but not ready to acknowledge yet.

A random abduction meant that whoever had her had probably already killed her.

The very thought of her no longer existing made his world cease spinning.

They were just at the beginning of their journey, they deserved a chance to see if they could make it work. To have that chance ripped away from them didn't just seem unfair it seemed cruel.

Before they could delve into that horrific possibility, his phone began to ring. Relief coursed through him when he saw the name on the screen. If anyone could help them now it was this man.

"Tex, I'm putting you on speaker," he said as he hit answer. John "Tex" Keegan was a former SEAL who had lost part of his leg and was now a computer genius who had helped him and his team along with most of the other teams on more than one occasion. "The whole team is here along with Detective Jonah Jagger, Lavender's brother-in-law. Please tell me you have news for us."

"I have more than news," Tex's southern accent drawled.

"You going to keep us in suspense, man?" King demanded.

"Nope, on the contrary, I'm sending security camera footage to all of your phones right now. I was able to find the last known location of Lavender's car. It was across the street from the park and about halfway up an adjacent block."

"Lavender hates parking, she probably chose that spot so she wouldn't have to worry about it, she could just pull into the curb," Night said softly.

"I sent local cops straight to the area as soon as I located it. Her car is still there, and the phone is smashed and was partially hidden under the car. There's a medical facility across the street from where her car was, I got access to their security cameras and it caught the whole thing," Tex told them.

"The whole thing?" he asked uneasily. Knowing Lavender has been abducted and watching it happen were two different things, and he wasn't sure he could handle the latter. "What are we going to see?" he asked. As all their phones dinged with Tex's message, he felt like he needed to prepare himself before jumping in and watching the footage.

"Someone pulls up behind her as soon as she parks. The car was following her, they knocked her over the head, dragged her body into their car, stomped on the phone, then drove off." Tex paused and Night knew there was more to it.

"What else?" he demanded.

"Watch the footage, see if you see the same thing I did," Tex said.

With hands that shook, he opened up the message. Leaving the call connected, he opened the video and watched as Lavender pulled up, a large black SUV pulling in behind her. Lavender got out, her attention fixed firmly on her phone and she didn't see the person jump out of their vehicle and run up behind her, hitting her over the back of the head with what looked like a rock.

Lavender dropped, and even though he thought he had

JANE BLYTHE

been ready to see it happen, he couldn't not gasp at the sight of her falling limply to the ground where she lay unmoving. His hand curled so tightly around the phone that he was surprised he didn't snap it.

"Oh," Spider said, sounding surprised.

Forcing himself to look at the assailant and not at Lavender's still form, he saw what the others had seen. "It's a woman. A woman abducted Lavender."

"Damn," Jonah muttered, and they all looked over to see that the cop's face had paled.

"You know who it is?" Night demanded.

"Yeah." Shocked brown eyes looked over at him. "That's my ex, her name is Carmen Boscoe. Carmen became obsessed with me, tried to break up Marigold and me when we first started dating, even broke into her hotel room and tried to attack her. She was sent to a psychiatric facility, I thought she was still there. We talked about how Marigold and Lavender are identical. I think Carmen took Lavender thinking it was my wife."

∼

4:10 P.M.

Carmen hummed as she bustled around the nursery, getting everything ready for the impending birth of her child.

She wanted everything to be perfect when he or she came along.

She hoped it would be a boy, a tiny little Jonah, with the same big brown eyes and messy brown hair. The same smile and crinkle around his eyes when he smiled, he'd be tall and big and strong, with a huge heart.

Everything would be perfect once he came along. Jonah

would come back to her, he'd apologize for leaving her, and for getting her locked up. Those years she'd spent in the psychiatric hospital had been the worst of her life. She'd longed for Jonah, needed to hear his voice, enjoy his touch, relish in his love, but instead she had been shoved into a small room, monitored every second of every day, and had to listen to doctors try to convince her that she was wrong.

But she wasn't wrong.

Jonah loved her, if it wasn't for Marigold Vaile, he would be with her right now.

The woman had ruined everything, but Carmen would get her revenge.

Hanging the mobile above the crib, she stood back and looked around the room. It was looking good, but it wasn't finished yet. She'd bought nursery furniture, a crib, and a changing table, along with a matching dresser, bookshelves, and rocking chair. There was a toy chest under the window that was already overflowing with toys, several stuffed animals sat in the crib, and she was planning on removing the closet door and putting baskets in there with more toys. Her little baby would never want for anything. She still needed to buy books and clothes, and she was going to stencil a woodland motif on the walls. She needed to find a design she liked and then collect the supplies, but she had plenty of time to get it done, the baby wouldn't be coming for another seven months.

Waiting was hard and something she had never been particularly good at. All she wanted was to hold her and Jonah's little baby in her arms. She'd waited so long for this, and she was ready for it to be over, for the baby to be here. Once it was born, she could take it to Jonah, and then finally he would come back to her. She'd made a mistake before, not giving him the child he craved, but she was going to make up for it, she was going to give him what he wanted.

She wasn't crazy.

The idea that anyone thought she was made her angry.

No, furious.

Four years of hell being locked away from the world, from her life, treated like she was a stupid little child, watched and monitored, condescending orderlies everywhere she turned.

But she had played the game.

Telling them what they wanted to hear was the easy part, convincing them that she wasn't a threat to anyone was the hard part. While she would never lay a hand on her precious Jonah, she would take out his wife. As soon as the baby came along she would get rid of the redhead, but not her children. As much as she hated the idea of Jonah having children with another woman, that little boy and baby girl were her baby's siblings, and she would take them in and love them as her own.

Smiling, she danced around the nursery, pausing at the crib to scoop up a teddy bear, cradling it in her arms as though it were a baby.

Soon it would be a baby in her arms.

She would love that child with every fiber of her being, cherish every second she got to spend with it, dote on it hand and foot, offer it everything its little heart desired.

Dropping down into the rocking chair, she held the teddy against her breast as she gently rocked, imagining her baby's tiny head there, suckling her breast, drinking her milk as she sustained its life.

Perfection.

Thumping from the other room interrupted her fantasy, and with a scowl she stood, throwing the bear into the crib as she stalked out the door and into her bedroom. Kneeling on the smooth hardwood floors, Carmen reached under the bed and rolled out the special box she had built just for Marigold.

As soon as she had the box out from under the bed, she slid up the little window she'd put in to make it easier to handle feeding Marigold and giving her water and vitamins for the baby.

Carmen wished she could carry her and Jonah's child herself, but sometimes you didn't get what you wanted, and at least in seven months, she would be holding their baby in her arms.

"Why are you thumping around in there?" she demanded as she looked down into a pair of gray eyes that haunted her dreams. She hated those eyes, hated the woman they belonged to, hated that this woman had stolen Jonah away from her.

But she would get him back.

She would get back everything she had lost.

"Please, I'm scared that something will happen to my baby if you keep me trapped in here." The pleading tone of Marigold's voice only served to anger her.

Thumping a fist into the box, causing the other woman to jump in fear, she growled, "That is *my* baby. Mine and Jonah's, not yours."

"What? Jonah? Oh no ..." the other woman gasped and trailed off, staring up at her with terror etched into her features. "Are you Carmen?"

"Of course I'm Carmen. Don't be playing stupid, we've met, you know who I am," she reprimanded.

"You think I'm Marigold," the woman said, almost in a thoughtful manner, as though speaking more to herself than to Carmen.

"I *know* you're Marigold," Carmen corrected.

"You don't know."

"Know what?"

"That Marigold has a twin sister. I thought you were in a hospital getting help."

"I don't need help," she yelled, slamming her fist into the box again and taking great satisfaction in seeing the woman startle.

"Okay, okay," the woman soothed. "Sorry. I don't want to make you angry, but I'm not who you think I am. I'm not Marigold, I'm her sister Lavender."

Carmen scoffed. "You really think I'm that stupid?"

"I don't think you're stupid, you had no reason to know about me. I live in California, I just came back here because I found out I'm pregnant. The father of the baby is my best friend, I … uh … I thought he didn't want the baby, and I got scared. I needed to spend some time with my sister, she's the only family I have. But Eric, the baby's father, came out here to see me, he's a good man, and deserves to be a part of his baby's life, or at least to know what happened to it. Please, Carmen, please don't keep me here, don't let anything happen to this innocent little baby."

She just stared at the woman. Did she honestly expect her to believe a word of that? Identical twin sisters, it was all so cliché.

Obviously, seeing that she wasn't convinced, the woman kept talking. "I made a lot of mistakes, Carmen, I know you know what that's like. I made mistakes, did things I'm not proud of. I wasn't a good sister to Marigold, I was selfish, let her shoulder the burden our parents dumped on us. I left her to go gallivanting off around the globe, moving from city to city, having fun and dating guys, I let her down. I tried to make up for it by giving my life to helping those in need, but I ended up getting held hostage and rescued by the most wonderful man in the world. I thought I knew what he wanted, I made decisions based off that, but I made a mistake. I kept this baby from him. That was wrong of me, but my baby doesn't deserve to suffer for my mistakes. Please let us go, Carmen. I know about you and Jonah, how he wanted kids and you pretended you did too only you were taking birth control so you couldn't get pregnant. I know that he ended things with you when he found out, but that doesn't mean he doesn't care about you, and he wouldn't want you to do this."

"Don't pretend you know about me and Jonah. He loved me," she screamed.

"I'm sure he did, but things changed. He loves my sister now. They have two children together, two sweet little babies that they adore. He wouldn't want you to do this, Carmen, he wouldn't want you to try to hurt the woman he loves, and he wouldn't want you to hurt me and my baby. Please, this baby isn't yours, and it isn't Jonah's. It's Eric's, and I just want to go home to him. Please let me go." The woman was crying now, tears streaming down her cheeks as her eyes begged for mercy, as a string of pleas continued to fall from her lips.

Mercy.

When had she been shown mercy?

When she had been dumped by the man she loved?

When she had been humiliated when he turned her down after she told him she wanted him back?

When she was dragged out of a hotel room in handcuffs?

When she was told she was insane and needed to be committed?

No one had shown her any mercy, and she wasn't going to show any now.

"It's not your baby," she screamed, "it's mine and Jonah's, and I'm going to keep it and use it to get him back."

That was what she needed. She just needed to go back to when everything was perfect, when she and Jonah were married, and he'd wanted to have a baby with her. If she could just get back to that moment in time then everything would be okay.

～

4:40 P.M.

Night was itching to get in there.

The last half-hour seemed to have passed with excruciating slowness. Once they knew who they were looking for it hadn't taken long to track down where Carmen Boscoe was hiding out.

It appeared that the woman had been released from a psychiatric facility around four months ago. Her family had helped her get a job, working as a cashier at an uncle's gas station. She had rented her own house, and from the little Carmen's mother had given them, she appeared to be happy and adjusting well to her new life.

What her family hadn't known was that she had obviously been stalking her ex and his family.

Carmen must have decided that if only she could get Marigold out of the way, she could get Jonah back, only she had mistaken Lavender for Marigold and taken the wrong woman.

Which meant that Lavender could already be dead.

If Carmen had found out that she had the wrong twin, she had no reason to keep Lavender around. Lavender had nothing to do with Jonah and Marigold and their relationship, she was just a loose end, and one that could be quickly and easily terminated.

Right now, he didn't even want to consider the possibility that they were too late.

Lavender had been gone for more than eight hours,

plenty of time for Carmen to have learned the truth about the twins and disposed of the wrong one.

"Try not to think the worst," Spider said, placing a hand on his shoulder and squeezing. "We don't have any evidence that Lavender is dead, so we're going to go in there assuming we're performing a rescue."

Night nodded, in his heart he prayed that he would know if Lavender was already gone, but his head said there was no way to know one way or the other. "Thanks for leaving Abby to come here."

"Who do you think was the one that insisted I come?" Spider asked with a grin.

"She okay?"

"Yeah, she'll be discharged tomorrow if everything goes according to plan, but she's on bed rest until the end of the pregnancy. She's going to be okay, man, whether you'd been yelling at her or not, it probably would have happened. Let's just focus on getting your girl back."

Looking out the car window, he saw Jonah approaching and prayed it was good news, he opened the door and climbed out. "We good?" he asked Lavender's brother-in-law.

"My chief said you guys are good to be part of this," Jonah replied.

Relief flooded through him. He'd been going to be involved in going in after Lavender regardless of whether they got the official okay or not, but this made things easier. "Let's get moving."

"I'm taking the lead, Night. I know you want to just go running in there and grab your girl, but Carmen is unbalanced, and she's obsessed with me. I'm sure I can keep her talking long enough for us to get Lavender out, but unbalanced means unpredictable, we need to move slowly, play into her delusions, at least until Lavender is safe."

"Fine," he said shortly. He wasn't going to argue about it,

nor was he going to do anything to endanger Lavender. All he wanted was to get in there and confirm she was alive and then get her someplace safe.

Jonah nodded approvingly, then motioned to his partner and Night's team. Everyone gathered around, and Jonah gave them a quick rundown. "Carmen's car—the same one we saw in the footage of Lavender's abduction—is parked in the driveway of the house she's renting. We haven't seen anything to indicate that she's aware we're watching her. We have confirmation from a neighbor that she hasn't left since arriving back there around lunchtime so we're fairly confident that Carmen is home. We are assuming our victim is in there somewhere, we know she was injured—knocked unconscious—during the abduction, but we have no idea of her current status. Getting her safely out is the priority. I'm going to focus on Carmen, try to keep her talking, try to take her down gently, the rest of you will locate Lavender and take her out."

His team had done plenty of rescues, none had been done on US soil, but the principle was the same. Protect the innocent. Lavender had been through enough. She'd suffered twice at the hands of violent psychopaths, she deserved a happy ending.

Weapons in hand, they moved quickly and quietly down the street to Carmen's home. The house was in the same block, just a couple of houses down, from the home she had shared with Jonah when they had been married. It was clear that despite what she had told her doctors she wasn't over her ex. Far from it. Instead, it seemed like she wanted her old life back and was prepared to eliminate any obstacles to making that happen.

The house was a ranch on a small lot. According to the floor plan they'd gotten from the owner, there were two bedrooms on the left side of the house, a master bedroom in the front, a second bedroom at the back, a bathroom, and a study were on the right side of the house, and in the middle was the living area.

Depending on where Carmen was when they went in, she would see them immediately. That didn't bode well for Lavender because it meant that Carmen could eliminate her just because she could, or it could get Lavender stuck in a situation where she was used as a human shield. It wasn't ideal, and he wasn't pleased about it, but it wasn't like he had a choice, he couldn't change the floorplan just to make this an easier rescue.

They breached the house easily and found the living room empty, and while he was initially thankful for small mercies, the sound of an angry voice screaming, mixed with the sounds of crying echoed through the house.

Lavender crying.

His heart wanted to run to her, comfort her, reassure her, make sure she was okay, but his head knew that one wrong move could end her and their baby's lives.

Following Jonah, they both headed in the direction of the voices and paused at the door to the master bedroom. Carmen Boscoe was down on her knees beside a large wooden box. She was looking inside it which could mean only one thing.

Lavender was in there.

Fury burned through his veins at the sight of her restrained in such a way. She'd been locked in a cage by Cage Anderson, she'd been thrown in a hole by a bunch of greedy terrorists, and now she was locked in a box because of a case of mistaken identity.

"Carmen."

The woman spun around when she heard Jonah's voice. She scrambled to her feet and took a step toward him but stopped when she saw that he had a gun pointed at her.

"What are you doing, Jonah?" she asked.

"Is Lavender in there, Carmen?" Jonah asked.

"Lavender? That's Marigold, and she's carrying our baby," Carmen protested.

The woman was clearly crazy, but they didn't have time to deal with that, he needed to get Lavender out of that box. Her tears had stopped when she'd heard Jonah's voice, she had to know that she was safe now, that she just had to hold on a little longer, but he hated knowing that she was in there even for another second.

Jonah took a step closer. "No, it's not Marigold. My wife is at home with our children, that's Lavender, Marigold's twin sister. Lavender is pregnant. This is Eric, he's the baby's father. We need to get her out of there, make sure that she and her baby are okay. Don't you think that would be a good idea, Carmen?"

"No," Carmen said, pouting like a toddler. "I don't care about this Lavender woman, or Marigold," she spat the word out like it tasted bad in her mouth. "I care about you. About you and me. I want to give you a baby, the baby that you wanted."

"But that baby isn't yours to give away," Jonah told her. "That baby already has a mom and a dad. What we had is over, Carmen. We weren't in love, we got along, we had fun, but we didn't love each other. That's why you didn't want to have a baby with me. Just step over here, put your hands on your head, and we'll get you out of here. Get you the help that you need."

Jonah's voice was calm but also comforting, and for one second Night thought that everything was going to be okay.

Then his world stopped spinning.

Carmen scowled at Jonah, then a look of disconnect came over her face, and he knew it was going to be bad.

"Okay," Carmen agreed, "just let me unlock the box so she can get out."

When Jonah nodded, she knelt down beside the box, pulled something from her pocket which at first he thought was a keyring, but then she flicked a lighter at the same time she shoved the box Lavender was trapped inside under the bed. She touched the lighter to the mattress, which immediately caught alight.

"I'm not falling for your tricks, Marigold will die, and then you'll be mine," Carmen screamed.

Flames began to dance on the bed, Lavender's screams mingled with Carmen's ranting, and Night saw everything that he had been dreaming of slip through his fingers.

~

5:05 P.M.


One second she was hopeful that all of this was about to end, she'd heard Jonah's voice, knew that they had found her, knew Eric was there—that he had come for her—and thought that she was going home.

And then everything had changed.

Carmen had shoved the box back under the bed and then done something that Lavender quickly realized was to set the bed on fire.

The flames seemed to consume the mattress, and even from down here she could feel the growing heat.

She was trapped.

It wouldn't take long for the fire to burn through the mattress and then next in line was her box.

She was going to be burned alive.

There wasn't enough time for smoke to claim her first which meant that she would feel everything.

And what was worse was that Eric would hear every second of it.

He'd hear her screams, he'd have to stand there and watch the flames claim her and their unborn child.

He'd blame himself.

She knew that.

It wasn't his fault, but Eric was a protector, and he knew that part of the reason she had left and not told him about her pregnancy was because of his own words telling her he didn't want a baby with a woman he didn't love, and the way he'd withdrawn from her after they'd slept together, leading her to believe he didn't care about her.

She didn't want this to destroy him.

She loved him enough to want him to be able to move on with his life, fall in love, have a family, finally let go of the guilt he carried around for what happened with Abby and Spider, and Jackie and the baby. She wanted him to be free.

Forcing herself to calm down enough that she stopped screaming and hitting her battered hands against the wood, she closed her eyes and tried to shut out everything else. This was too important not to do. "Eric, it's not your fault. I'm sorry. Sorry I didn't tell you right away about the baby, and sorry I got scared and ran. I'm sorry I wasn't paying attention today, I didn't know she was following me. I was listening to your messages, I didn't know she was there until she hit me. I'm sorry, Eric, I'm sorry that you aren't going to get to meet this baby, and I'm sorry that you're going to have to watch us die, but please don't blame yourself, be happy, that's what I want for you." Lavender finished on a sob, her eyes opening just in time to see the mattress above her shoved away.

"You are not going to die today," Eric's voice roared and the next thing she knew she was being yanked sideways.

Eric's face appeared in the small window, and he reached a hand inside and gently caressed her cheek.

"You're here," she cried, tears streaming down her face, and the sense of claustrophobia that she had been battling ever since she woke up in there now felt like it was about to smother her.

"Hold on, honey, I'll have you out of there in a moment."

With one final caress, he withdrew his hand and Lavender had to chew on her bottom lip to keep herself from protesting, begging him to keep touching her because she needed to feel him to keep from falling apart.

"Close your eyes, sweetheart, and try to move to your right as much as you can, cover your face with your hands," Eric instructed and assuming she would do as he said he waited barely a second before something slammed into the box.

Lavender had been expecting it, thought she was prepared for it, she knew it was only Eric busting her out, but still her body reacted with a violent shudder. She was pushed to the very edge of what she could handle, and one more little shove was going to send her shattering into a million pieces.

It took another two hits, and then finally Eric was throwing open the lid and snatching her up into his arms. One of his hands covered the back of her head, and he gently pressed her face against his shoulder as he carried her out of the house.

She started to shake when the cold air touched her bare skin, but she didn't care, she'd gladly sit down in a snowbank if it meant being free of that box.

"I need a blanket," Eric called out as he managed to keep ahold of her while also opening the door of a car. He slid into the backseat, and she tightened her hold on him thinking he was going to put her down, but he didn't, he settled her on his lap, wrapping the blanket around her.

She was still crying, her face pressed against Eric's neck as all the fear and confusion over her pregnancy and her relationship with Eric, mixed with her terror over believing that Carmen was going to kill her poured out of her.

"It's okay, sweetheart," Eric soothed as his hands smoothed up and down her arms, trying to still the tremors wracking her body. "How's your head? Nausea? Dizziness?"

"Both," she whispered, not lifting her head.

"Concussion, we'll tell the medics that as soon as they get here. Are you hurt anywhere other than your head?"

"My hands," she said, cradling her aching hands in her lap.

"Let me see them." Eric parted the blanket to get access to her hands, and when he saw them he gasped. "Lavender," he said softly, dismayed.

"I … I lost it a little … when I first woke up … I tried to get out … it was silly … never going to work," she explained haltingly. Now that she was safe the pain in her head and hands grew.

"Silly?" Eric growled, setting her hands down and tucking the blanket tightly around her. Then he framed her face with his hands and looked her straight in the eye. "You fought, there is nothing even remotely silly about that. You weren't going to give up, that's strength." He leaned down and touched his lips to her forehead, holding them there for a long moment before he lifted his head. His eyes met hers and then dipped to her lips before meeting her gaze again.

He wanted to kiss her.

Pain forgotten for the moment, her heart fluttered in her chest. Eric still wanted her, she wanted him more than anything, maybe it wasn't too late for them.

When she gave a small nod, Eric's lips met hers, and he

kissed her softly, sweetly, but there felt more to it than just a kiss.

There was also hope.

"I'm sorry," Eric murmured against her lips.

"I'm the one who's sorry," she countered.

"We have a lot to talk about," he said.

"We do," she agreed. There was something in his voice that said he was withdrawing, putting some emotional distance between them and immediately she felt panic flare inside her.

Was she wrong?

Did he not want her?

Was the kiss just a result of realizing how close he had come to losing his baby?

A knock on the window drew both their attention away from each other, and she saw Spider standing there, two paramedics about a yard behind him.

Spider opened the car door. "EMTs are ready to transport Lavender to the hospital."

The hospital was the last place she wanted to go right now. Eric was right, they did need to talk, and she knew she wasn't going to be able to concentrate on anything else until they did. Her entire future—and that of her baby—hinged on that conversation. Once it was done and she knew where Eric stood, then she could start making plans. However it turned out, she was determined to be the best mother she could be.

It didn't look like she was getting a choice in the matter though. Eric climbed out of the car, still holding her in his arms, and set her on the stretcher. She expected him to walk away, go off with his team—who she was touched to see had come all the way out here for her—and then call her later to set up another time to talk.

But he didn't.

Confusing her further, he helped get the stretcher into the back of the ambulance and then followed it in, staying out of the way while the medics bustled around her, taking her vitals, starting an IV, and checking the wounds on her hands as well as the one on the back of her head.

When one of the medics left, closing the doors behind him, to get into the driver's seat and the other moved back, jotting down notes, Eric moved closer, sitting beside her and resting a hand on her wrist, just beneath the bandages the EMTs had wrapped on her hands. His touch was warm, comforting, but she resisted how it made her feel because she didn't want to get too used to something that might be snatched away.

As though sensing her anxiety, he leaned down and kissed her forehead. "Close your eyes, sweetheart, turn your mind off and rest. We will talk, but right now the most important thing is making sure you and this baby rest and heal."

His free hand briefly touched her stomach, and she had to wonder whether he was being so nice to her purely because of the baby or because he did have feelings for her.

Exhausted from fear and stress Lavender knew that in this Eric was right, at the moment what she needed was sleep, so she closed her eyes, let her mind release all of the worries swirling around inside it, and floated off to sleep.

# CHAPTER 18

February 13<sup>th</sup>
1:24 P.M.

"You can drop me off at a hotel if you want. You don't have to bring me here," Lavender said tentatively as he opened the car door for her.

That wasn't happening.

Night had almost lost her and their baby, it had been too close. If he hadn't decided to fly out to talk to her, if he had believed she'd blown him off, or if Carmen had killed her when she realized she had the wrong sister. If the fire had spread more quickly, so many things could have gone wrong, and that left him barely able to breathe normally.

There was no way he was letting Lavender go, she and that little baby growing inside her were his now, and he would protect them with his life.

But before they got to that they had a lot to talk about.

The last two days had flown by, and Lavender had spent

most of the time in the hospital, being released last night. She'd spent the night at her sister's house, and he'd spent it in his rental car in their driveway, unable to leave her there.

As in physically unable to.

He had tried. He'd gotten into his car after leaving her inside with her family and turned the engine on, but knowing she was in there was like having an invisible rope tied from her heart to his. When he'd asked her to fly back out to California with him he'd expected her to say no, which he would have dealt with, and made plans to come back and see her as soon as he could, but shocking him, she'd agreed.

So this morning they had flown back here with the rest of his team, and now she was here, at his place, where she belonged.

"You aren't going anywhere else but here, sweetheart," he told her as he took her elbow and helped her out of the car. When it looked like she was going to argue, he added, "Besides, with both of your hands out of commission you need to be with someone who can help you."

"I can manage on my own," she said firmly, jutting her chin out defiantly.

Yeah, she could.

Lavender could survive on her own, but he wanted more for her than to just survive, she'd been doing that for four years now, but that was over.

"I don't want you to just manage." He kissed the tip of her nose, not missing the hope that lit in her eyes. He wished they'd been able to talk before now, but they hadn't had a moment alone. Marigold and Jonah, and his team had been in and out of her hospital room nearly constantly, and for this talk they needed time and space.

Inside, he steered Lavender to the couch in the living room, helped her take off her coat, then when she sat down he picked up her ankles and turned her so she could rest her legs on the cushions. For the next couple of minutes, he fussed around her, grabbing the pillows from the bed for her to lean against, covering her with a blanket, making her coffee, getting her painkillers, and putting some soup on to heat since she hadn't eaten anything since breakfast.

By the time he returned to the living room with bowls of soup, he found her watching him with a bemused expression. "What?" he asked.

"Nothing, just never seen you fuss like this before."

That was because he'd never had anyone to fuss over. "I just want to take care of you."

Lavender's gray eyes shuttered. "We need to talk."

"Yeah, we do." But not like this, not with her sitting there preparing herself for whatever blow she thought was coming. Yes, he'd been angry when he learned she was pregnant and hadn't told him, but she'd apologized, and he knew he was as much to blame for her decision as she was. Lifting her legs, he sat down beside her on the couch, resting her calves in his lap.

"I'm sorry," they said simultaneously, and then both chuckled, breaking the tension.

"You apologized already," Night reminded her. He would never forget the sobbed words she'd said while thinking she might be about to burn to death.

"Doesn't seem like enough." She shrugged, her gaze fixed on her bandaged hands. She had three broken fingers and had badly damaged the nails on four fingers and a thumb. While none of the injuries were life-threatening, she had come precariously close to losing her life. In light of that, it didn't seem worth it to be angry about anything else. It didn't mean they didn't have to work through this to move forward though.

"You made assumptions about me not wanting a baby," he told her.

"To be fair," she said, risking a glance up at him, "*you* told me that you only wanted a baby with someone you loved, so yeah, I assumed that you wouldn't be over the moon to receive the news you were going to become a father."

"You're right, I shoulder my share of responsibility for your decision to run and not tell me why. But you made assumptions about my feelings for you."

Her gaze darted up to meet his again, the confusion there he wanted to kiss away all over her face, but he couldn't fix this with hot sex, it could only be fixed by words.

"What *are* your feelings for me? Maybe if I'd known, I wouldn't have freaked and run. What happened between us on Christmas Eve changed things between us. No," she corrected herself, "that's not true, it made me see what I'd known for a long time but never addressed. I feel more for you than just friendship." Having said her piece, Lavender held herself perfectly still as she awaited his response.

"Good." Night nodded, relieved to hear her say it out loud. "I'm falling for you. I freaked on Christmas Day when my sister and Spider showed up, realized how it would look to them like I was taking advantage of you, and I was worried you thought the same thing."

"I didn't. That night we spent together was the most amazing of my life. I wish you had talked to me, asked me what I was thinking," she said wistfully.

He did too, but he couldn't go back and fix it. All he could do was not let this opportunity pass him by. "You're right, I should have, but by the time I realized that it was already too late. I was going to talk to you that night at dinner, but you'd disappeared. I looked for you on the roof, but you weren't there, and then we got called out."

"You didn't text to tell me you were going. You *always* tell me when you're going so I can make you promise you'll come back."

He smiled sadly at their silly tradition. "I should have texted, but Abby told me how you were upset and I didn't want to make things worse. The first thing I did when I got home was go straight to your place only …"

"Only I'd already packed up and gone."

"I was so confused, I knew I'd messed up, I just didn't realize how badly until that moment when I stepped inside your place and saw all the boxes and knew you were gone. I thought it was too late to win you back, and then …" he trailed off, knowing he needed this last answer before they made it official. "If Abby hadn't backed you into a corner and forced you to tell me about the baby before it was born or she would, would you have told me?"

Lavender sighed. "I was trying to do the right thing. I didn't want to be selfish, I was terrified of the idea of being a single mom and crushed that you weren't falling in love with me like I was with you, but more than that, I didn't want you to hurt, and I thought it would hurt you to find out you had another unwanted pregnancy. My head said to keep it quiet, not tell you, not put you in the position of having to feel obligated to me, but my heart said you had to know. It wasn't fair to you or the baby to keep you in the dark forever, and my heart …"

"Your heart always wins," he finished for her.

She smiled at him, a genuine smile and she was watching him with hopeful eyes. "Yeah. So where do we go from here?"

"We date, get to know each other as boyfriend and girlfriend with the understanding that I will be asking you to marry me before this little baby makes its arrival." He reached over and rested his hand on Lavender's stomach, she immediately covered it with her own bandaged hands. "Because make no mistake, I am falling in love with you too."

Deciding he had waited long enough, Night hooked an arm around her waist and pulled her sideways so she was sitting in his lap, then finally he was kissing her like he'd wanted to do every single day since that wonderful night they'd shared.

The first hurdle might be over, but he still had a lot of work to do, a lot of wooing to do, and he couldn't wait to get started.

# CHAPTER 19

February 14<sup>th</sup>
9:02 A.M.

Something soft touched her forehead, and stuck between sleeping and waking it took Lavender a moment to figure out what it was.

She smiled when she realized it was Eric kissing her and blinked open her eyes to see him perched on the edge of the bed beside her.

"Morning," he said when he saw she was awake.

"Morning. What time is it?" Still working through the effects of the concussion, she'd gone to bed at around nine last night, unable to hold her eyes open any longer. Eric had set her up in his spare bedroom, and although part of her had been disappointed that he hadn't wanted her in his bed, she had understood. They might be having a baby together, and they might have been friends for four years, but them as a couple was still new and it was perfectly reasonable for him to want to take things slowly.

"Just after nine," Eric replied.

"Wow, I slept for twelve hours straight." She probably shouldn't be surprised by that. She'd been sleeping a lot at the hospital, but while there, and even while she was at her sister's house, she hadn't had that feeling of safety that she got knowing Eric was sleeping in the next room. He'd watched over her in Afghanistan, made her feel safe despite the danger she knew they were in, and he made her feel safe here, he really was her very own superhero.

"You needed it." Eric's hand cupped her cheek, his fingers gently caressing her skin, and when his eyes dipped to her lips and then back up to meet hers she answered by parting her lips. That was all the invitation he needed, and his mouth swept hers up in a kiss that had her body melting into a puddle of goo.

How amazing would it be to wake up to kisses like this every morning?

How amazing would it be to make love to this man every night before she went to sleep?

How amazing would it be to spend their entire lives together?

She whimpered a protest when he straightened, ending what could have been an amazing morning love-making session before it could even begin.

She really had to stop thinking the word amazing, it made her sound like she was in middle school, but Eric like this, all sweet and sexy and in her bedroom, made her lose her ability to form sensible, logical adult thoughts.

Eric smiled—that panty-melting smile that almost had her begging him to rip off his clothes and her clothes—and smoothed her hair. "I have the whole day planned for us, and if we don't get moving now we won't get everything done."

"The whole day, huh?" she asked, sitting up, not an easy task with both of her hands partially out of commission. "Don't you have PT this morning? In fact, if it's already nine, shouldn't you already be there?"

"I'm not going today."

"You're missing it again? I just assumed now we were back here you would be going this morning."

"I took today off. We're just starting out as a couple and after everything you've been through I didn't want to leave you alone."

"Well, I guess I better get dressed then," she said, pushing back the covers and swinging her legs over the side of the bed. Just as she was standing, she saw a bunch of boxes stacked all around the room.

Her things.

Somehow Eric had got a bunch of her boxes here, and she was pretty sure she knew how.

"You sent the guys to my place, didn't you?" she asked.

"I wanted you to have your things around you. I thought it would help you feel more settled, especially as you're dealing with a lot right now."

"And people say you're just a big, tough SEAL, who knew you could be such a sweetie," she teased as she stood up, standing on her tiptoes to kiss his cheek.

"Yeah, yeah, yeah, I'm a regular teddy bear," Eric said with a grin and an eye roll. She knew that he wasn't the most sensitive guy around and yet at the same time he had always been sweet with her. He'd listened and talked through things with her so many times that he had definitely earned his title as her best friend.

"You're my teddy bear," she said and kissed his cheek again.

"Go on and get out of here before I change my mind and throw you back down onto the bed," Eric said, swatting at her bottom as he gently nudged her in the direction of the bathroom. "Call out if you need any help."

She'd kind of mastered using the bathroom with both hands injured. Her broken fingers were taped up so she could remove the bandages to do her business then bandage them back up when she was done. Marigold had helped her shower properly after leaving the hospital, and yesterday after their talk she'd taken a quick shower, but she was probably going to need to wash her hair again tonight. That wasn't something she thought she could do on her own which meant that Eric was going to have to help her. That wasn't a bad thing she thought with a grin.

After finishing up in the bathroom, she shrugged on the jeans and lavender sweater Eric had laid out on the bed he'd obviously made while she was in the bathroom. She couldn't do up the button on her jeans or get her socks and shoes on by herself so she went in search of Eric. She found him in the kitchen talking on the phone, he immediately hung up when he saw her there, and she wondered what that was about.

"I can't do my jeans up, or do my shoes," she announced.

"No problem, sweetheart, I got you." Eric did her jeans for her then put his hands on either side of her hips and lifted her up, sitting her on the counter while he took the socks and shoes from her arms. He picked up one of her feet, studied it for a moment before lightly brushing his thumb across her toenails. "I love how you always paint them this color," he said.

"Lavender is my favorite color," she said a little breathily.

"I know." He grinned before slipping her sock on and then her shoe, doing the same to her other foot. Then he set her down on her feet and held out her coat. "I thought we'd go for a walk along the beach before I take you to lunch."

"That sounds wonderful." Lavender had never been fussy with where she went on a date because she'd traveled the world, lived in some amazing cities, she'd done everything from walk the Champs-Elysees and had dinner at the Eiffel Tower, to romantic gondola rides in Venice, to hiking through the rainforests of the Amazon, she didn't care where she went or what they did, it was all about who she was doing it with. And there was nobody she would rather go on a date with than the man standing beside her.

With butterflies in her stomach that she hadn't felt in a long time, maybe because with all the men she'd dated before she'd known that what they had was only temporary while this thing with Eric had the ability to become as permanent as things got, she followed him out to the car.

The day was cold, with a biting wind, but as they strolled along the water's edge, Lavender couldn't think of any place she would rather be. This was better than any country she'd ever visited, it was better than castles or pyramids or safaris, they were fifteen minutes from her apartment, walking along a beach she'd been to dozens of times, but everything was perfect.

"You too cold? Want to go back to the car?" Eric asked, standing closely behind her as he rubbed her arms.

"No, I'm not ready to leave yet," she replied.

Without another word Eric sat, bringing her down with him. He leaned her against his chest, sitting between his bent knees, his arms wrapped snugly around her, his chin resting on her shoulder as they both watched the waves crash against the shore. The sky was a mixture of gray clouds, making the ocean appear gray too. It was turbulent and rough and echoed everything she had been feeling since that day she had been knocked unconscious and shoved in a cage and realized the man she thought she was falling in love with was nothing but a monster.

So much had happened in these last four years, some of it good, like meeting Eric and making lifelong friends, but a lot of it had been bad, and she didn't just mean being held hostage by terrorists or nearly killed by an unbalanced woman. It was the feelings she'd had about herself that had been the hardest to deal with, but for the first time in a long time she felt hope.

Like the worst was behind her.

That she didn't have to throw herself into a dangerous country to prove she could be selfless, she could do it by being the best mom, the best friend, the best sister, maybe even one day the best wife she could be.

A beam of sunlight shone through a crack in the clouds, streaming directly over where she and Eric were sitting.

"Perfect," she whispered.

"You say something, honey?"

"Perfect, I said that this was perfect," she said, snuggling closer.

"With you in my arms, everything is definitely perfect," he agreed.

~

12:32 P.M.

"You don't really have to feed me you know, my hands might be sore, but I can manage cheese and crackers," Lavender said with a giggle as he held out the cracker.

"I told you before, babe, I don't want you to ever *manage* anything again," he reminded her, moving the cracker closer.

She rolled her eyes but couldn't wipe the grin off her face as she opened her mouth and took a bite. After walking along the beach and sitting watching the waves, he'd brought her to their special place for lunch. Night had debated the idea of doing something fancier, like taking her out for a candlelit dinner at the most expensive restaurant he could find, but when he thought about it, he decided that simple was definitely better when it came to the two of them as a couple.

Since they had been friends for so long, they had skipped the getting to know you phase of dating, and he figured they had also skipped the needing to impress one another stage. Lavender didn't need him to spend hundreds of dollars trying to make the day perfect, all she needed was the two of them to be together.

So he'd brought her up to the roof of the restaurant where she had worked, only since it was their first date, he'd made sure that it was special. He'd asked his friends to set things up, stringing fairy lights around, and candles, and flowers. They'd set up a blanket for the two of them to sit on and a picnic lunch of some of Lavender's favorites, and he was pretty pleased with his idea when he saw the smile on her face when he brought her up.

Night was quickly realizing that he would do whatever it took to make Lavender smile like that.

How had he not seen it earlier, not realized how special she was and how important to him she had grown to be?

It had taken almost losing her twice in as many months for him to realize that she was the woman he wanted to spend his life with. Not just wanted to spend his life with, but could actually see them together. See them getting married, welcoming this little baby into the world, buying a house, having more kids, growing old, and still enjoying spending every day side by side.

This was it for him.

*She* was it for him.

He was actually … nervous … wondering if she felt the same way. He thought that she did, she'd said she was falling in love with him, but he knew that she still had doubts about whether his feelings were because of her or because of the baby. There was only one thing that was going to soothe her fears.

Time.

And speaking of time, they had somewhere to be.

"What has you looking so serious?" Lavender asked, reaching out to touch his cheek with one of her uninjured fingers. She'd been lucky in that she'd broken her pinkie finger on each hand and the one next to it on her left hand, so she could still use her thumbs and her other fingers. It also told him that she had awful form when it came to punching, something he would have to rectify as soon as she was fully healed. He intended to drill her in self-defense until she was confident in her abilities to defend herself.

"Just thinking that we better get packed up here because we have somewhere to be at one," he replied.

"Part two of the date, huh?"

"Technically, part three," he teased. "Part one was the beach, which unless I'm mistaken, you enjoyed."

"It was perfect. The beach is beautiful no matter the time of year, and while I love sitting in the sand or swimming on a gorgeous hot summer's day, the beach in winter is different, darker, wilder, more beautiful somehow."

"I'll have to remember that," he said, tucking away that piece of information sure it would come in handy through the years. "And part two was lunch, which given how much we've both eaten I think I can say was another win."

"Oh yeah, you can't go wrong with cheese," Lavender said, placing a hand on her stomach which only made him more excited for part three.

"So, I think you can safely assume you'll love what I have planned for us next." Reaching out, he grasped her elbows and helped her stand, but she resisted when he went to lead her toward the door.

"Shouldn't we pack everything up first?"

"Don't worry about that, the guys will come and get it all."

Lavender giggled. "Your own personal clean-up crew."

Night grinned back at her. "That was exactly what Chaos said, only he wasn't laughing, he was complaining."

"Your team would do anything for you, even help you set up this amazing picnic lunch date."

"My team would do anything for you too," he reminded her. "And not just because we're together, but because they care about you, they're your friends every bit as much as they're mine."

"I know," she assured him, stepping closer so she could wrap her arms around his waist and rest her cheek against his chest. "I'm lucky to have them, but not as lucky as I am to have you. Thank you again for believing that I wouldn't run out on you and for finding me and saving me from Carmen."

She'd thanked him several times already, but even one thanks hadn't been necessary. "I will always believe in you, always come after you, always save you." Night kissed the top of her head and then gently grasped her chin and tilted her face back so he could kiss her properly.

Although he would have loved to be able to take his time kissing her, touching her, making her come, he had already decided that kissing was as far as they were taking things until Lavender told him she was ready for more, and even if she was ready right this second they really did have to go.

Night took her back downstairs, bundled her into his car, and started driving. When she realized where they were going, Lavender looked over at him in confusion.

"You're taking me to the hospital for our date?" she asked.

"The OB-GYN," he corrected.

"But we already know that the baby is okay," she said. An ultrasound was done at the hospital to ensure the baby had survived the trauma Lavender had endured. And unlike with

Jackie's pregnancy, the idea of anything happening to this baby left him ice cold and struggling to breathe.

"I know, but you were stressed and in pain, traumatized, and I wasn't there. Now that you're staying here you need a doctor, this is Abby's, and she was able to squeeze us in for an appointment today after I explained everything you'd been through. I told you that we're in this together, I should have been there with you for the first appointment." He paused and pressed a finger to her lips when she opened her mouth, he was sure to apologize again for leaving and not telling him she was pregnant, but he didn't want apologies. "I'm not saying that was your fault only that I want to do everything right from here on out."

Lavender relaxed and smiled. "Then this is definitely a perfect part three of our date."

They went inside, checked in, were sent to an exam room where Lavender changed into the gown, and Night found himself pulsing with nervous anticipation. He couldn't be still, which for a SEAL who had spent many an hour in a cramped, dirty spot, surrounded by danger, waiting for the perfect second to act, was not normal.

But this was different.

He was about to see his baby for the first time.

His *child*.

He'd never been to any appointments with Jackie. She'd been seven weeks along when she found out she was pregnant, they'd been married by the following week, then he'd been sent off on a mission, and she'd miscarried three weeks later. Familiar shame filled him, but he pushed it aside, Jackie was happy, and he couldn't be more thrilled that Lavender was having his baby.

"Good afternoon, I'm Dr. Betta," a pretty middle-aged woman greeted them. Lavender chortled at the name, and the doctor grinned. "I think with a name like mine it goes without saying I'm the best OB-GYN around."

"Thank you so much for fitting us in," Lavender said. "We know the baby is okay, but the daddy didn't get to be there when they did the last ultrasound."

"Considering the circumstances I was more than happy to rearrange a few things and see you both," Dr. Betta assured them. "So, are you ready to see your baby?"

"Yes," was all he could manage to get out. As Lavender pulled up her gown and the doctor smoothed gel across her stomach, his heart felt like it was just about ready to come bursting right out of his chest.

This was really happening.

Lavender was really pregnant, and he was really seven months away from becoming a father.

She held out her bandaged hand to him, and he clasped it as gently as he was able.

Then a moment later a beating sound echoed through the room, and a grainy black and white image appeared on the screen.

"That's ... that's ... that's our baby," he stammered, not ashamed to admit that he had tears brimming in his eyes. He'd never seen anything more amazing than the sight of his child growing inside the woman he was falling in love with.

"Congratulations, mom and dad, everything looks healthy and perfect," Dr. Betta told them.

"Perfect," he agreed. Leaning down, he crushed his mouth to Lavender's thanking her without words for this amazing gift.

CHAPTER 20

March 13<sup>th</sup>
3:40 P.M.

Lavender roamed around the apartment feeling ... lost.

It had been a month since Eric brought her back to California and moved her into his apartment. Everything had been going well, they'd gone on lots of dates, spent lots of evenings cooking for each other, and then curling up on the couch in each other's arms watching TV. She was fully healed, although a few of her nails hadn't quite finished growing back yet, everything was progressing fine with her pregnancy. She was closing in on three months along and thankfully hadn't suffered much with morning sickness past those first couple of weeks.

Everything was perfect ... and yet it wasn't.

Eric wasn't shy about touching her, he'd hold her hand, or put his hand on the small of her back, put an arm around her shoulders, hug her, hold her, even kiss her, but that was it. He hadn't once over the last month made any move at all to take things further than a few kisses.

At first she'd thought he was giving her time to adjust to them being a couple, to living together, to deal with everything that had happened to her, but now she wasn't so sure.

Now the doubts were starting to creep in.

Was he attracted to her?

Was this all just about the baby and not the two of them being a real couple?

Because if that was all it was, he didn't have to keep her living here to be part of the baby's life. She would never stand between her child and its father. They didn't have to be a couple to co-parent. They would work out a custody arrangement that worked for all three of them. She still had the lease on her apartment and it was only ten minutes away from Eric's, it would be easy enough to shuffle their baby between the two homes.

Only that wasn't what she wanted.

She wanted it all, a commitment, a marriage, more kids in the future, but other than telling her that very first night when they finally talked, Eric hadn't mentioned anything else about the two of them getting married, and it was starting to make her nervous.

He'd been gone on a mission for the last six days and the time alone had given her time to think.

*Too* much time to think.

Lavender had debated packing up her things—which had bit by bit started to find their way around Eric's house—and moving back to her place, but so far she hadn't gone through with it. There were pictures on the walls, throw cushions on the couch, the spare room she'd been sleeping in had suddenly had her old bedroom furniture and furnishings all set up one day when they came back from a day out. Seeing all of her things in Eric's home should infuse her with confidence about where he saw the two of them heading, but it didn't.

She needed the words.

Needed him to touch her.

Had to know that this was about more than a shared child.

She was on the brink of tears when she heard the door to Eric's apartment open. She turned around and drank in the sight of him. He looked tired. There were little lines around his eyes that hadn't been there when he left and scruff on his chin that said he hadn't had a chance to shave in a while. It was obvious that this mission hadn't been an easy one and while she longed to go to him, offer whatever comfort she could, Lavender knew she could never ask. He could never tell her about what he did when he was gone, and she was okay with that, she could still be there for him any way he needed.

But she didn't move.

Because she wasn't sure where things stood between them.

Eric's brow creased, and he took a step toward her, flicking the door closed behind him. "Are you crying?"

"No," she lied, quickly brushing at her eyes.

He took another step closer, his eyes full of panic now as he glanced from her face to her stomach and back again. "The baby?"

"Is fine," she quickly assured him.

Relief washed away some of the stress on his face, but he didn't come any closer, obviously aware of the fact that something was wrong. "If it's not the baby, then what's wrong? And don't tell me nothing," he warned, "you were crying when I opened the door just now."

Lavender chewed on her bottom lip and looked anywhere than at the man who meant so much to her. She'd loved this last month, loved all the little things he did to make her feel special, the way he planned out their dates down to the tiniest of details, loved the way they had become so attuned to one another's thoughts and needs, and yet … she still had doubts that he truly wanted her in a way that had nothing to do with obligations.

"You're scaring me, sweetheart," Eric said as he stalked toward her, reminding her of a predator about to pounce on its prey. He stopped right in front of her, his large body would be menacing if she didn't know without a shadow of a doubt that he would never hurt her. The only thing she was risking by being with him was her heart.

"I'm g-glad you're back," she said lamely. "You don't look hurt."

"Nice try, sweetheart," he said, nudging her chin to make her look up at him. He was giving her a half-smile, but it didn't reach his eyes. "Tell me what's wrong. Now."

"Nothing is wrong … exactly. I just thought that maybe it was time I moved back to my old place."

Eric stepped back as though she'd slapped him. "You're not happy here?"

"No, it's not that," she quickly assured him, uneasy seeing how uncertain her big, strong superhero looked. This was Eric, he was a SEAL, he saved people for a living, he was never uncertain. "It's just that we've been moving so slowly and I wasn't sure if you still wanted me here."

"Then I've obviously been doing this all wrong," he said, stepping toward her again and wrapping his arms around her, lifting her feet off the floor as he clutched her tightly, his face buried against her neck. "This is how I expected coming home to go. I thought you'd come flying across the room, throw yourself into my arms, and I could hold you like I've wanted to ever since I left. What put these doubts in your head, sweetheart?"

"You never touch me," she admitted. "I mean, you hold me, and you kiss me, but you never do more than that, and I was afraid that meant you were only with me because of the baby. I know how much you want it, Eric, I'm not saying you don't. It's just you don't have to be with me to be a part of its life. I'll never run away again, I want this baby to know its daddy and how wonderful he is. So if you don't want me that's ... that's okay." It wasn't, but she would find a way to be okay, she didn't want to be with a man who didn't really want her.

"Is that what you want?"

"No. I want you, but if you don't want ..." her words were cut off when Eric's mouth claimed hers, kissing her until all her doubts melted away ... almost.

"I told you before, and I'll say it again, I will be marrying you before our little one makes his or her appearance, I was only holding back because I didn't want to push you. You lived through two traumatic ordeals in the space of two months, I wanted to give you time to process and be ready for more because, baby, I want to give you more. You were all I thought about while I was gone, and on the plane flying back, I was counting the seconds until I could see you, touch you." One strong arm kept her anchored against him while his other touched her face, tracing her skin as though he wanted to commit it to memory. "When I saw you standing there crying, I thought the worst, I thought history was repeating itself in the most cruel way. But, sweetheart, even if the worst happened and we lost that little one, I would still want to be with you."

"You're sure?" She searched his eyes for any signs that she was an obligation and not what his heart desired, but she saw none and relaxed.

"Sweetheart, I have never been more sure of a single other thing in my life." Eric kissed her mouth and then his lips were everywhere, her cheeks, her chin, and her neck where he paused to nibble at the sensitive spot above her pounding pulse. "You ready for this?"

"I've been ready since the day you brought me here, Eric. Yes, I lived through two horrific ordeals, but you were there for me when I needed you, you make me feel safe and protected, you make me feel hopeful for the future, and you make me feel like I can be the person I want to be." Lavender paused and dragged in a fortifying breath. "I love you, Eric "Night" McNamara."

Eric groaned, his eyes, when he looked at her, glittering with need and shining brightly with every single thing he felt for her. "I'm happy to hear that, sweetheart, because I love you too, Lavender Vaile. And now I think it's time that I show you how much."

~

4:21 P.M.

Potential heart attack avoided, now Night's heart was pounding for a very different reason. When he'd arrived home, desperate to erase some of the horrors that the mission had turned into, all he had wanted to do was drag his woman into his arms and hold her. But when he'd seen her crying, noted the way she stood still as though her feet were nailed to that particular spot on the floor, he had thought the worst.

For one horrifying second, he had believed that he had lost everything he wanted.

That sense of loss had quickly morphed into one of fear when he felt Lavender pulling away from him.

He had been trying so hard to do everything perfectly, give her time and space to deal with what had happened without him drooling all over her like some horny adolescent, but it was clear his intentions—however well-meaning —had in fact allowed a small crack for her doubts to sneak through.

No more.

Never again would this woman doubt his love for her. He was going to worship her body the same way he worshipped the ground she walked on.

Nuzzling her neck, Night carried her through to the bedroom, his bed where she should have been from the night he brought her home, and laid her down on the mattress.

"You're beautiful, you know that?" he asked as he stared reverently down at her.

Self-consciously, she ran a hand through her hair which was pulled up into a ponytail. "I haven't even showered yet today, and I'm not wearing any make-up, and ..."

He cut her off with a kiss. "You are gorgeous, outside and inside." He rested a hand above her heart. The steady beat reminded him how lucky he was that he hadn't lost her in the hundred ways he could have, and that it was his job to protect her from here on out, make sure she never hurt again. "But I will make a mental note that when I finally let you out of this bed it will be to carry you into the bathroom so we can take a shower, wouldn't want you to be dirty." He winked and then dipped his head to kiss her neck again.

Lavender moaned and tilted her head to the side to allow him better access, and while he kissed her, his fingers worked at unbuttoning her shirt, exposing the most perfect pair of breasts he had ever seen.

"These are perfection," he said as he took them into his hands, enjoying the feel of them, all that smooth, creamy skin. "Only thing better than touching them is tasting them," he whispered in her ear before moving down her body enough that he could take one of those pretty little nipples into his mouth.

Lavender moaned again, her fingers curling into his hair, and he did what he'd been dreaming of ever since that one night they had spent together, he feasted. Moving from one to the other, making sure to keep his hand busy on the one his mouth wasn't devouring, Eric licked, nipped, and suckled until Lavender was squirming beneath him.

"You know I haven't been able to get your taste out of my mind," he said as he kissed his way down her stomach, ignoring her small mewl of protest as he stopped playing with her breasts.

"We only spent one night together," she reminded him, her voice breathy.

"One night I remember every single second of." Sliding an arm under her waist, he lifted her hips off the bed so he could free her leggings and panties, then set her back down and stripped her clothes off. "Feels like I've been waiting forever to do this again," he said as he touched his lips gently to her center. Her hips flew up off the bed, silently begging for more, and he was only too happy to oblige. "I got you, baby."

Just like he had done with her breasts, he licked, nipped, and suckled until Lavender was a panting, wriggling, groaning mess beneath him. Ready to give her what she needed, he slipped a finger inside her, plunging deep.

"Oh ... Eric," she moaned.

"You ready to come, baby?"

"Yeah ... yes ... please," she begged.

Adding a second finger, he began to move his fingers in and out as he continued to tease her swollen little bundle of nerves with his tongue.

"Eric, please, more," Lavender said.

Curling his fingers around to hit that sweet spot buried inside her, Night sucked hard on her bud, and Lavender cried out as she came apart. He continued to use his hand and his mouth on her, drawing out every ounce of pleasure that he could. By the time she sagged against the mattress, spent and sated, he was so hard he knew that he wasn't going to last long once he got inside her.

"That was ... don't even have words," she murmured. "You going to do something about that now?" She asked, nodding at the bulge in his pants.

"Oh yeah," he said, stripping off his clothes. Since Lavender was already pregnant there was no need to worry about a condom, not that it had really done them any good last time anyway. He stretched out above her and took her mouth in a kiss he hoped infused every ounce of love he felt for her.

"Love you, Eric," she said as he positioned himself at her entrance.

"Back at you, sweetheart, and you won't ever doubt my love for you again." In one thrust he was buried deep in her tight, hot body. "You feel so good."

"So do you," Lavender murmured. Her head was resting on the pillow, red waves fanned out around it, her eyes were closed, a look of rapture on her face.

She was stunning.

And she was his.

Forever.

Slowly, he started to move, wanting to draw this out for as long as possible because Lavender deserved more than hot, quick, teenager sex. So he took his time, lazily pulling out then pushing back in as he kissed her.

He was close, but Lavender wasn't there yet, and for all his parent's faults they had taught him to always take care of the woman in his life. They'd meant opening doors and pulling out chairs, but he thought it applied to the bedroom as well.

"Come on, baby," he said, shifting his position a little.

"It's okay, I already came."

"And you'll come again before I do or I won't come at all," he said, cutting off whatever protest she would have made by kissing her.

As he continued to thrust in and out, Night reached between them to touch her still swollen bud. It didn't take long before her internal muscles clamped around him as she moaned into his mouth as pleasure overtook her.

Once his girl found her release, he finally allowed himself to find his own, and it exploded inside him with a ferocity he had never experienced before. It seemed to go on and on, wave after wave of pleasure, washing away the dirtiness of his mission, the shame of his past actions, and the near loss of the woman of his dreams.

By the time it finally dissipated enough that he could see again, he looked down into Lavender's beautiful face as she stared up at him with open adoration.

"I love you, Eric," she said, touching his face.

Catching her fingers, he brought them to his lips, kissed every one of them, paying special attention to those that had been broken as she tried to fight for her life. "I love you back, sweetheart, forever. I'm ready to build a life with you, have you here waiting for me when I get home from a mission, support you as you decide what you want to do with your life, raise this little baby with you. I know this might not be the most romantic time to ask you to marry me, but, Lavender Vaile, will you be my wife?"

Her face crumpled, and for a second, he thought he was right and this was the worst idea ever to propose while he was still buried inside her, but then she threw her arms around him, overbalancing him and nearly allowing him to crush her with his weight.

"Yes, yes, yes, a million times yes. I would love to marry you and spend the rest of our lives together," she gushed, kissing him all over his face before finally on his lips.

Pulling out of her, he went over to his dresser, opened the top draw and pulled out the ring.

Lavender gasped. "Has that been there the whole time you were gone?"

"Baby, this has been there since the day I found out you were carrying my child," he told her, returning to the bed and dropping down onto his knees beside it. "I might have been angry at first that you kept it from me, but the second I knew about the baby I knew that we would find a way to work through everything and be together. I should have seen it earlier, now looking back I can see that we were always meant to be, all those times we talked, how easy it was to tell you anything, you were it for me from the moment four years ago that I saw you crying and pulled you into my arms. It might have taken us a long time to get here, but we're here now, and I can't wait to see what the rest of our lives look like."

"I am too, Eric. For the first time in a long time I'm excited for the future because you're in it."

Taking her hand, he slipped the ring onto her finger. "Our future can be anything we want it to be, it can be everything we want it to be, and I can't wait to experience every second of it with you."

Lavender smiled, laughed, and then started to cry. "You

think you're ready to start that future together with another round of mind-blowing sex?"

That wasn't what he had expected her to say, but it made him both laugh and start to grow hard again. "You betcha," he said as he rolled her underneath him, making her squeal in delight.

# CHAPTER 21

April 1st
7:31 A.M.

"Mmm," Lavender moaned as something hot and wet closed over her nipple. Sleepily, she blinked open her eyes to see Eric's dark head at her breast doing amazing things to her with that mouth she loved so much. She loved it when it teased the most intimate parts of her body, loved it when he kissed her and made the rest of the world fade away, and loved it when he said the sweetest words to her making her feel loved and cherished.

Almost three weeks had passed since they had gotten engaged, and it had been the best weeks of her life. They'd started looking for a bigger place, one that they would share, something near Abigail and Spider so that the cousins could grow up playing with each other. Things hadn't been perfect, they'd argued a couple of times, but they always made sure that once they both cooled down, they talked and fixed the

SAVING ERIC (SPECIAL FORCES: OPERATION ALPHA)

problem before it could grow and get out of hand. But even on the very worst of days, she was beyond thrilled to be engaged to and expecting a baby with such an amazing man.

"Don't stop," she protested as his mouth moved from her breast.

"Not stopping, baby, only pausing," he said as he tossed the covers aside and nudged her entrance.

There was nothing she loved more than the feel of him inside her, their bodies joined together just like their souls were. But there was one other thing she loved almost as much as sex.

Reaching between them, before he could enter her she wrapped a hand around his long, hard length and squeezed.

"Uh, baby, you keep doing that, and I'm going to come mighty quickly," he warned.

"Good," she purred as she put her hands on his shoulders and pushed him back until he was on his knees and then she crawled closer, taking him in her hand again. He was hot and pulsing and almost impossibly big. Sometimes when she looked at him, she could hardly believe that he fit inside her body.

Only the evidence of it was growing inside her.

And it was imprinted on her mind and her heart.

Now she enjoyed playing with him, watching the tense way he had his jaw clamped together because he didn't want to fall apart until he was inside her, but this time he wasn't getting a say.

She was in control.

And he *was* going to come for her.

Lavender trailed her fingertips up the length of him, from base to tip, her touch so light she knew it wasn't enough to give him any release. He didn't say anything, just watched her with that tight jaw and eyes that said he was clinging to restraint because he could see that this was important to her.

Slowly, she began to increase the intensity of her touch, curling a hand around him and sliding it up and down, pausing every so often to squeeze him. Lavender could tell he was close, hanging onto resolve by a thread.

A thread she intended to snap.

While continuing to use her hand, she leaned down and swirled the tip of her tongue around his tip, and that was all it took, he came in thick spurts that landed on her bare chest and belly.

"You pleased with yourself?" he asked as she leaned back on her heels.

"Yep," she agreed, touching the evidence of his desire for her.

Eric growled and snatched her up into his arms and rolling himself off the bed in one smooth move. He carried her into the bathroom, turned on the shower, and as soon as the water heated he set her on her feet. Grabbing a loofah, he drizzled some of her lavender fragranced body wash onto it and dropped to his knees in front of her.

"Do you know how much I love seeing this on you?" he demanded.

Lavender nodded, the look on his face said he was about to devour her and she couldn't wait, thinking of anything else was near impossible.

"I don't think you do, caveman or not, this is my mark on you, I'm going to wash it away now, but neither of us is ever going to forget."

She could hardly breathe as anticipation coursed through her, but still she nodded because she knew that Eric wanted a response.

Eric began to wash her, starting with her stomach and then working his way down both of her legs, refusing to give her any relief by touching her where her body wept for him. He did her arms and chest and then turned her around to face the tiled wall while he did her back. When he was done, he stood, crowding her against the shower wall and it was all she could do not to beg him to fill her up.

Instead, he just stood there, his growing erection pressed against her back, his fingers trailing up and down the length of her spine, slowly, deliberately, making her pay for teasing him, and she stood there and took it until she was so delirious with need that she arched back against him.

"Please, Eric," she begged.

"Spread your legs," he whispered against her ear making her shiver despite the warm water raining down upon them.

She did and felt him move so he was nudging her entrance just as he had been in the bed earlier, only this time she wasn't going to interrupt him. She couldn't. She needed him to be inside her too badly.

One of his large hands curled around her hip, the other grabbed both of her wrists, pulling them above her head and holding them there.

Then in one firm thrust he was inside her. She loved this angle, him behind her, hitting deep inside her with every thrust, making her feel nearly impossibly full. Without even thinking about it she moved, meeting his thrusts, but he froze.

"Stay still," he warned, pulling almost completely out of her until just his tip was still inside her.

Lavender stopped moving, and Eric began to thrust inside her again. She wanted to move with him, meet him thrust for thrust, but Eric had allowed her to take control before, do with him what she wanted, and it was her turn to let him take over now.

So she chewed on her bottom lip and stood still and just allowed her body to feel each and every sensation Eric pulled out of her. She rested her head against the tiles, felt her legs start to tremble, and then just when she thought she wasn't going to be able to hold on for another second pleasure hit her. She cried out as it rolled over her, picking her up and carrying her along for its ride, moving through her body, until even her fingers and toes tingled with that amazing euphoria that nothing else could match.

Eric's arm had moved to around her waist, and he was holding her against him, keeping her from sliding to the floor which she almost certainly would have done if he hadn't held her up.

"How does that get better every time we do it?" she asked as she rested her head back against his shoulder and traced a pattern with her fingertip on the arm holding her.

"Because you're amazing."

"You're pretty amazing yourself."

"And together we top the amazing charts," Eric teased, a laugh rumbling in her chest.

When he reached to touch her between her legs she reluctantly pushed him away. "We have that lunch with your team today," she reminded him.

"So?"

"So if you keep doing that we're not going to make it," she said, sighing in delight when one of those long fingers of his teased her opening before slipping inside.

"Well, if you want to stop," he said, withdrawing his finger and making her mewl a protest.

"I guess we can spend a little longer in the shower and skip breakfast," she said.

"I thought that's what you'd say." Eric resumed what he was doing, sliding a finger inside her while his thumb went to work on that magical little bundle of nerves that could unleash indescribable pleasure on her.

It wasn't long until her head was falling back, her eyes fluttering closed, as bright white dots began to dance on her closed lids. Eric added a second finger, and then a third, his thumb pressing harder and faster against her little bud, and then those white dots burst into a mass of rainbow confetti, each colorful little piece carrying a little piece of ecstasy throughout her body until she thought she was going to spontaneously combust from the pleasure.

Shaking and feeling completely unraveled from two world-shattering orgasms, Lavender snuggled back into Eric's hold. Each day they spent together seemed to be better than the one before it, and they still had so many amazing things to come. Their baby would be coming in less than six months, they'd be finding a new place and moving, and they'd be getting married on Mother's Day in May. It had been Eric's idea. He'd said it seemed fitting since this was her first Mother's Day, claiming they had to celebrate it even if the baby hadn't arrived yet.

They had a whole lifetime to share together, all the ups and downs that would come with marriage and a family. She was ready and willing to face every one of them, secure in the knowledge that she and Eric would be facing them together.

The ups and downs of life weren't the only things they would be sharing, a lifetime of amazing orgasms like the ones Eric had given her this morning was also a big part of their future.

Yeah, they could be a little late to the BBQ.

11:53 A.M.

"So you two finally decided to show up," King teased as they walked through Spider and Abigail's house and out onto the back deck. "Don't think we don't know why you're late and what you two kids have been up to."

Beside him, Lavender's cheeks turned as red as her hair, and Night swatted at his teammate, getting him in the shoulder with just enough force that it would hurt. "Just because you didn't have a woman in your bed last night, King, doesn't mean you get to embarrass the lady."

"Sorry, ma'am." King shot a grin Lavender's way.

She rolled her eyes at King but giggled and snuggled closer against Night's side, and he knew she didn't really mind his team teasing her about the fact that the two of them were a couple very much in love who found it difficult to not touch each other.

"It's fine, King," Lavender said. "And we are sorry we're late. How you doing, Abs?" Lavender left his side to go and join his sister on the porch swing.

"Tired and bored and more than ready for this baby to come out," Abby replied, then looking at her stomach begged, "come out, please come out, I can't take much more of this."

It had been a long and difficult two months for Abigail, confined to the house, either in bed or on the couch, but she was now officially in the eighth month of her pregnancy, so she was almost there.

When Chaos opened his mouth, no doubt to make a joke of some sort at Abby's expense, Spider shot him a look that clearly screamed shut up. Abigail was exhausted, mentally and physically, not to mention full of pregnancy hormones, and was teetering on the edge. The last thing she needed right now was insensitive jokes.

Spider had been spending as much time as possible with his unhappy wife, and Night and Lavender had been by to see her as often as they could, and he completely understood Spider's protectiveness of her. Now that he had a fiancée and his own baby on the way, he knew what it was like to be completely responsible for another person. Lavender was smart, independent, and capable, but she was his, and he would rather suffer the fires of Hell than allow anything to cause her even the slightest bit of pain.

Chaos wisely decided to forgo the pregnancy jokes. "You guys are dropping like flies, falling to the opposite sex."

"I know," King quickly agreed. "Spider has a wife, a house, and a baby on the way. Night is engaged and has a kid on the way. Chaos is ... ow," King exclaimed when Chaos reached out and kicked the legs of the chair he was sitting tipped back on, with an arm resting on the porch railing, sending it toppling onto the wooden deck with King in it. "What the Hell, man?"

"Oops, sorry," Chaos said, shooting daggers at King, and Night wondered what that was about. It wasn't like Chaos to lash out at a team member, SEAL or not, Chaos was one of the most charming and easygoing guys Night knew.

"Oh, right, yeah, sorry, man," King said as he picked himself up, shooting a guilty look Chaos' way, and while Night was sure all of them were curious as to what that was about none of them brought it up, the look on Chaos' face was enough to keep them quiet.

For now.

Sooner or later Chaos would spill all, the man was an open book, he had never been known to keep a secret longer than twenty-four hours.

"Well, after that interesting interlude, I think it's time to start up the grill," Shark announced. The large man levered himself out of the chair that looked more like a child's chair in relation to his large frame and headed to the grill.

"What do you want to eat, honey?" Spider asked Abigail.

She made a face and shook her head. "Nothing for me."

"You have to eat," Spider reminded her.

"I know, but I'm just not hungry right now, okay? I'm just really tired."

"All right," Spider agreed as he reached over and put the back of his hand on her forehead. Spider was obviously worried about his wife, and Night couldn't blame him. Not only had the last couple of months of this pregnancy not been easy on either of them, but Abby looked off today, pale and drawn like she was in pain but didn't want to admit it.

"How about I make us a salad," Lavender suggested. "Honestly, I'm not that keen on the meat either, this little one is on a fruit and vegetable kick, and a salad would be easier on your stomach and still get a little food in you so you keep your strength up."

"Yeah, sure, okay," Abby agreed. "I'll come with you."

"You're meant to be resting," Spider said.

"I know, Ryder, okay, I'm not stupid, but I just need to move for a moment. I'll sit on a chair at the kitchen table and watch her, okay? I wish this baby would hurry up and come out, I can't take another second of your fussing," Abigail snapped.

Taking her outburst in stride because he knew she was just worried and frustrated, Spider said nothing, just helped her stand and watched her follow Lavender inside. "She's not the only one who wishes that baby would hurry up and come out," he muttered, dropping into the porch swing.

Before any of them could say anything else, Shark's phone rang, his eyes going wide when he saw the name on his screen. "It's Evie," he announced to the group.

All eyes turned to Fox.

Fox stared at Shark for a beat, his mouth hanging open. "Evie? As in my Evie?"

Shark nodded then touched accept. "Hey, Evie, what's up?"

While Shark listened, the rest of them tried to figure out

what was going on. Evie was Fox's ex-wife, the two of them had been divorced for going on two years now, and while Evie still hung out with both Abigail and Lavender he had no idea what would have her calling Shark.

Surely the two of them weren't ...

No.

Absolutely not.

None of them would go after another guy's ex on their team, and definitely not Shark. If it was King she was calling then maybe, but definitely not Shark. If she was calling him it had to mean she was in trouble and needed help.

Shark listened patiently to whatever she was saying, his usual calm and stoic face giving nothing away.

"Slow down, honey, so I can catch all of what you're saying." He listened for a moment before saying, "Can you repeat that last part." Another pause. "And you're sure?" He listened again before saying, "Okay, I'll meet you there, probably in about fifteen minutes, don't go anywhere." He hung up, slipped the phone into his pocket, stood, and then seemed to notice they were all watching him expectantly. "What?"

"Why is my ex-wife calling you, Shark?" Fox asked. Their highly intelligent and usually cool under pressure leader stood and stared down the larger man.

"Because you're her ex," Shark said simply.

"Are you two together?" Fox fumed, and Night tensed ready to jump in if this came to blows.

"No," Shark replied.

Fox stared at him for a moment, and Night knew he wasn't the only one ready to jump in if their team leader lost it, but finally Fox deflated. "Is she in some sort of trouble?"

Not one to mince words or play games, Shark nodded. "She is."

"Then I'm coming," Fox said, already starting for the door.

Shark grabbed his arm to hold him back. "She didn't call you, man, I'm sorry, but I don't think you should come."

"Too bad, I'm coming whether she likes it or not. I'll take my car and stay in it while you talk to her, she won't even know I'm there, but I'm coming."

Shark gave a single nod as though he greatly approved of this plan. "Good. Let's go then."

Before they could leave, the back door flew open and Lavender stood there, her face panicked. "Abigail is in labor. I think her water just broke."

"What?" Spider scrambled to his feet so quickly he nearly stumbled in his hurry to get to his wife. "We're still a few weeks away from her due date."

"I think we all knew she wasn't going to make it," King said as they all headed inside.

"She's lucky she made it this far," Chaos added.

"Hey, honey, I'm right here," Spider said as he scooped his wife into his arms.

"I'm scared, Ryder," Abigail whimpered.

"I know, honey, but it's going to be okay. It's baby time." Spider grinned, looking both terrified and thrilled by the prospect.

Although this wasn't a mission and they weren't about to attack an enemy, Fox doled out orders, "Spider, Night, King, and Lavender, you guys take Abigail to the hospital, Shark, Chaos and I will go check on Evie, and then we'll come by to meet our new little niece or nephew. We're a family, we take care of each other. Let's get this done."

They were a family, and while he would be the only blood relative to this new little addition, the others would be every bit as much an uncle to Spider and Abigail's baby. They'd get her to the hospital, and the others would figure out whatever problem Evie had found herself so stuck in she had reached out to her ex-husband's team.

The next time they welcomed a new member to their family it would be his and Lavender's baby. As they all hustled out the door, he wrapped an arm around Lavender's shoulder, he didn't think she realized it because she thought that he was the one who had saved her, but she had saved him from a life of shame and guilt, helped him to set the past behind him, to right the wrongs he'd made as best as he could, and given him the family he'd thought he would never have.

As far as he was concerned, she was his own personal superhero every bit as much as he was hers.

**Find out about Owen "Fox" LeGrand's ill-fated marriage in the next book in this action packed and emotionally charged military romance series!**

**Saving Owen coming summer 2021**

ALSO BY JANE BLYTHE

*Saving SEALs Series*
SAVING RYDER
SAVING ERIC

**Broken Gems Series**
CRACKED SAPPHIRE
CRUSHED RUBY
FRACTURED DIAMOND
SHATTERED AMETHYST
SPLINTERED EMERALD
SALVAGING MARIGOLD

**River's End Rescues Series**
SOME REGRETS ARE FOREVER

**Detective Parker Bell Series**
A SECRET TO THE GRAVE
WINTER WONDERLAND
DEAD OR ALIVE
LITTLE GIRL LOST
FORGOTTEN

**Count to Ten Series**
ONE
TWO
THREE

FOUR

FIVE

SIX

BURNING SECRETS

SEVEN

EIGHT

NINE

TEN

## Christmas Romantic Suspense Series

CHRISTMAS HOSTAGE

CHRISTMAS CAPTIVE

CHRISTMAS VICTIM

YULETIDE PROTECTOR

## Conquering Fear Series

(Co-written with Amanda Siegrist)

DROWNING IN YOU

OUT OF THE DARKNESS

## Other

PROTECT

COCKY SAVIOR

# ABOUT THE AUTHOR

Jane Blythe is a *USA Today* bestselling author of romantic suspense full of sexy heroes, strong heroines, and serial killers! When she's not weaving hard to unravel mysteries she loves to read, bake, go to the beach, build snowmen, and watch Disney movies. She has two adorable Dalmatians, is obsessed with Christmas, owns 200+ teddy bears, and loves to travel!

To connect and keep up to date please visit any of the following

Email – mailto:janeblytheauthor@gmail.com
Facebook – http://www.facebook.com/janeblytheauthor
Instagram – http://www.instagram.com/jane_blythe_author
Reader Group – http://www.facebook.com/groups/janeskillersweethearts
Twitter – http://www.twitter.com/jblytheauthor
Website – http://www.janeblythe.com.au

*There are many more books in this fan fiction world than listed here, for an up-to-date list go to www.AcesPress.com*

*You can also visit our Amazon page at:*
*http://www.amazon.com/author/operationalpha*

### Special Forces: Operation Alpha World

PJ Fiala: Defending Sophie
Nicole Flockton: Protecting Maria
Alexa Gregory: Backdraft
Michele Gwynn: Rescuing Emma
Casey Hagen: Shielding Nebraska
Desiree Holt: Protecting Maddie
Kathy Ivan: Saving Sarah
Kris Jacen, Be With Me
Jesse Jacobson: Protecting Honor
Silver James: Rescue Moon
Becca Jameson: Saving Sofia
Kate Kinsley: Protecting Ava
Heather Long: Securing Arizona
Gennita Low: No Protection
Kirsten Lynn: Joining Forces for Jesse
Margaret Madigan: Bang for the Buck
Trish McCallan: Hero Under Fire
Kimberly McGath: The Predecessor
Rachel McNeely: The SEAL's Surprise Baby
KD Michaels: Saving Laura
Lynn Michaels: Rescuing Kyle
Olivia Michaels: Protecting Harper
Wren Michaels: The Fox & The Hound
Annie Miller: Securing Willow
Kat Mizera: Protecting Bobbi
Keira Montclair, Wolf and the Wild Scots
Mary B Moore: Force Protection
LeTeisha Newton: Protecting Butterfly
Angela Nicole: Protecting the Donna
MJ Nightingale: Protecting Beauty
Sarah O'Rourke: Saving Liberty
Victoria Paige: Reclaiming Izabel
Anne L. Parks: Mason
Debra Parmley: Protecting Pippa

Lainey Reese: Protecting New York
KeKe Renée: Protecting Bria
TL Reeve and Michele Ryan: Extracting Mateo
Elena M. Reyes: Keeping Ava
Deanna L. Rowley: Saving Veronica
Angela Rush: Charlotte
Rose Smith: Saving Satin
Jenika Snow: Protecting Lily
Lynne St. James: SEAL's Spitfire
Dee Stewart: Conner
Harley Stone: Rescuing Mercy
Sarah Stone: Shielding Grace
Jen Talty: Burning Desire
Reina Torres, Rescuing Hi'ilani
Savvi V: Loving Lex
Megan Vernon: Protecting Us
Rachel Young: Because of Marissa

### *Delta Team Three Series*
Lori Ryan: Nori's Delta
Becca Jameson: Destiny's Delta
Lynne St James, Gwen's Delta
Elle James: Ivy's Delta
Riley Edwards: Hope's Delta

### *Police and Fire: Operation Alpha World*
Freya Barker: Burning for Autumn
B.P. Beth: Scott
Jane Blythe: Salvaging Marigold
Julia Bright, Justice for Amber
Anna Brooks, Guarding Georgia
KaLyn Cooper: Justice for Gwen
Aspen Drake: Sheltering Emma
Alexa Gregory: Backdraft

Deanndra Hall: Shelter for Sharla
Barb Han: Kace
EM Hayes: Gambling for Ashleigh
India Kells: Shadow Killer
CM Steele: Guarding Hope
Reina Torres: Justice for Sloane
Aubree Valentine, Justice for Danielle
Maddie Wade: Finding English
Stacey Wilk: Stage Fright
Laine Vess: Justice for Lauren

### *Tarpley VFD Series*
Silver James, Fighting for Elena
Deanndra Hall, Fighting for Carly
Haven Rose, Fighting for Calliope
MJ Nightingale, Fighting for Jemma
TL Reeve, Fighting for Brittney
Nicole Flockton, Fighting for Nadia

*As you know, this book included at least one character from Susan Stoker's books. To check out more, see below.*

## SEAL Team Hawaii Series
*Finding Elodie*
*Finding Lexie (Aug 2021)*
*Finding Kenna (Oct 2021)*
*Finding Monica (TBA)*
*Finding Carly (TBA)*
*Finding Ashlyn (TBA)*
*Finding Jodelle (TBA)*

## Delta Team Two Series
*Shielding Gillian*
*Shielding Kinley*
*Shielding Aspen*
*Shielding Jayme*
*Shielding Riley*
*Shielding Devyn (May 2021)*
*Shielding Ember (Sept 2021)*
*Shielding Sierra (Jan 2022)*

## SEAL of Protection: Legacy Series
*Securing Caite (FREE!)*
*Securing Brenae (novella)*
*Securing Sidney*
*Securing Piper*
*Securing Zoey*
*Securing Avery*
*Securing Kalee*
*Securing Jane*

## Delta Force Heroes Series

*Rescuing Rayne (FREE!)*
*Rescuing Aimee (novella)*
*Rescuing Emily*
*Rescuing Harley*
*Marrying Emily (novella)*
*Rescuing Kassie*
*Rescuing Bryn*
*Rescuing Casey*
*Rescuing Sadie (novella)*
*Rescuing Wendy*
*Rescuing Mary*
*Rescuing Macie (Novella)*
*Rescuing Annie (Feb 2022)*

## Badge of Honor: Texas Heroes Series

*Justice for Mackenzie (FREE!)*
*Justice for Mickie*
*Justice for Corrie*
*Justice for Laine (novella)*
*Shelter for Elizabeth*
*Justice for Boone*
*Shelter for Adeline*
*Shelter for Sophie*
*Justice for Erin*
*Justice for Milena*
*Shelter for Blythe*
*Justice for Hope*
*Shelter for Quinn*
*Shelter for Koren*
*Shelter for Penelope*

## SEAL of Protection Series

*Protecting Caroline (FREE!)*
*Protecting Alabama*

*Protecting Fiona*
*Marrying Caroline (novella)*
*Protecting Summer*
*Protecting Cheyenne*
*Protecting Jessyka*
*Protecting Julie (novella)*
*Protecting Melody*
*Protecting the Future*
*Protecting Kiera (novella)*
*Protecting Alabama's Kids (novella)*
*Protecting Dakota*

*New York Times*, *USA Today* and *Wall Street Journal* Bestselling Author Susan Stoker has a heart as big as the state of Tennessee where she lives, but this all American girl has also spent the last fourteen years living in Missouri, California, Colorado, Indiana, and Texas. She's married to a retired Army man who now gets to follow *her* around the country.

www.stokeraces.com
www.AcesPress.com
susan@stokeraces.com

Made in the USA
Middletown, DE
21 July 2023